Praise for *From the Memoirs of a N*

A *New York Times* Editors' C.

"Delicious . . . You'll be twisting a lip upward at the Bellowesque brio of Gilvarry's language. . . . A left-handed love letter to America."
—Daniel Asa Rose, *The New York Times Book Review*

"In this funny debut, flashy Filipino fashion designer Boy Hernandez sees his American dream become a nightmare when he's ensnared in a terrorist plot and shipped to Guantánamo. Gilvarry nails the couture scene, but Boy's rough journey from Manolo to Gitmo is no joke."
—Andrew Abrahams, *People*

"Like *30 Rock* at its most gleefully savage . . . [This] cocktail of themes—immigrant on the make, post-9/11 burlesque, sybaritic send-up of fashion and hipster Brooklyn—goes down smoothly because Gilvarry writes with authority, if often with tongue firmly in cheek . . . It's not false praise to say that *From the Memoirs of a Non-Enemy Combatant* anticipates our reality."
—Jacob Silverman, *The Daily Beast*

"One of the best celebrations and condemnations of American fear and ambition since Bellow's Augie March was doing the celebrating and condemning."
—Brock Clarke, author of *Exley* and *An Arsonist's Guide to Writers' Homes in New England*

"Sharply written and wryly witty, touching on the sensitivities and paranoia of post-9/11 America. . . . A timely and touching triumph."
—Stephanie Turza, *Booklist*

PENGUIN BOOKS

FROM THE MEMOIRS OF
A NON-ENEMY COMBATANT

Alex Gilvarry is a native of Staten Island, New York. He's the founding editor of the Web site *Tottenville Review*, he has been named a Norman Mailer Fellow, and his writing has appeared in *The Paris Review*. He lives in Brooklyn, New York, and Cambridge, Massachusetts.

Alex Gilvarry

FROM THE MEMOIRS OF A NON-ENEMY COMBATANT

PENGUIN BOOKS

I would like to express my deepest gratitude to Hunter College and the generous Hertog Fellowship, and to the Norman Mailer Writers Colony. My sincerest thanks to Seth Fishman, my agent, for his smarts and dedication, and to Liz Van Hoose, my editor, a protector of words. Thank you to my friends and colleagues for their tireless support, to Dr. Juan and Selfa Peralta, and to Ashley Mears.

PENGUIN BOOKS
Published by the Penguin Group
Penguin Group (USA) Inc., 375 Hudson Street, New York, New York 10014, U.S.A.
Penguin Group (Canada), 90 Eglinton Avenue East, Suite 700,
Toronto, Ontario, Canada M4P 2Y3 (a division of Pearson Penguin Canada Inc.)
Penguin Books Ltd, 80 Strand, London WC2R 0RL, England
Penguin Ireland, 25 St. Stephen's Green, Dublin 2, Ireland (a division of Penguin Books Ltd)
Penguin Group (Australia), 707 Collins Street, Melbourne, Victoria 3008, Australia
(a division of Pearson Australia Group Pty Ltd)
Penguin Books India Pvt Ltd, 11 Community Centre, Panchsheel Park, New Delhi–110 017, India
Penguin Group (NZ), 67 Apollo Drive, Rosedale, Auckland 0632,
New Zealand (a division of Pearson New Zealand Ltd)
Penguin Books, Rosebank Office Park, 181 Jan Smuts Avenue, Parktown North 2193, South Africa
Penguin China, B7 Jaiming Center, 27 East Third Ring Road North, Chaoyang District, Beijing 100020, China

Penguin Books Ltd, Registered Offices: 80 Strand, London WC2R 0RL, England

First published in the United States of America by Viking Penguin, a member of Penguin Group (USA) Inc. 2012
Published in Penguin Books 2012

1 3 5 7 9 10 8 6 4 2

Copyright © Alex Gilvarry, 2012
All rights reserved

THE LIBRARY OF CONGRESS HAS CATALOGED THE HARDCOVER EDITION AS FOLLOWS:
Gilvarry, Alex.
From the memoirs of a non-enemy combatant : a novel / Alex Gilvarry.
p. cm.
ISBN 978-0-670-02319-6 (hc.)
ISBN 978-0-14-312306-4 (pbk.)
1. Fashion designers—Fiction.   2. False arrest—Fiction.
3. Guantánamo Bay Detention Camp—Fiction.   I. Title.
PS3607.I4558F76 2012
813'.6—dc23
2011032993

Printed in the United States of America
Set in Bodoni Book   Designed by Francesca Belanger

For Peter and Vilma Gilvarry
and for
Gloria Reyes

FROM THE MEMOIRS OF A NON–ENEMY COMBATANT

With Footnotes and an Afterword by Gil Johannessen

EDITOR'S NOTE

With the exception of footnote annotations, the author's acknowledgments, the editor's afterword, and a supplemental article included with permission, all material herein has been reprinted verbatim from the confession of Boyet R. Hernandez, composed from June through November 2006.

*Since everything is in our heads, we had better
not lose them.*

—Coco Chanel

ACKNOWLEDGMENTS

The patsy of this wrenching tale would like to extend his thanks to several people without whom I would cease to exist.

To my editor, my dear, dear friend in exile, esteemed fashion editor at *Women's Wear Daily*, my Virgil, my gondolier, my guide through a hell unimaginable—Gil Johannessen, *salamat*.

To Philip Tang, Rudy Cohn, and Vivienne Cho, oh those wild rooftop parties at the Gansevoort. To John Galliano and Rei Kawakubo for their whisperings in my ear. To Catherine Malandrino, you gave me color, you gave me life! To Coco, Yves, Karl, for their invention and their reinvention—the wheel on the bus was never the same again, yet round and round it goes.

I would be remiss if I did not mention my attorney, Ted Catallano, of Catallano & Catallano & Associates. (If it were not for Ted, where would I be today? Not in the figurative sense, but where would I be, physically? Perhaps in some black site in Egypt being waterboarded naked or slapped with menstrual blood while my interrogator takes a dump on a copy of the Qur'an. If my imagination seems a little graphic, for heaven's sake, do pardon me, for I have been through a great ordeal.)

Before I lay into every U.S. government agency that has defiled me (DoD, DHS, ICE, INS, CIA, FBI) let me give a big *salamat* to the

New York Police Department, those strapping boys in blue, the true heroes. Never once did they cause me any grief.

For Abu Omar, Shafiq Raza, Moazzam Mu'allim, Hassan Khaliq, Dick Levine. Riad Sadat, for translating his poetry into English so that my heart could palpitate outside of Camp Delta. They took our imagination, but they couldn't take our words.

For all at OhCmonMove.org.

To Lieutenant Richard Flowers, who I only met once, but whose small bungle set the world off its axis.

I would like to acknowledge playwright Michelle Brewbaker's *The Enemy at Home or, How I Fell for a Terrorist*, to which this memoir is neither dedicated nor immune. Three acts of didactic rumor and defamation, soon to be published by Farrar, Straus and Giroux— shame on you.

For Olya, Anya, Dasha, Kasha, Masha, Vajda, Marijka, Irina, Katrina, etc.—the maddening dream of your bare white asses kept me alive.

To Ben Laden (no relation), my publicist, old Irish gelding in arms.

To the only people who will still have me! My purgatory and homeland—the Republic of the Philippines, where I was spat into this world, eight pounds two ounces, January 11, 1977, under martial law, the little dark bomb of Boyet Ruben Hernandez.

To you, dear reader, my life *is* in your hands.

To my enemies: It ends now.

—B. R. H.

New York City, 2002–2006

Every man needs aesthetic phantoms
in order to exist.

—Yves Saint Laurent

You Made Me

I would not, could not, nor did I ever raise a hand in anger against America. I love America, the golden bastard. It's where I was born again: propelled through the duct of JFK International, out the rotating doors, *push*, *push*, dripping a post–U.S. Customs sweat down my back, and slithering out on my feet to a curb in Queens, *breathe*. Then into a yellow cab, thrown to the masses. Van Wyck, BQE, Brooklyn Bridge, Soho, West Side Highway, Riverside Drive—these are a few of my favorite things!

My story is one of unrequited love. Love for a country so great that it has me welling up inside knowing it could never love me back. And even after the torment they've put me through—tossing me into this little cell in No Man's Land—would you believe that I still hold America close to my heart? Stupid me, Boy Hernandez. Filipino by birth, fashion designer by trade, and terrorist by association.

So here I wait for my combatant status review. Not a college literary journal like the one my ex, Michelle, used to publish her poems in, but a real-life tribunal starring me . . . on trial for war crimes.

It's true that I knew some very bad people. Though it is my opinion that everything must be digested in context. If I am to be released, as I have so often demanded, then hard facts contrary to my accuser's egregious mistake must be presented in a clear and chronological fashion. And so my special agent here has given me the chance to write out my true confession (to be used as formal evidence in my tribunal). A pen and legal pad have been provided to me. "Spare no detail. Leave nothing out" were my special agent's instructions. "You can start with your arrival in America."

According to the *New York Post*, where I once graced the columns of Page Six—my name in bold, next to Zac Posen and Stella McCartney—I'm the "fashion terrorist." An émigré candy ass turned hater of Americans and financier of terror. (My special agent has shown me select headlines from the moment I was extraordinarily rendered here. The papers really think I'm their man.) I was a fiction from the beginning. We see only what we want to see, do we not? And when what we want to see isn't there, we create it. Tah-dah! If I could somehow put all the pieces of my "secret life" together according to what's been said about me in the tabloids, it would go something like this:

Fed up with being the immigrant turd that gets flushed over and over and won't go down, Boy Hernandez finally worked up the nerve to take aim at America. Be it the White House, the Empire State Building, or a Boeing 747 out of Newark bound for Tallapoosa, Missouri.[1]

---

1. "Fashion Coup," *New York Post*, June 4, 2006:
HERE'S ONE TO brighten your Mercedes-Benz Fall Fashion Week. Federal officials say that Fashion Terrorist Boy Hernandez is headed for Gitmo. Let's hope this junior designer likes bright orange jumpsuits, because that's what he'll be wearing 24/7.

The President authorized Hernandez's one-way ticket to the maximum-security compound by the bay on Wednesday, setting a new precedent in the War on Terror. Hernandez will be the first Guantánamo detainee captured on U.S. soil.

Big-ass, bald-faced, barbed-wire lies.

My first day in America, September 13, 2002, was the most eye-opening day of my life. I never had any foul intentions, especially toward the city that took me into her unbiased arms, wrapped me up in her warm September skin, and gave me a big maternal smooch. *Mwah!*

New York City was a utopia.

By contrast there was Manila, my hometown. I grew up on the north end in a wealthy suburb. Tobacco Gardens, corner of Marlboro and Kools (no kidding). Though I didn't come from tobacco money. My parents had a private practice, which made us middle-class at best. Hernandez y Hernandez, Ear, Nose, and Throat. I left the suburbs at seventeen to attend fashion school at FIM.[2] It was there that I began to choke on my own city's mistakes—the crowded motorways, barrios, dirt, and smog gave me a bad case of acne and an all-consuming desire to get the hell out of there. And Manila was no place for a serious designer of women's wear. One had to go to New York or London. After graduation, I couldn't imagine staying put. What is it that they say? Home is where you hang yourself.

The Fashion Terrorist had been living illegally in the Williamsburg area since 2002. Like many other illegal immigrants from Mexico, Hernandez dodged officials for years.

His independent women's fashion label, *(B)oy*, was expected to be a major ATM for Hernandez as of next season. Sources say that once *(B)oy* took off, the proceeds would have backed terrorist sleeper cells. Their whereabouts are still unknown.

"We don't know where they plan to strike," said White House correspondent Mike Anspa. "Be it the White House, the Empire State Building, or Tallapoosa, Missouri, it doesn't matter. Put us on the board. We got one."

(*see related* "Panic in Tallapoosa," page 13).

2. Fashion Institute of Makati, Makati City, Manila.

From the arrival terminal at JFK I directed my cabbie to drive me to the foot of Manhattan, Battery Park. I had studied my maps! I had always dreamed of seeing the Statue of Liberty on my first day in America, no matter how impractical it was from my point of arrival. I wanted it to be a part of my first memory. Just like in the immigrant narratives I had read as a teenager. Oscar de la Renta, Diane von Furstenberg, etc. "Give me your tired, your poor, your huddled masses yearning to breathe free . . ." I was being sentimental, I know. But what rebirth is complete without a proper baptism? Seeking out Lady Liberty was my way of christening myself an American, and a New Yorker to boot.

We hit the Van Wyck (pronounced "Wike," said my guidebook), which took us through an unsavory part of Queens. Now, from what I saw of it, Queens was a desolate place, much unlike what I would come to know as the city proper. Panel homes gave way to industrial factories; on-ramp gave way to on-ramp. It wasn't until we rolled along the BQE, passing a massive cemetery with thousands of ornate tombstones, that I realized Queens too had its own filthy beauty. As my taxi approached a little bridge I couldn't pronounce, there it was on my left:[3] Manhattan. The skyline I had glimpsed from the plane when the captain tipped his wing. The skyline I had seen all my life on television and in films. A skyline that was as much a symbol of my dreams in fashion as it was a symbol of America and its financial prowess. A skyline that called out to me, "Come and get it, sucka!"

---

3. His right, actually. And it's the Kosciuszko Bridge, connecting Maspeth, Queens, to Greenpoint, Brooklyn.

My driver took me in. The city beckoned me at every pothole struck. I traced a finger along my map as we went over the Williamsburg Bridge. And then . . . "Delancey Street," called my driver, "where one comes to pick up drunk young fare." He was a knowing guide, pointing out the neighborhoods as we went. Chinatown, Little Italy, SoHo, City Hall. "First time in the city, I take it?" he asked.

"Yes," I said. I was giddy.

"Just keep your head up and your eyes open," he said. "You'll be all right."

We were downtown, cruising along Broadway, entering the north tip of the financial district. Fulton, Church Street, Maiden Lane. Buildings surrounded me on all sides. I could no longer see the sky. Instead of out, the city just went up and up.

To my surprise, Battery Park was not shaped like an alkaline Duracell. All those things I saw in the movies regarding New York's hard edge, like the winos, the drugs, the graffiti, the muggings and murders, the racial strife—these weren't anywhere to be found. I did see my first New York bum sprawled out on a park bench. But he was not begging. He was listening to his own portable radio, propped up on a pushcart full of bottles and cans. There were office mates on lunch—men and women flirting with each other behind sunglasses. There were black women cradling white babies and white women cradling Asian babies and Asian women cradling Eurasian babies. Every diverse American and his mother! I hurried past with my luggage to the water's edge. New York Harbor. *Breathe.* The river was a blue-green bayou. I watched a water taxi play chicken with a tugboat, while the Staten Island ferry—the

John F. Kennedy—came from behind and threatened to crush them both. I leaned my torso over the railing so I could see Lady Liberty. She was in mourning. A black veil covered her face.[4] Yet she held her torch high, uncovered, as if leading a fleet of ships into battle away from industrial New Jersey. I closed my eyes and listened to the choppy water. I leaned out until my feet were lifted off the ground, and I held my balance over the guard railing by my hands and waist alone, floating, surrendering to the harbor. A foghorn blew in the distance where there was only clear sky.

I listened.

For description's sake—to paint a picture of your fashion terrorist as he was in his twenty-fifth year—I am a modestly proportioned man of five foot one. At the time I was in peak physical condition. I was progressing in my yoga practice. I could stand on my head for fifteen-minute intervals, do twenty sun salutations, and still balance myself in *Virabhadrasana* one.[5]

This is the man I *was*.

I kept my hair shortly cropped and would shave a faux part down the left side of my scalp and through the corresponding eyebrow, classically fashioned after the major hip-hop artists of the 1980s. My Nike high-tops added an extra inch or two to my stature, but let's skip all pretensions and just stick to the bare facts. I'm a small man! I'm even small for a Filipino, a people notorious for being slight of frame. Myself, I have often been confused for an overgrown, mustachioed child.

There I was, leaning out over the railing with my eyes closed.

4. According to the National Park Service, the Statue of Liberty was undergoing restorations at the time.
5. Also known as Warrior 1.

I can still hear the breeze off the harbor, the children's voices echoing from a nearby playground, the rustling in the trees a mere decibel above the city's bustle. I dreamed of the splash I would make during one of New York's upcoming seasons with a collection of my own. The ripples would travel around the world to London and Paris and Milan. People would know my name. Back in Manila I had already shown one collection of knitwear during Philippine Fashion Week. A few pieces even got picked up in boutiques around Makati and Cubao, but I wasn't all that well-known. Back home you did runway with designers who were former beauty queens and minor celebrities—Miss Mindanao '95 and contestants fresh off *Pinoy Big Brother*[6]—and the buyers tended to stick to celebrity branding. One needed to be in New York in order to be taken seriously. And now that I had reached my destination my mind was swooning with possibilities. It took the wail of a street musician's tenor sax to bring me back down to earth.

I hailed another taxi and headed for the apartment of Dasha Portnick, an old friend I knew from Manila, where she'd modeled my first show. She was letting me use her place while she was away in Thailand doing a skin-whitening campaign for Oil of Olay. Dasha was a stunning, dark beauty, but at twenty-six she was already considered too old for the New York market. So whenever fashion week came around, she purposely booked a high-profile job abroad. Since there was an unquenchable thirst for dark-haired white girls in Southeast Asia, it was there that Dasha made

6. Philippine edition of the reality television show *Big Brother*, wherein twelve contestants are chosen to live in the same house under video surveillance. Many contestants go on to pursue careers in acting, pop music, fashion design, or in some cases all three.

her living. In fact, before I left Manila, her face had been plastered on billboards along the South Super Highway for some new cosmetic band-aid that wrapped over one's nose.

I had Dasha's address written down on the back of her modeling card, right next to her hips, waist, and bust. The cab let me out in front of her building on Ludlow Street, one of those glossy high-rise structures that loudly pronounced itself against the old-world tenements of the Lower East Side.

The doorman greeted me as I stepped into the lobby, my luggage in tow. He was a friendly Hispanic who kept a nice trim mustache. I introduced myself as Dasha's friend, and he in turn handed me a spare set of keys. "Wait a sec," he said at once, "I almost fuhgot." He produced a folded note from under his station and gave me a little wink, as if something had been understood. "Have a good night, guy," he said.

"Thanks, guy," I said, repeating him. Both cabbies had also called me "guy." I was quickly learning how to converse with New York's working class.

Boy,
    Welcome. Here is your key. Top lock is broken. Please don't overwater the ficus. And don't mind Olya, she's cool.

                    Ciao,
                    Dasha

    P.S. Make sure Olya doesn't overwater the ficus either. I already told her, but she's so forgetful you know?

This was the first I'd heard of Olya. But I wasn't at all bothered. Only when I was working did I demand complete solitude.

On the tenth floor at the end of a long carpeted hallway, I knocked on the apartment door and waited. When there was no answer, I let myself in. All the lights were off and the blinds were drawn. I left my things in the kitchen and went to the bedroom, where I found Olya, topless, wearing nothing but her panties. She was fast asleep on her back with her legs in a side twist. Olya had a fantastic blond bob, though her body was rather pale and hollow and lacked the healthy luster of her hair. Her breasts were small and anticlimactic. In the corner of the bedroom was the ficus, sprouting from a pot of muddy water.

I thought about covering her, but she had the sheets and comforter lodged between her legs. If she woke up with a complete stranger hovering over her, who knew how she would react? I reasoned the best course of action would be to reenact my entrance and make a lot of noise. This would surely rouse her, I thought.

Silly, I know, but I went through the motions once again. For the second time I knocked on the door. When I felt certain she wasn't getting up, I inserted the key into the lock, jiggled the door handle, dropped my suitcase in the kitchen, and slammed the door behind me. I called out, "Hello?" Still, there was no answer. "Hello?" I said again, much louder.

"Who's there?" said Olya. She had a calm, throaty voice.

"I'm Boy. Dasha's friend. You must be Olya?" I called into the room.

"One minute, baby." She began to cough, then hack a little. Waiting in the kitchen, I was greeted with the pleasant smell of a cigarette being smoked in bed.

Olya came out in a red oriental robe, pinning her hair up with bobby pins.

"You're her friend from Asia?" she asked.

"The Philippines."

"That's the one I always forget."

Olya opened the fridge, removed a bottle of San Pellegrino, and guzzled.

"She mentioned me?" I asked.

Olya belched. "'Scuse. She said something. You're staying a few days, yes?"

"About a week."

"Eh? A week?"

"Is something burning?"

"Then we'll have to share the bed. That's what Dasha and I do. Only don't get the wrong idea about it. We're not lezzies."

"Oh, I didn't think that. It's just that Dasha never mentioned she had a roommate. You can imagine my surprise, meeting you here under these circumstances."

"Typical Dasha. We have an arrangement, you know. I sublet from her whenever I'm in town."

I found out later that Olya paid Dasha rent for half the queen-size mattress. During fashion week there was a room shortage in modeling agency apartments, so many girls had to double up. The price of glamour comes at an encroaching cost, as Dior once said.[7]

"I swear I smell something burning."

"Oh fuck," said Olya. She ran into the bedroom, taking the bottle of San Pellegrino with her. "Fuck, fuck, fuck." From the

7. It was Cristobal Balenciaga who said this.

doorway I watched her sprinkle the soda water onto the bed, extinguishing whatever small flame she had ignited with her cigarette.

"Is everything okay?" I asked.

She reemerged from the room and closed the door behind her. "I burned another hole in Dasha's sheets. She'll kill me."

"Is the fire out?"

"*Of course.* I can't believe this. I'm so stupid."

"Don't say that. They're just sheets. We'll replace them."

"Fuck her."

Olya was a Pole by origin, just fifteen when she was first scouted in her small town of Kozalin by a German who took her to Milan, Tokyo, Paris. He showed her the world, and she fell in love with him. But once they got to New York, with Olya set up at Ford Models, he left her and eventually made his way back to Berlin to pursue a career as a drum-and-bass DJ. "I see him at parties," she said. "He's a dick now. But he got me out of Kozalin, so I suppose I owe him something."

She knew all the major cities and was a tremendous help to me as I navigated my way. She marked in my guidebook how to get to Ground Zero, how to get to Saks from Barneys, then to Bryant Park from Times Square. She enlightened me about the monthly metropass, scams by persuasive men at the turnstiles—"Don't ever pay them for swipe"—and where the closest subway station was. "Far," said Olya. "If you have casting, you have to leave like forty-five minutes early to get anywhere."

And so I spent the rest of my first day getting lost, making transfers, missing connections, falling in love. New York's subway system is a rubber band of sexual tension, stretched and twined around the boroughs, ready to snap. I frolicked in this salacious underground, where every motion had meaning—every leg crossed, every glance up from a paperback, every brush of a shoulder or rump was a kiss blown in my direction. The porcelain Chinese beauties on and off at Canal; the thoroughbred Eastern European models of Prince, castings a-go-go; the NYU coeds of Eighth Street, plump and studious. Oh, and the sexpot hipsters at Fourteenth, right off the L, like cattle, their eyes drowned in eye shadow, looking as if they had never missed a party, nor would they.

My first meal I ate at an establishment called Steak Chicken Pizza Grill, Forty-second Street. Its sign was lit up like a carnival and called out to me, American food eaten here. I was aware of the tackiness of the eatery upon entering. Its sign, menu, and patrons were a testament to a class of people I wanted nothing to do with. But let me tell you, it was the best meal I had ever tasted. The blackened burger, thick tomato, crisp iceberg, and lone fry, which somehow snuck its way under the bun, each lent a delight to the other. And the slice of authentic New York pizza, reheated by a Mexican, handled from oven to tray by a Pole, and rung up by an Italian—"Here you go, boss"—complemented the burger beyond my wildest dreams. I consumed more than my small body could digest. And what a feeling! Like I'd just fueled up on unleaded and had gasoline pumping through my small intestine.

The city could be hard on its own. It took everyone in as orphans, but if you didn't pull your own weight, you could be squashed. I learned this after that most memorable dinner, as I was standing outside Steak Chicken Pizza Grill, studying the fold-out map of my guidebook. I was to go east on Forty-second to get to Bryant Park, the site of New York's fashion week. Twice a year it became the beating heart of the industry, and I wanted to walk its grounds in order to feel it pulsing beneath me. When I looked up to get my bearings, I saw a man about my age, a South Asian. Our resemblance was remarkable. Like me he was five foot one, nearly a foot below the average New Yorker. He seemed to share my same build, though one couldn't really tell because he wore a giant menu over his torso. He was an advertisement for the Sovereign Diner. I began my approach in order to get a better look at his face. His eyebrows were overgrown and had formed a prominent unibrow, whereas I plucked mine daily. He had my mustache, a neatly trimmed whisper, just the right dash of masculinity. But it was looking down the length of the cardboard menu—2 EGGS, HAM, SAUSAGE, OR BACON $2.95—that I saw the biggest tell of all, the trait which bound us together as brothers of this world.

His hands.

His small, dexterous hands.

His hands were just like mine. And in his hands were menus, replicas of the giant board he wore like armor. "Take one, take one," he said, rapidly. "Take one." And then, "Please." This was his job, to stand in front of the Sovereign Diner distributing menus. Had he come here hoping for something better? Of course he had. What he got served, however, was hard-boiled reality, the city's ruthlessness, and he had to wear it every day, bearing the brunt over his shoulders as a sign.

PANCAKE SPECIAL $4.95.

I took one of his menus and at the next corner threw it away with a hundred others. Bryant Park had suddenly lost its appeal. Instead, I went back to Ludlow Street to spend more time with Olya.

Look at how far she had come. The beauty and generosity this little Polska had was bursting from every invisible pore! She shared her Icelandic yogurt and showed me all of the cable channels. We talked about movies, fashion, drive, ambition. She promised to take me with her to the week's castings and introduce me to other models and designers, with the intention of getting me a job on a show somewhere. When we retired to the bed, she kept me up, tired as I was, in order to practice her English language skills. She was preparing to take a TOEFL exam and planned to study at Baruch College in Manhattan. Olya read to me the opening pages of *The Catcher in the Rye*. I had read the book in high school, but hearing it through Olya's Polish accent, with her poorly timed inflections, gave it a new place in my heart. "If *you really* want to hear *about* it, the first thing you'll probably want to know *is where* I was born, and *what* my lousy childhood was like, and *how* my parents were occupied *and all* before they had me . . ."

I wanted to make love to her then, but I am not an animal. You see, I respected the boundaries of our new friendship. A girl who would share her bed with a total stranger didn't deserve to be taken advantage of. Plus, she had a new boyfriend, Erik, who she talked about constantly.

I had no delusions. In a city that could reduce a virile young man to dressing up as a menu on Forty-second Street, pleading, "Take one, take one, please, take one," I understood the force I was up against. One needed friends much more than lovers and enemies. This city was cutthroat. This city, crossed with the exclusivity of the fashion industry, was a closed network to new talent. This city wasn't hard on its newcomers—it was goddamn relentless. Don't believe me, take a look outside the Sovereign Diner, and surely a walking, talking menu will be there—feast your eyes! Under that menu is a human being whose English is good enough to have any job, but too many obstacles stand in his way, poor menu. Sure, the financial skyscrapers, the sprawling bridges, the underground love tunnels, the people in their park-side penthouses—these were physical proof of the impossible. Manhattan was a testament to everything being out of God's hands and within Man's. Dreams could be realized on these streets. Olya was hot smoking proof. But mostly, dreams were crushed in this city (menu man prime example). Ninety-nine percent of the time.

I knew a sign when I saw it, all right.

Apropos of No Man's Land

How did I end up in No Man's Land? It has been two weeks since the Overwhelming Event of May 30, 2006. That's right, just two weeks ago I was back in Brooklyn at work on a new line of women's wear out of my studio in the toothpick factory. (It really was a former toothpick factory.) My latest collection was to be bought and sold in Barneys alongside Philip Tang 2.0, Comme des Garçons, Vivienne Westwood. Gil Johannessen had called my collection a "bildungsroman" in the pages of *W* magazine. A compliment. I had finally broken into Bryant Park after six seasons in New York spent struggling to get editors and buyers to show up at my showcases. I had come of age as a designer, and I was ready for the big leagues. Then, faster than you can say Sunni insurgents, it was all taken away from me. Bandits, Homeland Security's henchmen, came bursting through my door in the middle of the night, ripped me from artistic slumber, and told me very explicitly to put my hands behind my head, and that I better pray to Allah that there's no one else hiding in my shit hole, motherfucker.

I've asked for a lawyer. They keep delaying. One thing they're very good at in No Man's Land is delaying. I've shouted it from my cell, frantic; I've cursed it for days in a row—"Bring me a lawyer!" Still nothing happens.

My cell is approximately six feet by eight feet. I measured it heel to toe. The walls are steel mesh, and my bed is a metal plank affixed to one side. There is a barred window that brings natural light, though the outer pane is opaque. There is a squatting-style toilet—an Arab toilet—and a sink built low to the ground.

I am administered comfort items. One standard-issue blanket, one towel, one rubber exercise mat (my mattress), one inch-long toothbrush, one travel-size tube of toothpaste (Colgate), one roll of toilet paper, one plastic water bottle (Freedom Springs), one set of flip-flops for the shower. I receive religious paraphernalia: one standard-issue Qur'an (mine is in English; it once belonged to a D. Hicks,[1] his name written on the inside flap like a child's), one foam prayer rug, one white skullcap, one plastic vial of oil (patchouli). These items are completely useless because, as I keep telling them, I'm no Muslim! I was baptized a Catholic, and I'm barely that anymore.

The man who guards me from 0600 to 1800 hours is from Fort Worth, Texas. I had never before met a Texan. His name is Win. I've wondered if that's his real name or if he's given me a nom de guerre. Win.

In here I go by a nom de guerre of my own: Detainee No. 227.

Win wants to be a lawyer someday. He's still quite young, only twenty, with an associate's degree in economics. His plans are to finish college back in Fort Worth and then use what's left of his

---

1. David Hicks, the Australian. Hicks renounced his Islamic beliefs early on as a prisoner at Guantánamo Bay. He was released in April 2007 and returned to Australia, where he served out the remaining nine months of his sentence. Even though their detainments overlapped, the two men never had any contact.

GI scholarship to go on to law school, studying the Constitution and arguing cases in mock trials.

"Mock trials?" I said.

"Yeah, mock trials. Fake ones," he said. "Something they do in law school to prep you for the real courtroom. There's a judge, two counselors, just like in real life, and you argue the case to the best of your ability. Sure it's fake, but you don't know what the outcome will be. No one knows, and so that's what makes them seem real. No one goes to jail or anything. At the end of the day, everyone gets to go home."

"What kinds of cases?"

"Every kind, I imagine. Criminal cases, murders, civil suits, you name it."

"And each man gets a fair hearing?"

"Oh sure. But it's still fake. No one really did anything in mock court. It's practice."

"I've never been to Texas," I told Win.

"It ain't nothin', really. Though there are a lot of other jarheads here who'll tell you different."

"That's what they call Texans?"

"That's what they call marines. Jarheads, grunts, leathernecks. Texans are Texans."

"Leathernecks."

"No one says leatherneck anymore."

The man who relieves Win at 1800 is named Cunningham. He's from a place called Government Mountain, Georgia. Cunningham's not much of a talker. He's a true jarhead, high and tight. He sits in his chair with his feet up on my cell door for the most part and rocks back and forth on its hind legs, reading a

magazine. Everything I do gets recorded in a logbook. Cunningham keeps the logbook at his side on a little table. He writes down
whatever I do at night. The time I sleep. The time I eat. If I take
a squat, this goes in the logbook.

He is very good at pretending I'm not here. He can go for hours
like this, flipping through magazine after magazine.

Just the other night, while I was lying on my bed watching
Cunningham read a *Maxim*, I caught a glimpse of my past on the
cover. It was Olya. My darling Olya, who once shared a bed with
me so openly and who would remain a dear friend over the years.
I couldn't believe it was her. Olya has walked the runway for every
major designer—Marc Jacobs, Carolina Herrera, Lanvin in Paris,
Burberry in London—and now here she was spread-eagle on the
hood of a flaming Pontiac in a cheap patent-leather bikini. "The
Hot Rod Issue" boasted a most offensive cover font. It's been
months since we last spoke, not because of anything that happened, but because I had been extremely busy with my collection
before the Overwhelming Event landed me here. Cunningham
turned the magazine on its side to look at a two-page spread,
which I found especially irritating.

"May I take a look at that when you're finished?" I asked him.

"Nope."

He continued to look at the pictures, ignoring me. As I said,
he's very good at that.

I stood and went for a leak, knowing very well that Cunningham would have to stop reading and jot it down in the logbook.
Which he did. But now I ached to get a better look at Olya. He
had to share it with me! *He must.* I paced my cell back and forth,
trying not to stare too hard at the magazine. Cunningham ignored

me as best he could, but soon enough I got him to pay attention. He let out a suggestive sigh.

"You know, I know her," I said to him.

"Who?" he said.

"Her. Olya. The girl on the cover."

"You don't know her," he said, as if it was totally impossible for a man like me to have known a girl like Olya.

"Of course I do. I'm a designer of women's wear in New York. Olya is a friend. She's even worked for me on several occasions."

"Bullshit."

"We're friends," I said.

This made him laugh.

"You really don't know who I am, do you?"

"Sure I do," he said. "You're a designer of women's wear in New York. Now go back to where you were before on the bed."

"You don't believe me," I said.

"Go lie back down."

I did as I was told.

Cunningham noted our exchange in the logbook.

"I want that book when I get out of here," I said.

"When you get out of here it'll be my gift to you."

Some time went by when I tried to think of nothing.

"What's she like?" Cunningham finally asked me.

"Who?" I said.

"Olya."

"Ah, yes. Olya. She's very beautiful."

"What else?"

"Lovely personality." I wouldn't give him the satisfaction.

"What does she look like for real?" he said.

"When I knew her her breasts weren't quite as full. They must have matured."

"What else?"

"What do you want to know?"

"Did you fuck her?"

"I refuse to answer that."

"You see. You don't know her. You're a liar."

"Just because I didn't fuck her doesn't mean I don't know her." I waited, and then I admitted, "We slept together. For a week, actually. But nothing ever happened."

"Let me guess," he said. "Because she didn't have a dick."

"Because we were friends. I don't expect you to understand."

"I know what I'd do if she were my friend."

"That's the very reason you can't be friends with a girl like that."

"Is that so?" he said. "I know what I'd do. Have her peel open my banana."

"You would."

"Then I'd look under the hood. Take my time. Rev her up. Check out her headlights."

"You lost me. You were talking about a piece of fruit?"

Cunningham went back to flipping through his *Maxim*. I sat back down on the bed and tried to think of something else, to no avail. It was now very important to me that Cunningham believe I knew her. I can't explain why, but I needed him to acknowledge that I was telling the truth.

"I can tell you her real name," I said, surprising even myself.

"What?"

"If you're so interested in Olya, maybe you'd like to know her real name."

"It's not Olya?"

I shook my head no.

"What is it, then?"

"You won't believe me anyway."

"Fuck you. Tell me."

"You'll only think I'm lying."

"Okay. I believe you. Okay? I believe you were some big shit in New York. Now spill it."

Cunningham was no longer ignoring me.

"I'll tell you if you let me look at that magazine," I said.

"Not a chance."

"Then never mind."

After a moment's hesitation he caved. "Okay. But you look at her spread only, and then you give it back. If you don't give it back, I'm gonna call the CO. And then you're fucked."

"That's all I would want. Just her spread."

"Tell me her real name first."

"Her real name is Olga," I said. "Olya is just a nickname for Olga."

"Olga?" He looked disappointed, flipping the magazine over to look at Olya's image on the cover.

"That's her real name."

"Olga is a terrible name."

"But she only goes by Olya. She has since she was a little girl. But you don't have to believe me," I said.

Despite his mean streak, Cunningham was a man of his word. He slid the *Maxim* through the slot in my cell door as promised. He was suddenly very interested in what I knew.

And so I began to tell him more about Olya. If a character witness is needed at my tribunal, let Olya Rubik be the first to swear by my harmless intentions. She knew me from my very first day in America. She introduced me to models and stylists as I tagged along with her on castings. She walked in nearly every one of my shows, my debut in Bryant Park included. When I needed a fit model on short notice, Olya was always there. She adored my clothes, my sense of style, and remained loyal and true over the years. Cunningham was only interested in our nights in bed together, and so I told him about how she read aloud the story of Holden Caulfield, the severely depressed boy runaway. I threw in what she wore to bed, the brand of cigarettes she smoked, her taste in men. "You think she'd be into me?" he wondered. Yes, I said. It wasn't a lie. Cunningham was very handsome. He could model catalog if he wanted to, I told him. Before I went to bed, I added one more memorable detail: the smell of her unwashed hair on her pillowcase at the end of a long day. Like dead roses.

The Canadian

Nay! I swear by the whole of New York City, by the begetter and all whom he begot, that I was created so that I could be tried with afflictions. For it says so right in my Qur'an. (Underlined courtesy of D. Hicks.) Now, as I've said, I'm no Muslim. In fact, with the exception of a weekly Vinyasa class I took back in New York, I've never gone in for anything spiritual. Glamour, fashion, sex, drugs—these were all too alluring for me. How could I subscribe to any organization that pointed its righteous finger at a hedonist?

Back in 2002, I had financial afflictions of a certain variety. These pains would come to haunt me for most of my career, and it would be my hunger for money, as they say when it comes to the immigrant mind, that would feed me into the hands of Homeland Security.

During fashion week I was still staying with Olya, and I snagged a few freelance gigs as a stylist's assistant. One was for the insurmountable Vivienne Cho, a designer of such elegant women's clothing that no one in New York at this time could topple her leaning tower of ready-to-wear. Behind her, in close second, was Philip Tang, who was a friend of mine from Manila. We both attended FIM, only Philip transferred after a year to Central Saint Martins in London, leaving me behind to fend for myself among all the other lame-os who were so intent on doing bridal wear for the rest of their lives.

Because of the impression I'd made on Vivienne I got hired on to do a few other designers' shows that week—Catherine Malandrino, who I absolutely adored; a young Zac Posen. Even Philip paid me to assist him during what became his most hectic season. He had received a grant from the CFDA[1] and was being courted by the president of Louis Vuitton – Moët Hennessy, Yves Carcelle. All of the supplies I needed to set up a workshop I was given by Philip at this time: a portable Singer, a form mannequin, a rotary cutter. The rest, thread and fabric and linings, I purchased on Fashion Avenue.

As the work petered out, I became intent on finding an apartment of my own. Since money was still tighter than the skinny jeans I wore around my size 30 waist, I settled for a tiny studio apartment in Bushwick, Brooklyn, right off the Kosciuszko stop on the J, M, Z. For anyone who worked in fashion, this was a kind of exile. Bushwick was a dangerous neighborhood on the cusp of hipster Williamsburg, my north star. It was unlike Williamsburg in that it refused to let go of its roots in high crime, to the dismay of the Corcoran Group real estate agents who were so determined to turn it into Bushwick *Heights*. Still, there were plenty of hipsters around cohabiting with the poverty-stricken natives, and I, fortunately or unfortunately, qualified as one of the former, because I was an artist and fashionable.

I first met Ahmed Qureshi, the benefactor, the mover and shaker, the bane of my existence, on the day I moved in. I was hauling Philip's form mannequin up the front stoop when a man in a white dishdasha opened the door. His gown was draped to his

1. Council of Fashion Designers of America.

ankles, and I saw that he was sporting a pair of fluorescent aqua socks, the once popular alternative to beach sandals.

"New tenant?" he asked. He was a foreigner too. Our skin color was the same deep sienna. From his accent I guessed that he was Pakistani. My family once had a maid from Karachi with similar inflections. But unlike her, this man had an additional British lilt that gave his speech a great deal of authority.

My own Filipino accent was slight. I spoke English with the rhythmic singsong of Tagalog punctuated by a California rise picked up from years of watching American television. Particularly the show *Beverly Hills, 90210.* Only when I was nervous, as I was at that moment, did my pronunciation stagger. I'd immediately slip into speaking like my parents—unable to pronounce the F or V consonants. I'd worked for years to correct this deficiency, but you can't fight who you are. "Just moobing in," I said. In my head I repeated the proper pronunciation. *Move. Moving. Moved.*

"Welcome to Evergreen Avenue," he said. "You'll find nothing evergreen about it. Who's this?" He tapped the mannequin I had tucked under my arm.

"Oh, this is a dress form. I'm a designer."

"Fantastic. I'm in the garment business myself. Imported fabric from Egypt, India, all over. Ahmed Qureshi. Pleased to meet you."

"Boy," I said, and we shook.

"Come, let me help you with your things."

"It's really not necessary."

"Don't be silly. A man extends his hand you should take it. After all, we're neighbors. I have the entire first floor."

I told him I didn't have much, just a few personal items like my suitcase, the Singer, a sewing kit, four or five bolts of fabric.

He grabbed what he could from the curb where the cab had dropped me off and followed me up to the second floor.

That first apartment wasn't much bigger than the cell I find myself in now. The kitchen boasted a cast-iron tub bolted to the hardwood floor. "Classical prewar," the Corcoran agent who rented it to me had called it. And for the price of six hundred dollars a month it came furnished with a full-size mattress, a bureau, and a decrepit old fan, all left behind by the former tenant. Because we were still in the midst of a heat wave this late in September, the agent threw in a preowned air conditioner as a signing bonus.

The little fan had been left on and was blowing hot air. Ahmed followed me in and placed my things down onto the floor. He said: "Your predecessor met a rather unfortunate end."

"Oh no. What happened?"

"He was executed. Right where you're standing now."

I sidestepped, instinctively.

"Two men broke in, tied him up in a chair, and ransacked the apartment. They found nothing. What do you expect? He was a street merchant. He sold little trinkets. Cell phone cases and the like. He didn't have anything. So they put two in his chest."

"Jesus."

"They left a note too, which they pinned to his forehead with a thumbtack. 'Go home Arabs' it said. The idiots. The poor guy was a Bangladeshi. And turning an ordinary homicide into a hate crime in this day and age will only get you an additional ten to fifteen. Am I wrong?"

"That's terrible."

"It's all true. Every word of it. This is the world we live in. I think that was his." Ahmed pointed to the fan, and it somehow took on a greater significance as it clicked twice and then jammed at the end of its 180-degree rotation. I turned it off.

"How did they get in?" I asked.

"How else? They broke down the door. I wasn't home, I was in Port au Prince with a young lady. Not my wife. But if I had been home I would have heard them. I'd have called the authorities. And who knows, that Bangladeshi could still be here today. Anyway, look at me going on. I'm scaring you. This kind of thing is a freak occurrence. In this building, ever since the homicide, we watch out for each other."

We shook hands. I didn't know if I completely believed the story about the Bangladeshi. As I would soon learn, Ahmed had a taste for embellishment.

Over the coming weeks I found work here and there for lesser designers through the connections I had made during fashion week. I dressed models and took Polaroids. I helped with impromptu shows, showcases, even trunk shows, ironing fifty pounds of crumpled dresses and pinning them on twenty Russian models in no time flat. It was all very repetitive, frankly, but I was excited by the contacts I was making in New York. Everyone worked or partied or slept with each other. The designers, the stylists, the makeup artists, the bookers, the models, the photographers, we were all part of an incestuous machine with one purpose: to create beauty.

Getting set up in Bushwick also enabled me to embark on my own enterprise: the collection I had been planning since I left Manila. I sewed at night and on my days off, starting with a fine-layered white dress, the skirt a matte satin over a soft wool slip.

The wool hairs adhering to the satin produced a natural clinging pattern. I felt I was on to something completely original.[2]

In Bushwick I was surrounded by struggling artists and musicians who came from middle-class backgrounds similar to mine. The neighborhood was an artsy barrio. We bartered things on the streets, gathered found objects. I acquired a full-bodied mirror from a man on McKibbin for a carton of Camel Lights. My worktable had once been someone's front door. It looked as if it had been kicked in by the cops. I loved the rough urban contrast to the elegant fabrics I'd cut on its surface. I was assimilating, you see. I wasn't just some fly-by gentrifier.

At night one could hear the real Bushwick come alive. Arguments abounded from the neighbors above or across the street: men calling women bitches, women calling men liars and cheaters, children wailing, and then all of them being momentarily drowned out by sirens.

One learned to tune all of this out.

Ahmed stopped by unexpectedly on a night when the couple above me were really going at it. It was late when he knocked, after ten, and I had been working since the afternoon and had no intention of letting up.

"You hear this upstairs?" he said. "How can you work through it?" He invited himself in.

"Should we do something?"

"Like what? There's nothing we can do. She'll call the cops, that's usually how it ends. Or she'll throw him out, and he'll be

---

2. Actually, this technique is known as *agugliatura*. Italian designers like Miuccia Prada have been doing it for years.

gone for weeks. What's the point, when she always takes him back? It's been going on for years." He helped himself to a look around my apartment. The cotton sheets strewn on my bed, my laptop, an iron steaming on my work table. Then there was the form draped in the fine-layered dress.

"Oh my, you really are in fashion. Are you a homosexual?"

"Excuse me?" I was so taken aback by his bluntness I grew defensive. "No," I said. "I like women. Blondes," I specified.

"Easy, I didn't mean anything by it. I know plenty of fashion people in my line of work, mostly male homos. I see that you're offended. Let me make it up to you. Since you're a designer—a talented one at that, as I can see from this lovely dress—allow me to offer you discounted fabrics at a bottom price. Consider it, when the time comes."

"Right. You said you were a fabric salesman."

"Of sorts. I don't like to put limitations on what I do. I have a finger in many pies. I do a little importing-exporting. I move things from point A to point B, with little interference from variable X. I'm a businessman. And yes, sometimes I have one of those fingers in the fashion pie. Lucky for you I have plenty of contacts in the industry. Especially in New York, London, and Dubai, the latter of which I am no longer welcome. A discrepancy with me and the sheikh's youngest daughter—a misunderstanding, naturally."

Each of Ahmed's stories seemed incredibly far-fetched to me at the time. But I never suspected I was dealing with someone who wanted to harm America. An arms dealer, please! I was a designer of women's wear. What would I know about arms? I saw through his stories, of course. I wasn't stupid. They were so obviously embellished, but his manner never struck me as dangerous. As he went on about the sheikh's youngest daughter and all the virgins he had had in Dubai, he claimed that he was also a wanted man in Yemen. "But who isn't these days!"[3] Ahmed made ridiculous comments like these all the time, and one had to learn to pay them no mind.

Especially when, say, dishes in the apartment above us were being smashed. We listened as a door slammed. The man was leaving. Suddenly there was a period of quiet that I wanted to take advantage of if Ahmed would only get out. But he turned to the form mannequin and began admiring my dress, rubbing the skirt with his dirty fingers.

"Careful, please," I said. "It's quite delicate."

"You're talented, Boy. I like the texture. What about men? I'm looking for a stylist myself."

"I'm concentrating on a women's line, solely. This is part of a new collection."

Ahmed swiveled the form around to inspect the back, with its V-cut opening that ran from the shoulders to the base of the spine. "Mmmm. This I like. I could do with a little more cleavage in the front, kind of like what you did here, but overall . . ."

"Well, it's unfinished. There's still a lot that has to be done."

"You ever design a suit?"

"In school," I said.

"Good. Because I want to commission you to make me two suits. The color I leave up to you, but they must appear Western, and radiate class. For this service I will pay you fifteen hundred

3. There is no evidence that Qureshi was a wanted man in Yemen, though the Dubai story bears some truth. The United Arab Emirates has had Qureshi on their watch list since 1999 for reasons unspecified.

dollars." Ahmed's hand had worked its way up to the form mannequin's breast, which he now cupped in his palm.

"That's very generous," I said. "But I couldn't. I'd be cheating you. Besides, you could go into Barneys and probably get two suits at that price."

"Yes, but they wouldn't be made for me. There would be other suits out there just like them. They wouldn't be originals. Call it crazy, Boy, but having possessions that are unlike any other in the world is very important to me. It's a symbol of status where I come from. A mark of prosperity."

"Really. Where are you from?"

"Canada."

As I said, I was able to overlook his lies no matter how blatant. I knew his kind didn't respond well to accusations. Our Pakistani maid at home had quit when my mother accused her of stealing washcloths out of our upstairs linen closet. The maid left the house that day swearing in her language, totally incoherent, except for one foreboding phrase she managed to utter in her poor English: "You'll pay por dis."

Besides, I understood Ahmed's desire for something original. I suffered a similar hang-up with Nike high-tops, and had gone to great lengths in the past to find pairs that were equally as rare—originals from the 1980s. Sometimes fashion is all about stature, and making the other guy feel inferior.

"I have to decline," I said, regarding the suits. "Please understand, but I'm very busy."

"Two thousand," he countered.

"There's so much time that goes into a thing like—"

"Twenty-one hundred."

"And it's been *so* long since I last—"

"Twenty-two fifty. Fabric included."

"Who knows if it would be any good?"

"Twenty-five. Including materials. And Boy, remember that I have plenty of contacts in the industry. In addition, I know how to return a favor. A true businessman. If you take the same care with me that you have given this gown"—Ahmed placed his arm around the form mannequin's waist, and they stood joined at the hip like two lovers—"you won't regret it."

"Two thousand five hundred dollars?"

"Look at me, you're gonna say no? You already hiked me up a thousand U.S. You know what you're doing. You're a businessman as much as you are a brilliant designer. You'll go very far. My mind's made up. Twenty-five hundred!"

I didn't want to design a suit, let alone two of them. I wanted to work on my own collection. But the money was significantly better than what I was making ironing dresses at trunk shows for upstarts I didn't really respect. Plus, I could get all of this done on my own time.

I suggested that we discuss fabrics another day, and then perhaps set up a time the following week to do a fitting. This was all still pretense, mind you. I didn't think he really had the money. And how could you trust a "Canadian" who was obviously from Pakistan or somewhere thereabouts?

"Listen, Boy," he said. "There's nothing to talk about. Classy and Western—the rest is up to you. Come by first thing tomorrow for the fitting," he said. "I have Wi-Fi and panini press. The whole ground floor of the building is mine."

On Memory

Those known knowns! If I may borrow a piece of logic from the U.S. defense secretary.[1] Those knowingly knowable knowns! They stand propped up in my way like roadblocks to the truth. A road I have been down over and over. I find myself in a dilemma of time versus truth, don't you see? At the present time in which I reveal these facts, I fear that they will be misconstrued, and taken in a manner that presents me as a liar, an ignoramus, or worse—terror's lackey, a coconspirator. Why should I be so afraid if I am completely innocent?

Because, because, because.

Because Ahmed Qureshi, aka Punjab Ami, the man who I naively took into my confidence as a fabric salesman, was arrested for selling bomb-making materials days before I was brought here to No Man's Land. My interrogator has revealed that Ahmed is being indicted for conspiring to acts of terror. "He will be convicted, and quickly," he said, during our reservation earlier today. (That's what they call our sessions together. Reservations. I am visited by a commanding officer, the CO, a day in advance, and

1. Now former U.S. defense secretary Donald H. Rumsfeld. "Reports that say that something hasn't happened are always interesting to me, because as we know, there are known knowns; there are things we know we know. . . ." –Defense Department briefing, February 12, 2002.

told that I have a reservation at such and such hour the following day. Being interrogated here is like trying to dine at Babbo.)

Yes, regarding Ahmed, there were certain degrees of doubt in my mind. Undoubtedly, yes. But as I sit here in my cell, filling in the blanks of the past few years, more blanks seem to crop up. One of the problems I'm having with the construction of this true confession is the remembrance of actual thoughts at the moment of their occurrence. It is impossible to remember exactly what I was thinking when I was thinking it. What was the exact thought that crossed my mind when I decided to leave my apartment and hop down the dilapidated staircase to meet with Ahmed on the matter of two suits? I wish I could just bite into a macaroon[2] like Flaubert,[3] and poof, it would all come flooding back to me like some irresistible dream. But I can't. This confession is composed of thought thoughts—those things we think we thought at the time we thought them. They are re-creations, composites of ideas we have reasoned and not the actual thoughts themselves. Because to remember an actual thought at the exact time it occurred in the brain would be utterly inconceivable. That is, unless I had that magical French cookie, but real life doesn't happen like it does in the books. In my world they shackle you to the ground and pump death metal into your ears till you recall being in your mother's womb, quite vividly, and that it was Dr. al-Zawahiri who did the C-section.

My interrogator understands all of this. He believes that for me to get at the true truth—the stuff of a surefire confession—I must

2. Madeleine.
3. Proust.

relive it again and again, play it over and over like a video in my head, and then expel it like a demon once I arrive at the closest representation. That's why he's made sure I have pen and paper with me at all times in my cell. Who knows when a moment of clarity will strike me?

I find it strange that my interrogator is so sympathetic toward my situation. Why does he treat me so? Maybe it is because he is part of a defeated minority himself. (He's a Greek, my special agent. Goes by the name of Spyro.)[4]

"Can I be honest?" said my Greek today. "I think you know more than you think you know."

He's a large man, my interrogator, with a taste for expensive suits. He obviously knows a thing or two about men's wear, so I must remember to be as specific as possible when I recount my forays into men's fashion with Ahmed Qureshi. My Greek's hairline has mainly disappeared, and the few curly black strands he has left up front mold together into a little patch resembling the Italian boot. Coincidentally, there's also a sunspot on his scalp right where Malta floats in the Mediterranean. He continued: "There are some things lodged so deep in our minds that we can't recognize them. Wouldn't you agree?"

"Come again?" I said.

"You know Dostoyevsky?"

"I've never met him," I said.

"You wouldn't have. He's dead," said Spyro.

This made me feel rather ignorant. Of course I had heard of

4. Special Agent Spyros Papandakkas of the FBI, lead investigator on the *Hernandez* case.

Dostoyevsky. *Notes from Underground*, *The Brothers Karamazov*, and the one about the idiot whose title escapes me.[5]

"You two have a lot in common," said Spyro. "He was sent to prison too."

"Lucky for him."

My interrogator is a real Russophile and will go on and on about Dostoyevsky and Tolstoy, as though these men were the greatest of all thinkers. He's even mentioned his admiration for the music of Chai Kaufsky.[6] I find it strange that an American investigator (of Greek heritage, no less) is so taken with all things Russian. But I'll admit that I too am an admirer of some of Russia's exports, particularly Alexandre Plokhov.[7] His militant, sexy outfits were quite an influence on my designs, as well as on my own personal style. I remember his store on Greene Street, with those thin little gothic sales boys and their angular haircuts.

"You know what Dostoyevsky once said?" he continued. "He said that there are things in every man's memory that he's afraid to divulge, even to himself. And he said it might even be the case that the more decent the man, the more substantial the accumulation of these memories." My interrogator looked down at his handmade shoes. Again I spotted the patch of hair on his broad forehead that formed the Italian boot. "When I was a kid," he said, "I threw a rock at a man's house just to do it."

A confession. "In the Greek isles?" I asked.

"In Perth Amboy, New Jersey," he said. "Anyway, it doesn't matter where. I broke a window. I didn't mean to. My brother was

5. *The Idiot* (1868).
6. Properly spelled *Tchaikovsky*.
7. Founder of the men's label Cloak.

with me. The thing was to hit the side of the man's house. We knew
him as our neighbor. I had nothing against him. It wasn't even
about him. It was about throwing a rock at a house just because.
When it was done, the man came over and told my father. He said
he saw me do it. He confronted me in front of my father. Of course,
I denied it. I lied. I had to. And then I lied to my father. I was too
embarrassed, because even I didn't know why I had done it. I
couldn't explain my actions. I threw the rock at the man's house
because it was there. Sometimes there are no reasons."

My interrogator removed a handkerchief from his pocket and
dabbed his forehead. The room was air-conditioned, but his excess
weight caused him to sweat a great deal.

"Forgive me," he said. "I started this story backward. Memory
sometimes works in reverse, don't you think?"

I didn't answer.

"Anyway, it was last Christmas when my brother reminded me
of this occasion, when I had thrown the rock at the neighbor's
house. He said, 'Don't you remember when you threw that rock?'
I said, 'What rock?' I didn't know what he was talking about. I
honestly couldn't remember. He told me the story again, as he
knew it. And again, I had no memory. I didn't think my own
brother was making it up, but I was convinced he was thinking of
one of his friends from when we were kids. I dismissed the story
without offending him, but for some reason it just wouldn't leave
my mind. And then, sometime after New Year's, it occurred to me.
I remembered. The rock in my hand. The throw across the road.
The shatter of the windowpane. My brother laughing. I recall the
particular time of day. My father's face when I swore to him I
didn't do it. I forget where I was when I remembered all this—I

could have been at the office, or on assignment somewhere—but suddenly my face went flush with embarrassment." Spyro stood up to take off his jacket. Then he sat back down, unbuttoned his sleeves, and rolled them up. He had a long scar running down the length of his left forearm. "You see, our tendency to make ourselves look better in disagreeable circumstances can be overwhelming. It can make us forget. What I'm most interested in is if there's anything you've forgotten."

And this is where we left off for the day. I was tasked to go back to my cell to remember all that I may have forgotten. Win wondered how it went with my Greek. "Fine," I told him. It seems that Spyro's intent is to inspire my confession. In a way, he wants the same thing I do. For all of this to be finished as soon as possible. For my confession to be submitted as evidence and for my tribunal to be underway.

And yet oblivion, not active remembrance, has become my sole means of survival after three weeks in No Man's Land. Not a day goes by where I don't try to forget where I am. It is not the guards who make this difficult but the other prisoners. Five times a day they pray. As soon as the sun rises, imagine! During prayer time I'll often sit up in bed, shut my eyes, and transport myself back to my former life. A fall fashion week in New York City. The white tents laid out across the lawn of Bryant Park. I venture in through the canvas flaps of the tent, past the ice sculptures of female torsos—nipples melting over avocado rolls, translucent vaginas dripping into mounds of pickled ginger. I navigate through the labyrinth of runways and the foray of flash photography, escaping backstage through an inviting satin curtain. Around my neck, a VIP pass: DESIGNER. Backstage is a different kind of frenzy, the workers scrambling to put on a show. I watch fifteen stylists do the hair and makeup of models too plentiful to count. Pulling, clipping, crimping, blowing, flattening, spraying. I summon up each model's face from my past. Olya and Dasha, Irina, Katrina, Marijka, Kasha, Masha—their white, cherubic young skin contrasted by such stark Eastern European bone structure. I inhale the aerosol of hairspray and am suddenly lifted off the ground, floating above the circus of backstage fashion until I hit the pillow-like ceiling of canvas above. I hold my breath, floating over a maddening sea of bare asses and thongs and hair, and look! There's Catherine Malandrino! Bonsoir, Catherine! Once I exhale, I free-fall and am deposited safely into a pile of Miu Miu handbags.

Open my eyes, and I'm still on my thin rubber mat.

Unlike one of Spyro's repressed memories, I can't just will away this cell, can I? And if I ever do get out of here, if I ever get my thoughts together in one plausible row, I doubt that I will ever be able to forget the memory of this place. The sounds alone will rattle in my mind forever. There is the chime of the razor wire outside. Dogs. Barking dogs coming from the other camps. Rats scurrying underneath our cells. Men are taken for reservations in the middle of the night, and so there are the sounds of their shackles, chains scraping along the metal floor. This of course wakes everyone on the cell block. We are kept between sleeping and waking. We are kept tired. There are the sounds of farts and belches from the other prisoners. Wailing, crying, yawning, grunting, every variation that can come from a human being. The night guards talk and pace the deck. A few times I have heard distant explosions. I thought we were under attack. Cunningham, my night guard, told me that the explosions were land mines left over from a forgotten war. They were being set off by natives of the island trying to flee for the confines of No Man's Land.

Imagine, people blown to bits trying to get in! Can such an act of brutality still be called irony?

Why am I in No Man's Land?

I've asked my interrogator.

The question still lingers in the air like the stench of a rat that has gone and died under my cell.

My fear is that we'll all get used to the stink.

Modus Operandi

Because I am guarded 24/7, I hardly ever interact with the other prisoners. Sure, they surround me on the prison block, but Win or Cunningham will prevent them from speaking to me. "Don't talk to him," Cunningham has yelled at my neighbor, who has tried to whisper things into my cell. Anyhow, the man doesn't speak any English. And even if we could understand each other, what would I say to him? Unlike you, I am innocent.

Even during rec hour I am kept apart from the other captives. Once a week we are let out of our cells and taken to the prison yard. It is called rec hour by the guards even though it only lasts fifteen minutes. The remaining forty-five are spent in transport to and from the prison yard. I am suited up with chains, my hands and feet, then moved outside to yet another cage of my own, while the others are piled together in communal chicken-wire confinement. During rec, Win, my day guard, is relieved from duty, and I am escorted by a different MP. Today, a woman.

The fencing overhead is covered with blue tarp. Rays of sun break through its little holes. It is mostly sunny in No Man's Land. We have not had a drop of rain since I've been here. And yet the air is disgustingly humid. Rarely a sea breeze.

Just beyond the prison yard is a dirt expanse. At one end is a soccer goal with no net. Off on the sidelines a stationary bicycle covered in dust. A deflated ball midfield. We're not allowed out of our cages, so the field is only there in plain view as a reminder of what we can't have.

It is clear by the way they look at me through my cage that the other prisoners have had some trouble adapting to my presence. They think I'm a plant, a mole, sent here to spy on them. And I don't even speak any Arabic. How could I possibly spy on them without knowing a word they are saying?

It all comes down to motive, I am told.

Motive is something my Greek and I discuss quite often, in fact. What was my main motive in getting involved with Ahmed? It is yet another question that lingers throughout our sessions, and one that haunts this true confession. I was a designer of women's wear, so why on earth did I decide to make two custom men's suits for a stranger? What was my motive?

They often say it turns the world round, and that in America it can be made hand over fist. I did it for the money! I was swayed by the necessity to pay my way, which quite honestly I had not been doing up until that point. Even though I was regularly booking jobs as a stylist, I was still living off the fat of my homeland—Momma and Dada; my two parents back home were sending me a monthly allowance of one thousand dollars. And I don't need to tell you that in 2002 this amount didn't go very far, considering the cost-of-living expenses in New York City. One needed to pay rent, eat, buy new clothes every season to keep up with ephemeral fashions, go clubbing, pay cover charges, tip, buy drugs for the after parties. I know this all sounds sophomoric, but such is the fashion industry. To make the necessary contacts and to develop an insider's network, a large amount of time and money needs to be devoted to nightlife. You need to put in the face time. And face time comes at a cost.

Let me here dispel the stigma of the scrappy dark illegal: the small man-child who waits in the shadows undetected while you finish your entrée. We do not all come to America with the sole intention of taking all the American jobs at a lesser hourly rate. That is a bias, a slander, a belittlement, and gratuitous! Like the fullest-blooded American, I knew that the key to my success was capital, and making Ahmed's suits for twenty-five hundred dollars would be profit, pure and simple.

Moreover, the earliest seeds of my passion for clothes lay in the business of suits. As a child I spent each summer working for my Tito Roño in Cebu. He was a tailor by trade. A family man. He had a wife and two adopted children from the provinces. He was also a closet cross-dresser. Once when he bent over I saw that underneath his trousers he had on a pair of women's panties. I immediately learned that my uncle was a little special, that he was incognito and hiding something from all of us. (By no means does wearing women's panties make one a homosexual. Yet I made the only judgment I could at that age—the same judgment my fellow classmates made upon me in the schoolyard.)

Lying on a steel desk in front of a large industrial fan, I watched my uncle work. Each day I held an ashtray for clients who stood still in front of a three-part mirror while Tito Roño wielded his measuring tape, the one he always wore around his neck like a doctor with stethoscope. If I was to look over while my uncle was taking an inseam, I could expect to catch sight of his pastel under-pants stretching past the point of no return—the space between the femur and the lower back where American college girls often get tramp stamps. Even his clients espied his little satin secret. Some of the men pretended it wasn't there, some looked to me for guidance, some smiled and just continued smoking their cigarettes, occasionally burning me with the ash they flicked in my direction. Yet all of them returned time and again, so loyal, so admiring of my uncle's way with suits.

So what was there for me to like? Not much. Tito Roño's shop was cramped and smoky. Rolls of fabric were piled into skewed towers, each one threatening to topple over like a heated game of Jenga. Even then I thought suits lacked the luster and pulse of the dress, the medium I would devote my life to.

I did understand, however, that my uncle was very well respected. The fact that he was *someone* at a time when I was *no one.* And that we were related, of all things, and that people would recognize me, the tailor's nephew, as I made my rounds about the city. All because of my Tito Roño, who wore women's panties. Here was *someone*, I thought. And I understood fashion as its cause.

Among some two hundred names in my uncle's Rolodex were several politicians, once high up in the Marcos administration, as well as a few film actors I recognized. They were the upper echelon of Filipino surnames: Rosaleses, Aquinos, Cuarons, even actual Marcoses, most likely relatives of the exiled ex-president.

These were the high times, the years when my uncle's shop thrived. Nearly a decade and a half later, as Ahmed stood before me with an offer I couldn't refuse, I felt those high times return to me.

I admit that on the evening of my encounter with Ahmed, after he left my room, I had my doubts. But any doubts about his character were overwhelmed by an awareness that I was about to make some good money. I suppose I was immature in matters of money. Sure, I had sold a few dresses here and there to boutiques back home, but I hadn't really turned a profit. My financial savvy was stunted. And for this I blame my parents. They spoiled me rotten as a child and as a twenty-five-year-old man. So however unlikely a true deal with Ahmed seemed, however much of a pathological liar he was, I couldn't discount the matter of twenty-five hundred dollars, the amount I was being offered to tailor the two suits. I kept thinking about the sum total, depositing the amount into my account and then withdrawing it in five-hundred-dollar increments day by day until I spent it all. It seemed like enough money to last me forever, even though it would last me only four days.[1] This was the American dream thrown at me, without asking.

I spent that entire night dreaming of ATMs scattered around Manhattan, their screens blinking at me: Would you like a receipt for this transaction? Or, would you like to make a balance inquiry? Long white scrolls of paper fluttered out of the machines and into the night air to form a light drizzle of confetti. Meanwhile, I skipped along Seventh Avenue, trying to catch the flimsy scrolls out of the sky while singing a show-tune rendition of the Wu-Tang Clan's "C.R.E.A.M." ("Cash Rules Everything Around Me / C.R.E.A.M. / Get the money / Dollar dollar bill y'all"). On one of these receipts I saw that printed very lightly in indigo ink was my birth name (Boyet Ruben Hernandez; I was named after my father, Dr. Boyet Hernandez Sr., Ear, Nose, and Throat), my account number, and an available balance of $2,500, the exact sum Ahmed had offered to pay me. The ledger balance, however,

---

1. Five days, at the very least, according to the math he cites above.

was much more extravagant: $250,000 or $2,500,000 or more. It was hard to make out the exact figures in this lucrative dreamland; all the zeros ran down the length of the receipt in an infinite trail.

I swear to you, I had no preconceived intentions besides making the dough to infiltrate the New York fashion scene.

I considered Ahmed's offer for all of one night, then did exactly as he commanded. The next morning I was headed down one flight of stairs to his apartment, neither in excited two-at-a-time leaps nor in slow, doubtful intervals. I moved at an average tempo, calm and collected. I was approaching this new business deal like a levelheaded professional, weighing in my mind both the pros and cons: on the one hand, my neighbor—a pathological liar (but not an arms dealer, I assure you!)—on the other hand, cash, cold and hard. These were the known knowns.

Now, it would be impossible to pinpoint my exact thought thought at the precise moment I arrived at Ahmed's that morning. But I do remember this, a most telling action: My hand froze, halted in the air, before I knocked on the man's door. There you have it—an outward sign of hesitation. Actions, or in this case inaction, can sometimes speak volumes, as I've told my interrogator.

And how could I have turned away? To abandon my course at this stage would have been cowardly. I am many things to many people, as you will soon learn, but one thing I am not is a coward. This man was my neighbor, after all. The least I could do was conduct the fitting. Imagine the embarrassment I would suffer by not showing up and having to see him around the building after. He lived on the first floor. I'd have to pass his apartment twice daily at the absolute minimum.

This *was* opportunity, as they say, and so . . . I knocked.

"I was about to start taking bets with Yuksel on how long you were going to stand out in the hall," Ahmed said. "I was watching you through the peephole."

Ahmed stood in the doorway in what looked like the same dishdasha he had worn the night before. The three buttons at his neckline were undone, revealing a nest of white chest hair in the shape of a large diamond.

I actually admired the gown's free-flowing elegance. It was airy and had a lot of movement. It somehow covered up the fact that underneath was a hairy, stinking man. This was fashion's power, after all. To disguise our most hideous weaknesses. I took a mental note of the way the dishdasha draped over his shoulders and belly and how, even though it was white, it was surprisingly slimming.

"Come in, Boy, please. Make yourself comfortably at home."

I entered the foyer. Ahmed wrapped his free arm around my shoulder and pulled me in for a friendly cuddle. His body odor was rancid.

"Are you a betting man, Boy?"

"I'm sorry?"

"Betting. Are you a betting man?"

"I suppose not," I said.

"How about horses? Do you like horses?"

"I like horses, yes."

"What am I saying? Everybody likes horses. I can get us an owner's box in Saratoga. You don't believe me?"

"No. I didn't say that."

"If I wanted to I could make a phone call and we'd be in

Saratoga instantly, betting on all the thoroughbred beauties. Ever
see those brunettes in their big fucking hats?" He spread out his
arms to demonstrate the width. "Like this."

"We're talking about the horses?"

"Ha! Yuksel, you see what I was telling you about this guy?
Yuksel. Yuksel!"

I heard someone gag and hack and spit in the far room. Then
I heard a stream of urine and deduced that Yuksel was a man.
The pee came from a considerable height.

The apartment itself was a horrific mess but sizable enough to
house a small sweatshop. The four original first-floor units had
been gutted to form one giant temple of disorder. Only a dilapidated wall remained as a division between two main rooms. The
foremost had several large wooden crates marked FRAGILE. Now, I
won't simply play the victim of my own tale. Here was a man who
I knew had been concealing something about his origins. Much
more than that, he was a Muslim in the year 2002. I tried my
damnedest not to give in to stereotypes, but with respect to the
truth—for this is a confession—I was not at ease in this man's
home. I won't go so far as to make accusations, but I did curiously
inquire as to the contents of those "fragile" crates, and the sacks
of earth that lined the walls in between small piles of sheetrock
and copper. "Cedar," he said of the sacks throughout the apartment. And in truth, yes, I picked up on their woodsy scent. It
overtook Ahmed's rancid body odor. As for the crates, I was told
they were packed with art. Paintings and sculptures by Pakistani
artists. "I can move anything within reason out of Pakistan," he
said, which confirmed my suspicion that he was Pakistani.

A carpet of bubble wrap with all of the bubbles decompressed led us into the far room, the living quarters.

"Pardon our appearance," Ahmed said. "We're renovating."

The centerpiece was a grand piano surrounded by a few upturned milk crates. In the back, next to the small kitchen area, was a bathroom visible through hollowed-out walls. I could see Yuksel in front of the toilet with his back turned, shaking off. He reminded me of a snake in a cage, a great boa. "Hee," he seethed as he looked at me over his shoulder. He was smiling. Ahmed said something to him in Arabic, but Yuksel didn't respond. Once he flushed and came out of the bathroom, revealing himself to me in proper daylight, I saw that the little devil was still smiling. A birth defect, I would later learn— a permanent smile that made him appear as if there were some joke going around. It made one feel very self-conscious, though in truth, he was a shy man, and moved past me quickly into the front room with his head down, concealing that demonic grin.

"Don't mind Yuksel. He'll be working in there while we have our breakfast."

"Is there something wrong with his face?" I asked, in the politest tone I could muster.

"He's just happy. Come, take a seat at the piano."

Ahmed went to the kitchen area, where he prepared some coffee. His odor began to dissipate. I sat at the piano as directed, resisting the urge to press on the keys. Even while not being played they seemed to produce music with their silence. I pressed my foot down on one of the pedals and felt the piano's drone.

"I play myself," Ahmed said. "Mainly show tunes. Go ahead, try me. And I'll tell you if I can play it."

I decided I would humor him. "How about something from *West Side Story?*"

He stopped what he was doing suddenly, and his face turned rather serious. It frightened me. "Dare is a place fur'uzz," he sang. "Anyplace fur'uzz." His fingers lightly tapped the air.

It occurred to me that this didn't prove he could play the song, or the piano. "Soomewheeeeerre. Soomehoooowww."

"Nicely done," was all I could think to say.

"See, I told you I could play anything."

"Indeed."

Ahmed poured the coffee and brought it over to the piano.

"Boy," he said, "since we're going to be in business together, allow me the privilege of your full name."

"I was named after my father, actually. Boyet Ruben Hernandez."

"It already sounds famous! As I said last night, I have no doubts about the limits of your success. You'll go far, my friend. Here's to you."

I raised my coffee, then took a sip.

"Now may I inquire—and forgive me if I'm being rude—where you are from. Wait, don't tell me. This is a little game I like to play. I call it 'country of origin,' just like it says on the passports. I will start with your accent, or lack thereof. I detect a slight U.S. colonization in your speech. You've learned an American English, not British, from a very early age. Perhaps even simultaneously with your native tongue. Your English is nearly flawless, but there is a slip in the pronunciation of your Fs as Ps. Only sometimes. It's your tell."

I must say I was insulted. I took pride in how I'd been able to suppress my native tongue. Ahmed came closer, beckoned me to stand, and began to size me up. "Then there is your height. You're a petite one. A man-child. But you have a big spirit. An unnameable proudness without a hint of entitlement." He latched on to both my arms and smoothed them over. "There are your hairless arms, and under your shirt, a chest bare like a woman. Your legs are smooth too, as if you just shaved in a warm bath moments ago." I swallowed the bitter taste of Colombian bean. He leaned in closer to where I could feel the baked air of his nostrils. He examined my face from the front and then the profile and said, "No beard, a whisper of a mustache. I know your people well. No one can say '*puck* it' with more brio than the *P*ilipinos. Am I right?"

I nodded, relieved as he let go of my arms. He patted me on the shoulders and returned to the kitchen.

"I spent a lot of time in your country in the early nineties. Manila and the southern provinces. It's a wonderful republic. My business takes me all over, especially to countries in economic and political turmoil. I don't have to tell you. Labor's cheap and the resources are for the taking. Ninety-three was my best year. I made a million dollars in Malaysia. It was very hard to do at the time. A lot of people said it couldn't happen. But I made my million. Ninety-four was not so good. I went through a painfully expensive divorce. It dampened much of the previous year's successes."

I should have stopped myself right there. I should have put down my coffee and excused myself. How could I have been so naive? For if I only knew then what I know now! That the U.S. Department of Defense does not take these things lightly. That an innocent conversation on origins could be used as sufficient evidence to be detained by the Department of Homeland Security, or as conclusive evidence of conspiring by DoD, depending on who you ask. I should have inquired into *which* southern provinces Ahmed had spent time in and, more specifically, had he ever been to western Mindanao (immediate red alert). Everyone knows that's where the Abu Sayyaf Group[2] (DoD-certified terrorists) rage jihad in an attempt to stake out an independent Islamic state in the middle of the Pacific. If only I had inquired, maybe I would have felt fear of this man, and I could have gotten the hell out. But I swear to you, I did not know then what I know now. According to the defense secretary's schema, my situation in Ahmed's living room resembled a known unknown—that is to say, I knew there were some things that I did not know, and that was okay by me, at the time. I saw no reason to pry into Ahmed's business or past.

"Sheela took the business and the flat in London," he continued. "She would have gotten custody of the kids too, but we never had any. It was better that way, for their sake. She had an incredible lawyer, a Jew. Israelson. They called him 'the Shovel.' I suspect she was balling him. I prepare the paninis now."

I was distracted by Ahmed's somber tone as he lamented over his marriage. He had me feeling sorry for him, and so I put aside any lingering suspicions. Instead, I turned my attention back to the piano, pressing the keys. What a simple man I was!

Ahmed shouted something from the kitchen that was hard to ignore. "Fucking Allah of prickdom! My hand! My fucking hand!"

"What happened?"

"I burned my fucking hand on the damned panini maker."

Yuksel came running in from the other room with his head

2. Abu Sayyaf, meaning "bearer of the sword" in Arabic, is a militant organization linked to Osama bin Laden and al-Qaeda, according to White House officials.

down. "Hee," he seethed. Ahmed shouted something at him in Arabic and Yuksel opened the freezer and brought out what looked like a frozen pork butt. Ahmed smacked it out of Yuksel's hands. The quick devil ran to the bathroom, then emerged with some gauze and a rusty first-aid kit. Now I felt sorry for Yuksel too. Even in a situation where someone had been severely burned he was incapable of showing any emotion besides glee. He must hurt on the inside, I thought, but how could he show this to the rest of the world?

"Boy, my apologies. Why don't you distract yourself while I bandage this inflammatory. Please, keep fiddling with the piano. Lunch will be ready in a moment. Perhaps when I am done nursing my hand I will play something for you, yes?"

Yuksel tended to the wound, applying ointment and wrapping Ahmed's hand with gauze.

"Gently, stupid," Ahmed instructed.

After Yuksel finished he was directed to the other room once more. I watched him pace back and forth from afar, muttering something under his breath. He had a damaged soul, I was almost sure of it. The memory of this reminds me of someone here in No Man's Land, one of the other prisoners who gets his own cage, as I do, during rec hour. This rabid dog ambles to and fro in almost the exact same manner. He's not quite right in the head and has been honored by the guards with a nickname of his own: Retard.

Despite the drama the panini burn had provoked, I found Ahmed's sandwich to be quite satisfying, though I couldn't help but notice that the panini contained a good deal of ham. What little I knew then of the Islamic community I had learned through television, watching the conflict between the Philippine army and the Islamic jihadists in the south unfold into mayhem. And so I wasn't too well versed in Muslim custom. I did know, however, that they prayed facing Mecca a couple of times a day, and that pork and booze were outlawed at some point in their history.

I watched Ahmed devour his panini. I looked back over to where the frozen pork butt had landed on the floor. Condensation was building on its plastic wrapping. My curiosity over Ahmed's dietary practices became too much. I just couldn't keep my mouth shut. I had to ask about the swine. "This is delicious, Ahmed. Is it ham?"

"Boar's Head."

"Mmm. Wonderful. Pardon my ignorance, but I thought as a Muslim you weren't allowed any pork."

"Ah, I know how I must appear. But Boy, please, don't be fooled by my dress. I do not fear Allah. And as for the Qur'an, I can't say that I'm much of a fan. This garb I am wearing is just my house gown. I'm no Muslim. Maybe once upon a time. Now I'm just a Canadian."

I let the last bit float in the air. Even though I had never met an actual Canadian, it was all too obvious that Ahmed was lying. So obvious, in fact, that I thought he was testing me to see if I'd call his bluff. It's hard to finger what I felt next, but I was suddenly compelled by something juvenile, and the only move that could put my unease at rest was to trap him in his own lie.

"What part of Canada did you say you were from?" I asked.

"I didn't." Ahmed's mouth was full, so he politely covered it with his hand. "Why? Are you familiar with the area?"

"Me? No. I've never been to Canada. I don't even have a proper winter coat."

"You won't need one. Layer. Layering is the key. I'm from a

little corner in Nova Scotia. A mountainous region where the sun stays up for six months at a time. At the end of this six months it goes down in a glorious sunset. Everyone comes out of their homes—huts and igloos, what have you—and we all watch it descend. It lasts for forty-five minutes or so. And then we have six months of night. Complete darkness. Crime goes up during this half of the year. Such is Canada."

"Fascinating," I quipped. "Doesn't sound like Canada at all."

"Rest assured. It is."

After a while I took to his BO the way one gets used to the aroma of a New York subway car. We collected measurements. Aside from Ahmed's bulbous gut, which was absolutely disgusting, he was actually in decent shape. I wrapped my tape around his body with haste. Arms, legs, inseam, chest, waist, neck. The figures began to shape the garment in my head. I envisioned the cut and color, then the inklings of a pattern.

Confident now in what I was doing, I stood behind Ahmed and spoke to him through the mirror that he had propped up against the piano. "I want the suit to be snug," I said. "Cinched at the waist. That doesn't mean tight. I want to retain the classical shape of the male torso but work with the contours of your body. I don't want the suit to look too young. It should be distinguished. I want it to mold with your age. Not work against it. A lot of this will rely on the right pattern and color."

"Yes, yes. I think that sounds wonderful. Go on."

"I want to try one suit double-breasted. You'll wear it with a wide tie. A suit for conducting business. Like you were saying last night. The second one will be completely different. Perhaps a one-button with a big opening. What do you think? You have a long torso, so we'll position the button a little higher than usual, above your navel." I showed him where. "It'll normalize your proportions and cover your stomach. You can wear it to a business meeting late in the day, and then go straight out for a fine dinner. It'll be versatile. Chic yet easy and uncomplicated. After dinner you can take off the tie and go out for a drink. At the bar, a woman brushes her nails against your lapel. 'Hard day?' she says. And then she leans her head on your shoulder and whispers something seductive into your ear. 'Let's get out of here.'"

"Boy, this is why I picked you. I knew you knew more than you let on. How did I know? I'm no idiot. And even if I were, I would still see that before me stands a fashion genius. Eh? When I saw that beautiful gown up in your room, I thought to myself, a man who can design such a thing of beauty must know a thing or two about everything else in between."

He then called over to his assistant in Arabic.

Yuksel reappeared with a white envelope. Inside was payment in full. Twenty-five hundred dollars in cash. Ahmed never handled money.

My memory fails me here. What I did with the rest of the day is one big blank. Funny how we can only remember certain things. It's what my special agent calls selective significance.

An addendum to my earlier theory on memory, vis-à-vis thought thoughts. To recollect everything in one's past is to hold oneself to an unreachable standard. It just can't be done. The sponge that is the mind will gather details that are interesting, odd, pleasant, etc. A new experience will have all sorts of these attributes, and so the mind remembers them with or without a conscious host (the person). We may not be able to recall these memories right away, as was the case in Spyro's reflection on his incident with the rock from childhood. And we certainly can't recall the darkest memories without meeting some sort of resistance, like trauma. It occurs to me now that in day-to-day existence events simply don't have much significance, and therefore we forget the majority of our lives.

My special agent seems to understand all of this. He's been very patient and accommodating.

Strange. I think in another life we could have been friends.

The Two Suits

I don't have to tell my special agent how suits are made. He's a very well-dressed man, as I'm sure I've mentioned. During our first reservation he wore a single-breasted light wool suit, quite breathable during the month of June. Now that it is nearly August he's switched into a light cotton summer affair. In the left breast pocket he keeps his silk hanky tastefully folded. The sleeves show just enough cuff. The jacket hemline rests perfectly at the top of his thighs. For a man of his size, proportions need to be balanced just right.

Back in 2002, I knew something about proportions. They were foremost in mind as I sketched out my ideas for Ahmed's suits. The two designs I settled on were throwbacks to the sixties: thin lapels, snug sleeves, pants cuffed above the ankles. The double-breasted suit would be cut with a light gray wool in a plaid pattern. For the other, the black one-button, I would stitch Ahmed's initials in gold onto the left breast pocket. It would be a little something extra for my new client, the defining touch of the jacket.

AQ, it would say.

Having merely collected ashes in Tito Roño's shop as a boy, I didn't quite know what I was doing when it came to menswear. It had been my own leap with the truth to tell Ahmed I'd designed men's clothing in school. I had made a men's three-quarter trench in Outerwear as a second-year but never a whole suit! So the task at hand was an exercise in imitation. I was borrowing rather than generating ideas of my own. To be perfectly frank, menswear was boring. I am a dress man, through and through, and it was dresses I kept returning to between fits and starts of composing Ahmed's suits.

The dress is a performance—its only responsibility is to the moment. It is elegant and ephemeral. It can't sustain a woman's body for very long. Women's changes are far too radical. In couture, some dresses can be worn for only a few hours, max. What's the saying? Elegance is a dress too dazzling to dare wear it twice.[1]

Whenever I finished a garment I needed to see it in action, moving around, before I could put it on the rack. This was all part of the creative process. I needed the opinion of a woman's body before I made my revisions. Each dress was a work in progress, even after the catwalk. Not until a dress landed in the showroom was it truly finished. Here is where I had already formed the habit of deferring to Olya. My darling Olya, who most recently appeared on the cover of *Maxim*. She was my fit model, coming all the way out to Bushwick to try on my clothes. By the end of September 2002, in addition to my white, fine-layered dress, I had enhanced two or three other looks from my Manila days that I wanted to see on her.

"I have to tell you, Boy, this is not so nice, this neighborhood," Olya said, on her third visit to my studio. She was getting undressed.

1. Said by a young Yves Saint Laurent.

"What do you mean? It's not so horrible. It's close to Williamsburg," I said.

I gathered the layered dress as Olya held out her arms. Together we put it on over her head. I zipped her up in front of the mirror and made some adjustments to the skirt so that it assumed its intended shape. This would become my inside-out dress, a hallmark of the (B)oy Fall Collection '04, though the resemblance would be apparent only to the most trained of eyes.[2]

"I saw a drug peddler outside," she said. "A hideous man with an eye patch. He was distributing pills from a prescription bottle. People formed a line, holding out their hands like it was holy communion."

"Oh that's just Roddy, he's harmless. It's methadone he's selling. It's prescription." It made me uneasy, imagining her prancing around Bushwick, but I was trying to make the best of it.

"Addicts make my skin crawl," said Olya.

"Try walking," I told her.

She paced the room in heels.

"You have any blow?" she asked.

"I'm out."

"We should get some if we go out tonight. There's a party at Spa. Steven Meisel will be there."

"How does it feel?"

Olya stopped in the mirror and looked at herself. "It's beautiful. I love it."

"Seriously?"

2. It was a variation of this dress that the actress-singer-songwriter Chloë wore to the 2005 Grammys, lifting Boy and his label into the public sphere.

"Yes. It's totally elegant, you know? Not like slut."

"How does it feel in the waist? Is it too snug?"

"No, it's perfect."

I felt so happy at that moment I started to weep, something I did whenever a real friend complimented my work. "I'm so glad you like it. Take it off and let's try on something else."

"Look at you, darling," she said. "You're such a bitch. Don't cry."

"I'm just so happy. I can't help it."

Someone knocked. There was only one person it could be. Ahmed had a way of interrupting the purest moments of my ambition.

"Oh shit," I said under my breath.

"Who is that?"

"Guess. It's probably Ahmed."

"Who's Ahmed?"

"He's a client. I'll get rid of him."

As soon as I opened up, Ahmed said, "You've been crying. What's the matter?"

"Sorry, I have a friend over. We're doing a fitting." I stepped back so that Ahmed could see Olya in the white dress.

"My dear," Ahmed said to Olya, "my most sincere apologies. Allow me to introduce myself, and then I will be on my way. I am Ahmed Qureshi, garment salesman."

"Olya, international model."

It was like they were speaking the same language. Olya held out her hand and Ahmed took it and bowed his head. With Olya so elegantly dressed and Ahmed in his same soiled dishdasha, the moment gave me an impression of a child's fairy tale. Ahmed, the foreign king, bowing down to Olya, the Polack princess.

"Enchanté, my dear," he said. "Allow me, if you would, to get a look at you in this most appealing gown."

"It's a dress," I said.

"Same difference," he said.

Olya did a 360, putting on a pouty face. She liked the attention.

"Careful, my dear. At this age my heart can't take such stimuli from a beautiful gel."

"Oy, you're big talker," she said.

This made him laugh. "Boy, this dress looks familiar." He snapped his fingers in rapid succession. "This is the one from the other night. I remember the open back. I see you took my advice and gave it a little more *umpff* in the chest. Pardon me, Olya. I don't mean to speak as if you weren't in the room."

"It's okay. I'm a professional."

"My dear, you're too much for me. May I borrow this man for one minute."

Ahmed and I stepped out into the hallway.

"I'm sorry I haven't gotten back to you," I said, "but I really don't have time right now. I have Olya here—"

"Two seconds," he said, nonchalantly.

"Okay."

"She is your gel?"

"My what?"

"Your *gel*. She's not your gelfriend?"

"Oh, my *girlfriend*. No, no, she's just a friend."

"She's beautiful. You should think about it. For you. Anyway, I'm not here to breathe down your back. The artist must work." Ahmed was always remarking on how great an artist I was, when really he didn't know a thing about me. He'd seen one dress. "I only have a small favor to ask. I have an engagement approaching. It requires my vital presence. Meaning to say, I'm expected to show my mug, and I have to RSVP by tomorrow and decide if I want the chicken or salmon plate. You know how these things go. The fish at these functions, what can you do? Anyway, it's a business-casual affair, tie optional, but I'd very much like to show up in one of your anticipated designs. It would mean a lot to me, Boy. And it would certainly make an impression on a few others in attendance. Some very important people will be in the room. So, what I mean to say is, I need a suit by Friday. Can you produce?"

It didn't seem possible with Friday only three days away. Although back at FIM I had squeezed out an entire thesis collection in three days' time. I pulled all-nighters dyeing fabric and sewing two looks a night. But this was a suit we were talking about. Suits took time. They had more layers, more structure, lining, pockets, padding. Not to mention I hadn't ever made one.

"No, I can't do it," I told him.

"I know what you're feeling, Boy. This is not what you signed up for. I know. I didn't intend to put you in such a position. But look, what is Friday? Friday is only a day. Wednesday, Thursday, Friday. Am I right?"

"I'm just not sure you'll get the quality you'd otherwise get if I had more time. For the money you're paying me it should be perfect. Two weeks. I can commit to two weeks."

"Beby, look at you. You're all flustered. Listen, two weeks from now is what? A Tuesday. I need a suit by Friday. This Friday. Something dressy. Yes? Friday would be essential. So how much?"

"It doesn't matter. It's not about money."

"Name your price, eh? Friday delivery. How much? Two hundred?"

I shook my head. "You're not hearing me. It's *time* I need."

"Three hundred? That's twenty-eight total, Boy. That's a fair price. Twenty-eight and I take a bath on the fabric. A twelve percent markup. You just have to deliver *one* by Friday, remember. Take your two weeks on the other. Hell, take more, what do I care?"

"No."

"Okay. Let's get creative. Three thousand for the whole caboodle. There. You just made five hundred, and I'm still considering it a favor to me."

He was a persuasive salesman. An extra five hundred dollars would basically cover another month's expenses in Bushwick. And the rest could go toward a deposit on a new apartment. I was desperate to move into Williamsburg, where I knew I truly belonged.

So there I was, looking after my own interests. But isn't that why we do anything? As citizens of modernity we're always trying to better our social status, right down to the smallest detail. Luxury, comfort, it's all a part of getting ahead. If that's a crime, then I'm guilty as charged.

"I'll need an overlock machine," I said.

"What's that?"

"It's a kind of sewing machine. And I'll need a button puncher and a new cutting board."

"Done. Expense it. I'll reimburse you."

"Fine. Three thousand plus the new equipment. I'll keep receipts."

"Receipts *reeshmeets*. Just tell me. We have trust, no?"

"Yes. We have trust."

"So just tell me, beby. We won't let money come between us. This is a special thing we have. It's casual. Don't worry about nickels and dimes. Change is for tolls."

Ahmed was beginning to grow on me. Perhaps this is more evidence of my naïveté, but he made it his goal to banish all the usual formalities that came with a business deal. With him it was your word, and nothing else mattered. No signatures. No contracts. He made you believe that a trust had been established from the very start. And from time to time he would check in on that trust by asking about its general welfare. He never wanted our thing to feel stiff or formal.

"All it takes is the right incentive, Boy. You'll get the extra five hundred plus damages when you deliver on our arrangement."

Back inside I found Olya wearing a black organza dress. She was putting on lipstick in the mirror. Tangerine. Whenever she was bored she would always put on more makeup.

"I liked your uncle," she said.

"He's not my uncle. Oh God, Olya, what have I done?"

"Whatever it is, I'm sure it's not as bad as you're making it out to be. You're so anxious, Boy. Just like my mother. The bitch. Always worrying."

"I'm so fucked. Where are my cigarettes?"

"You don't smoke."

"I do when I'm stressed."

"Here, then. Have mine." She reached into her purse, threw me a soft pack of Kools, and went back to doing her lips.

My first lesson as an American entrepreneur: learning to live with your decisions.

"I can't go to that party tonight, Olya. I have to work."

"Then can I wear this?" She turned to me in the dress. "It'll only be for a few hours."

"Will you bring it back unscathed?"

"What does that mean? 'Unscathed.'"

"Never mind. Just be careful."

"Unscathed." She practiced saying the word in the mirror and puckered her lips.

I opened the top half of my window and took a deep inhale of smoke. The air conditioner was on, making my hair follicles stand erect. I ashed out the window, but the ash just flew back in. Olya put on more makeup. Eye shadow, mascara, blush. A car drove by pounding gangsta rap at a new high, setting off every car alarm within a two-block radius. It caused the cracks in my walls to branch and blossom. This attention to every detail was a signal to me that I was experiencing the onset of a small panic attack. I sat down on the bed. Snap out of it, I said to myself, just as the thump of the bass beat faded into East Williamsburg. I worked on my *pranayama*.[3] Maybe a suit in three days was terribly inconvenient, but I wouldn't have agreed to it if it was not possible. Surely, somewhere deep in my subconscious, I knew it could be done. That it *would* be done. And it was this healthy optimism that I took with me to the garment district later that day. In other words, I wove the stress to my advantage, harnessed it like I had done in fashion school once upon a time. Amazing, the

3. Yoga breathing practice.

battleground that is the mind. A constant war of self-will with a counterinsurgency of doubt. We are our own worst enemies, ain't it the truth.

Over the course of the next three days I redrafted my designs, cut fabric, sewed into the morning hours. I tore open seams when they weren't good enough. I used everything I had learned, and then I threw it away—pants, sleeves, body—and taught myself how to do it right. When I thought I'd finished I would find a misstep, a connection that didn't make sense, and I'd force myself to reevaluate the entire construction; I would find the solution in the form. Design was a puzzle, but it had a formula of its own, and once I tapped this formula, the garment attained simplicity. Its beauty and perfection became evident. Even if it was a suit.

And I delivered the suit, by God. It took three days and nights, but I delivered! I felt it no small feat either, to complete my end of the bargain. I was out to prove I could make it on my own in America, and that first suit was a test. No matter how much talent you think you have, no matter how hard you studied in the bubble of the university, the open market of the real world sets the bar high. You have every right to doubt your abilities. In truth, doubt produces miracles. I should have called my first collection Doubt. Doubt is what would eventually get me into *W* magazine. Doubt is what would get me into the tent.[4] Such a funny thing, doubt. It's destined to fail. Its natural progression is to be overcome, and all sorts of forces will do it—faith, willpower,

4. Mercedes-Benz Fall Fashion Week 2006, Bryant Park (new designer's forum).

envy, greed, truth, lies, therapy. On October 4, 2002, as I sewed my first label onto the inside breast pocket of that jacket, I felt I had conquered my doubts. Even though the suit wouldn't be used in a collection, I couldn't help but feel pride over the finished task. It was proof. My little flimsy satin label stitched with black thread was proof. (B)OY. A suit was going out into the world that night to be worn, somewhere, at an undisclosed location, and it was proof of my existence.

Friday afternoon, Ahmed came by for the final fitting. I placed him in his new suit over what he had on—a knee-high tunic. For all my complaining about his horrendous odor and filthy appearance, the man had cleaned up nicely. His hair was neatly parted to one side and greased in place with Vaseline, and he had trimmed his spotty beard. A spicy cologne held his BO at bay, and together they created an earthy fragrance. The suit, however, is what transformed the man. Ahmed stood in front of the mirror, and I stood behind him, cinching and straightening. There was little left to do besides hem the pants.

"It's better than anything I've ever owned," he said. "Except for a dalmatian I had in London. Pogie. Goddamnit, how I miss Pogie. Sheela got him in the divorce. Her attorney, the Shovel, made it so. He passed away a few years ago. The dog, not the Shovel. Anyway, I will cherish this equally."

"The legs should come up a little." I marked them with pins. "Take them off and I'll adjust them."

"And my initials on the front pocket, what a gesture! Was I right about you or what?" he said, taking off the pants and handing them to me. "Talent. Grade-A talent."

"The initials give it just the right amount of flair. It's loud but not too loud. It'll bring attention to the clothes, but it won't over-whelm the clothes."

"I'm certain you've done your homework."

While I commenced hemming at my worktable, Ahmed returned to the mirror and continued to admire his jacket. He turned from front to side, buttoning and unbuttoning. He looked rather cartoonish, standing there with calves so thin beneath the swell of his belly. So rarely do you see a man's legs, and why not? I'm sure men would groom, moisturize, and tone their legs prop-erly if only they had the right garments to show them off.

The last time he wore a suit like this, he said, it was at his wedding back in the early nineties, when he was something to talk about on both sides of the Atlantic. These details of his life—Sheela, the dalmatian, and now his wedding—seemed incredibly murky, so I decided to exploit the moment to establish a proper time line while he still had his pants off.

"Tell me," I said. "How long did you live in London?"

"Many years."

"Was that before or after you lived in Canada?"

"Oh, time gets so convoluted at my age. One minute you're here, the next you're not. The amount of traveling I did in those days! My business kept me on my toes. I was between countries for years. The air over the Atlantic—that was home. I only became a citizen of Canada when I needed my operation. I couldn't return to England once the divorce was finalized. It was too painful. I felt like I had been kicked out."[5]

---

5. He was kicked out. Ahmed Qureshi was placed on British immigra-tion's watch list for falsifying papers (under the alias Ahmet Yasser). The UK

"Ouch. Health troubles on top of a divorce."

"They always come in twos, Boy. In the end it all worked out. Canada welcomed me with open arms, and I got my surgery. You won't see bifocals on this face anymore. I wear contacts now." He pointed at each eye as he said this. "These are the windows to the soul, my friend. Why shield them? That's why I never trust a man who wears glasses. Not with today's technological advances. I can't help but notice you have perfect eyesight."

"Oh, far from it. I wear contacts."

"But you don't wear glasses."

"I have them. I just don't wear them." I moved on to pressing the pants.

"And that's why it's so easy to trust you, Boy. You don't hide behind anything. You're an honest man. One doesn't need perfect vision to see that. I feel as if I can tell you anything. You should think of me the same."

"Why, thank you."

Looking back on what was one of our sincerer moments, I can't help but feel betrayed. I was beginning to trust Ahmed in some misguided way. Stupid me. I can sit here all day repeating, "I should have known better." But the fact of the matter is, I didn't.

I had him try on the pants again. He was beaming. I was suddenly reminded of why I became a designer—to see someone transformed, standing at attention with newfound confidence, to see them turn into someone better than the someone they thought

_____

deported him to Pakistan in 1996. As far as records show, Ahmed Qureshi was never legally married.

they could never be. Even suits, those boring garments my uncle had devoted his life to, were capable of inciting this. I knew there was something pure in what I was doing. All of my intentions were from the heart. Chanel once said that whatever is done out of love occurs beyond good and evil.[6] I believe that, I honestly do.

6. Coco Chanel was most likely quoting Friedrich Nietzsche.

My Life in Fashion

Never before in my life have I had to wear the same thing every day. My uniform is Day-Glo orange, the color of a prisoner. It's much too big and doesn't breathe. And so I tried to make do by removing the sleeves, which I did by hand. For removal of the sleeves I was punished. My dinner was withheld. Yes, that is how they've punished me. I was refused dinner. But I didn't care. Dinner is a packet, a ration, which is slid into my cell on a tray. Sometimes with a piece of bread or half a bruised apple.

Also, the extra material I had planned to tie around my ankles to taper these baggy pants was confiscated. However, they allowed me to keep my top. So for the remainder of the week I will be wearing my uniform without sleeves. It is much more breathable that way.

It is nearly August. Almost two months have gone by and still no lawyer. So I had Win read what I'd written so far, because of his interest in the law, etc. When I asked him how it makes me look—"innocent" was the word I was hoping for—he told me he was not allowed to say. But he enjoyed what he read, he said, in so many words. This pleased me, since over the two months I've known Win I've come to trust him, even though I've learned that trust is not something to just fall into with someone. (Cunningham too has grown on me, though his willingness to listen to my stories relies on how many models are involved.) What intrigues me most is that Win has not judged me as the others have. He tries not to call me by my number, though I suspect he's not permitted to call me by my name either. He doesn't call me anything. After he finished reading the part about the two suits, he confessed to me that he'd never owned a civilian suit. Earlier in the year at his grandfather's funeral he wore his military dress uniform.

"You must be proud to wear it," I said.

"When you're home it stands out a little. Everybody's always looking at you, wondering where you've been. People thank me for no reason. People come up to me and shake my hand."

"You're recognized for your service. What's so bad about that? I spent my whole life trying to get people to notice me for the same reason. When you go home, all you have to do is put on your uniform." I suddenly felt the time right to express my appreciation for the troops in Iraq and Afghanistan. I told Win that I respected him and his fellow soldiers for putting themselves in harm's way. It was true. Years ago I was a touch more ambivalent. Back in 2003 I stood alongside my then girlfriend, Michelle Brewbaker, on First Avenue in protest against the war. But I was more of a tourist than a participant. It was a cloudy, overcast day, and shoulder to shoulder, people took to the streets. I was there with the millions of others because it was an event that I wanted to be a part of, and because Michelle had asked me to be there. I listened to their chants, I joined in, I photographed their homemade signs, but I was still once removed from the cause.

In 2003, Win was only sixteen, a sophomore in high school. He ran track and played junior varsity basketball. Probably around the time I was marching along First Avenue, making my

way toward the United Nations with the masses, Win was sitting
in a classroom in Fort Worth, copying math equations off a chalkboard, determining the probability of something meaningless.
Maybe he felt just as ambivalent about the war as I did, which
makes it all the more embarrassing for me, since I was that much
closer to Operation Oily Deception.[1]

Win shrugged off my compliments. That kind of talk seemed
to make him uncomfortable. Regarding my written confession,
however, we had a meaningful exchange. Perhaps it was because
I had shared something personal with him that he felt compelled
to tell me his full name.

It's Winston. Which reminds me of the American cigarettes
my Tito Roño, the tailor, used to smoke when I was growing up.

Winston Lights.

Those Winstons turned out to be the only constant in my Tito
Roño's life. He hit a lull in the late eighties, when Cebu's family-
owned shops were overrun by Megamalls, and my uncle's fitted
suits were passed over for cheap quality Polo—clothes made by
the Third World, for the Third World. Cheap suits only partially
lined, or not lined at all, flooded the streets. Gone were the days
of flittering ash and pastel panties. While the acne blossoming on
my prepubescent face went unnoticed in my uncle's shop, he had
both his ears pierced and fell into a deep middle-aged depression.
He began to resemble a Filipino George Michael circa "Don't Let
the Sun Go Down on Me."

It was my auntie Baby who kept Tito Roño afloat in those
years. She was a moneylender, more feared than respected. There

1. Operation Iraqi Freedom.

was no bureaucracy with her. You didn't need good credit or proof of employment, because your word alone was enough. And so for a time the system worked, regardless of whether it was illegal or not.[2] Her line of street banking may have been unthreatened by the ever-looming financial collapse, but what her occupation lacked was the security of any Third World financial institution: men with guns. In late April 1990 my auntie was followed back to her suite at the Shangri-la from the Casino Filipino, where she had spent thirty-two hours at the mahjongg tables. She was recently separated from my uncle, although they were still on respectable terms. Housekeeping found her at the foot of the bed, her head covered with a black garbage bag, asphyxiated. She'd expired clutching a thousand-peso note (at the time, approximately twenty dollars U.S.) as if it were her dear life in hand.

I was thirteen when she died. There would be no more summers spent away from my parents helping my Tito Roño.

Both lives had come to tragic crossroads—one in a sorry, sulking state, the other in a brutal murder. But compared to my boring parents, the two doctors, my uncle and auntie had cultivated an element of risk. They had secrets and affairs and lived out of hotels and gambled and got offed. Eyewitness testimony said that my auntie's final hours at Casino Filipino might have very well been her finest. She was seen making bets as high as five thousand P (approximately one hundred dollars U.S.), laughing with friends, guzzling G and Ts, tipping waiters ten P (approximately twenty cents U.S.). I wanted a similar lifestyle for myself.

2. It was.

The thirst for novelty only increased when I returned to school in Manila that fall. Girls began appearing out of nowhere in a new, more developed light. I'd always known they existed, but not in this capacity. I'd been more concerned with myself, and with keeping that self entertained and distracted with whatever forms of American media I could lay my hands on. VHS tapes of blockbuster movies like *Batman* and *Superman* and American comics like, well, *Batman* and *Superman*. Not that these pursuits were themselves a waste of time. In retrospect it's clear comic books were what first introduced me to the proportions of the body. The robust pecs of a man, the hourglass figure of a woman. Although exaggerated, these images sparked an early interest in silhouette and form, in how clothes could be used to allure. I remember I liked the look of a superhero's leather cape, how it was always depicted in a gusty wind—a garment in action. Then there were the tight leotards that both the men and women donned, accentuating Catwoman's nipples and Nightwing's bulge. Much the opposite of the style I would later develop with women's clothing. My hobbies, as I thought of them then, had made me a loner of sorts. Before eighth grade I'd been much more inclined to sketch cartoonish bodies than hang out with real ones after school.

But then I discovered them. The girls in their plaid skirts, the uniform of a nymphet and that of our Santo Niño Prep. I began to notice how each girl's hips had started to widen, how their chests began to swell past those nubile bumps, and how their legs, hidden beneath white tights, promised something carnal.

Love first came to me in the form of Marianna DeSantos, a beautiful fourteen-year-old four months my senior. She was in my religion class. During chapel, with boys on one side, girls on the other, she caught me staring at her from across the aisle when we were on our knees saying the act of contrition.

We had our first date at the Megamall in Makati, where we went ice skating and took a long, romantic walk across Megawing 1 to Megawing 4. Marianna had her own personal driver, Romey, who chaperoned.

We found ourselves entranced, eye to eye, as we wandered into an arcade. There I explained to her the many intricacies of Mortal Kombat II.

"Left, Right, Up, Up, High Punch," I instructed. "See? See how I just ripped your head off." I was lost. I didn't know how to impress a girl, especially one of Marianna's magnitude, with her own chauffeur and everything. But then, I didn't really have to try, did I? Because as soon as my character went cannibal and bit the face off that decapitated head, Marianna went for my hand, placing it within hers.

"You're so smart," she said. Blood seemed to splatter down all around us. She gripped my hand tighter. Then she took her index finger and sensually tickled the inside of my palm. I learned much later in fashion school that this tickling of the palm was a signal for gay sex. But at the time we were both so innocent. What did I know?

"Do you wanna go with me?" Marianna said. She was very direct.

"What about him?" I indicated her driver. He was standing a few machines away, scratching himself.

"Who, Romey? Oh, don't worry about him. He's cool."

I looked at Romey, and he nodded over to us. It was as if he was giving me permission to go with her, right there in front of him, while he watched. He *was* cool.

"Should we go somewhere else?" I asked. I was extremely nervous.

"*Why?*" she said. "Where would we go?"

"You know, somewhere private."

"Look, we don't have a lot of time, Boy. I have to be home by four thirty. I have violin." And then she let go of my hand. It was the end of her seductive tickling.

Marianna was right. There wasn't a lot of time for us. I didn't know it then, but our love would last only that one weekday afternoon and the coming Saturday.

"You're right," I said. "You're so smart." I placed her delicate hand in mine. I was using what I had learned from her a moment ago. This was a skill that would come in handy much later as an immigrant in America.

My touch was all it took. Marianna rebooted her libido and forced herself upon me. We kissed. She sucked my lips, and I felt her teeth brace mine. She slid her tongue in my mouth as far as it could go. She kissed as if she *knew* our love would last only half a week. I reciprocated, battling her tongue, twirling figure eights in her mouth, all the while watching Romey, her driver, out of the corner of my eye.

We left the arcade holding hands. Everywhere I turned it seemed like other people were holding hands too, gazing into each other's eyes, tickling each other's palms, secretly transmitting their carnal desires to do it, right now, right away, right there in Megawing 4.

The following Saturday, Marianna DeSantos invited me over

in the late afternoon for *merienda*, or snack hour halfway between lunch and dinner. I hadn't been invited to a proper meal, and so my feelings were a little hurt, but still I thought, this was it, no more waiting. I was going to lose my virginity during *merienda*.

Our family driver, who was actually my cousin twice removed, dropped me off around four. Marianna lived in a gated fort in Pasay City by the American Memorial Cemetery. Her home was a mansion plus detached servant's quarters. A ten-foot concrete wall laced with barbed wire surrounded the property. Romey stood guard at the front gate with a shotgun slung over his shoulder. All of this high-end security made me jealous. Why didn't our driver have a firearm? My family should at least have pretended like we had old money that needed to be protected, even if our five-bedroom in Tobacco Gardens and the Mazda MPV I was driven up in screamed middle-class.

Once in the house I was instructed by one of several maids to go straight up. I took off my shoes by my foot heels and ran up the marble staircase that spiraled around the foyer in a great display of wealth. Then I burned carpet toward Marianna's bedroom, where I imagined her sprawled out on all fours across a daybed, waiting for me. She wasn't. She was on the carpet, lying on her stomach with her legs in the air. But what legs, kicking back and forth like some lazy Pilates trainer. I noticed something was different in her voice when she told me to close the door. She seemed preoccupied. In front of her, spread out like giant trading cards, were the glossy publications that would become my life. Thick and thin, text-light and image-heavy: *Elle, Vogue, Harper's Bazaar, W, Jalouse, I.D.* If memory serves me correctly, Marianna was flipping through the September issue of American *Vogue*, a five-hundred-page extravaganza. I remember the breadth of it, the weight. It looked almost biblical in its heft. She flipped through the pages at an incredible speed, skimming text and absorbing labels. And when a dress caught her eye she would slow down, hold the page still, and take a moment to consider why it spoke to her, a moment that transcended price and brand and the particular waif who wore it. It was between the individual and the clothes. All else meant nothing. This moment of catharsis is what we in the industry refer to as "in the zone."[3] It's when a designer takes it to the next level to create something fresh and hot and unforgettable. This may sound very subjective, but there's a definite logic to it. In fashion one gets that je ne sais quoi feeling.

"Pop a squat," she said.

I put down my tote bag and sat Indian style at the bank of the great pool of fashion magazines, next to my Marianna. She continued to flip through *Vogue*, basically ignoring me. The overwhelming number of heels and Gucci handbags in front of her had somehow sedated her libido. And this was fine by me, because I was excited to dig in myself. I chose an issue of *W*—what looked to me like an oversized comic—and sat there, reading.

Oh, dear fashion, if I could only remember exactly what I was feeling at that precise moment and re-create it here for the reader. But I can't, technically.[4] It was like a perfect dive, where the swimmer's focus is precise, his mind clear, his body controlled, the wind right, and so quickly he becomes one with the pool! That kind of Olympic utopia was a bug that hid deep in between the

3. A phrase first used by Yves Saint Laurent to Karl Lagerfeld. Paris, circa 1975.

4. See chapter, "On Memory."

lines of *W*, and I caught it. There wasn't one designer or dress that turned me on. It was the whole, not the individual parts. It was the highbrow celebrity culture interspersed among endless pages of ads for Givenchy and Dolce & Gabbana that appeared to be selling sex with androgynous models—the occasional nipple, the see-through underwear, the beauty of young life that seemed so unattainable yet so close, because you could reach out and touch it, it was right there! How could a young boy look at women's fashion magazines, you ask? How could he not? There was desire and fulfillment on every page. Action reaction. I don't know what I want; it tells me what I want. In that magazine alone were eighty pages of images—photos of beauty—broken by the occasional celeb profile, short and brief, followed by more beauty.

Fashion is not only a job, or a pretty face, or a dress that's so next level. It is a lifestyle. It is the only art form that we wear, head to toe, and the only one that automatically projects an image of the self, true or false—who's to say? It is how people see us. It is how we want to be seen. And in the end it is how we will be remembered; otherwise we'd be buried naked rather than in our best suit. "Look at him. He was an asshole, but what a dresser."

I devoured each magazine with a feverish hunger, and Marianna suddenly became concerned. "Are you okay? You're sweating," she said.

"Sorry, I get hot easily." I quickly changed the subject. "These magazines are great. Where did you get all of them?"

"They're fashion magazines. Duh? I got them at the fashion store." Even though Marianna had been born in Manila, she spoke English with the same California rise I had picked up from television.

"Where's that?" I asked.

She looked at me like I was contagious.

"Boy, you're an idiot. There's no such thing as the fashion store. I made it up. Duh? I was testing to see how stupid you were. FYI, you passed. Stoo-pid." She rolled on her back with the weighty *Vogue*, the bible, the one I wanted, and she continued to ignore me. It was strange to see her this way, very unlike the Marianna I knew from school and from our first date, when she had slipped me tongue in the arcade. What had I done to deserve this?

Rather than act out, I withdrew in kindness. Her treating me like shit gave me the urge to please her even more. How could I help myself? I loved these fabulous creatures! Girls gave me a sense of purpose.

"What are you looking at?" she said. She could feel me staring at her.

"I'm just looking at how beautiful you *are?*" I turned it into a question right at the end by adding the California intonation, unsure of myself.

"Really? You don't sound so sure, stupid. Are you sure? Or are you just being stupid?"

"I'm being sure."

"Of what? And how can you be so sure of it?"

"You're beautiful. It doesn't take a genius. Duh?"

This spoke to her. She put down the copy of *Vogue* and rolled over on her elbow to face me. "You're sweet. Want to make out?"

And like that I was on top of her, just like I had seen in the movies. Marianna was receptive to my moves. We kissed with the same intensity we had established in the arcade. Only now she placed my hand over her chest and added a sensuous thrusting. For the next fifteen minutes we dry-humped our way out of adolescence.

We never had our snack that night, and we never would. Something had transpired between us that broke us for good. Maybe it was that we had gotten too close too fast, but by Monday I was like a stranger to Marianna. She told me at lunch that she couldn't see me anymore; her mother wouldn't allow it. I asked her to run away with me to Cebu, where we could start anew living with my uncle. We could transfer schools, finish our studies, and still get into a good university. At this suggestion she told me, quite frankly, to stop being stupid.

By the time Marianna dumped me, my uncle had shut the doors to his shop in Cebu. He'd inherited all of my auntie's debt, and with no one to collect for her, Tito Roño was forced to give his business over to one Ninoy Sarmiento, a ruthless collector who'd floated my auntie whenever she needed the capital. I found out later that he had been one of my uncle's clients. I'd even held the ashtray for him on more than one occasion. Crime has no compassion, not even for the dead. What ruined my uncle completely, though, was the fact that he blamed himself for his wife's death.

I, on the other hand, turned what had befallen me into a minor victory.

That same week that Marianna broke it off, I begged my parents to subscribe to as many fashion magazines as possible. They looked at me like I was nuts, like I had spent one too many summers with Tito Roño, but they were accustomed to giving me whatever I wanted. *W*, American *Vogue*, *Elle*, *Harper's Bazaar*, *I.D.*—these would now be mine for the perusing. Whatever I couldn't get—*Women's Wear Daily* and a few other publications—I had to settle for their Asian counterparts. Soon I was rolling on my bedroom floor in my own pool of glossy high fashion: establishment icons Chanel, Dior, Karl Lagerfeld, Saint Laurent, Prada, Valentino, Versace, Givenchy; the new stars, like John Galliano, Vivienne Westwood, Marc Jacobs, Alexander McQueen; and the Japanese avant-garde, like Rei Kawakubo, Yohji Yamamoto, and Issey Miyake. It was like teaching myself a new language. I began sketching simpler silhouettes and bodies, much less detailed than my earlier comic book endeavors. I gave up supermen for supermodels. I sketched Linda Evangelista, Claudia Schiffer, Kate Moss, Christy Turlington, Naomi Campbell. This was the nineties, remember, the heyday of the supermodel. Soon my room became a shrine to high fashion. Every nook and crevice was covered with my sketches and spreads of fashion editorials hurriedly torn from magazines. I had pictures of the designers in action. Diane von Furstenberg dressing little Kate Moss. Karl Lagerfeld at work in his atelier. I remember very clearly one photo of John Galliano in a cerulean pirate's outfit. His heroic twirled mustache danced with the large feather in his cap as he stood arm in arm with five or six seminude models in a Vegas chorus line. Their breasts were covered with sequin pasties. Whorish black eyeliner masked their eyes. This was an extravagance beyond my wildest dreams! It spoke to me. It said, There are no limits to what Man can accomplish. (And I use "Man" in that all-encompassing sense.)

I remember the first look I put together. It was for my mother, who was a wonderful dresser with an impeccable sense of style. She was never afraid to wear color, and the palette of her closet was my introduction to bright, lush, crisp garments. I took a sleeveless dress and paired it with a lavender summer scarf—both of which she already owned. To this I added an accessory for her. It was a white hat, a beach hat made of straw paper with a wide, floppy brim—an ordinary style that could be found anywhere in the Philippines. But when I saw a similar hat on Christy Turlington on the cover of *Vogue* in 1992, I copied it. I tied a deep purple ribbon around the top, inserted a long white feather, a swan's feather, which I had dyed pink with a highlighter, and I manipulated the brim to take the same shape Christy wore on the cover of *Vogue*. I was able to create an exact replica of Christy Turlington's hat, and it was this hat that I paired with my mother's outfit. My mother, of course, was rather pleased with what I had done. As I said, she was unafraid to take chances. She wore this look to mass on Easter Sunday. And what did she get but compliments tall and large from all of her friends in the congregation.

It was by imitation that I was able to uncover my passion. And it was a constant desire to please others, to win them over, to woo, which drove me.

Love in a Time of War

Today I wore my sleeveless top outside in the yard. The younger men did not react well to my choice of outfit. Once they saw that I had altered my uniform, they immediately began shouting: *"Hamar!"*[1] *"Kafir!"*[2] The few who could speak English called out: "Hey, foggot! Look here, foggot." Like animals in a cage, these men. One kept yelling out over and over, "Wat don't he hev no slivs? Wat don't he hev no slivs?" He stomped around the communal cage, kicking the dirt with his white plimsolls. "Wat don't he hev no slivs?" The commotion only lasted a minute before the guards managed to quiet them down with threats of non-injurious acts.[3] But for me, it was too late. The prisoners had gotten out all they wanted to say. I walked circles in my cage. No longer tempted by the fresh air and the rays of sun, I simply wanted to go back inside.

This is not the first time I have been branded a homosexual, oh no. I am quite aware of what I represent to these men. They are completely repressed. Their notion of masculinity is being challenged by my presence. I wish to tell them that in a democratic society, like in New York, all men are of equal standing no matter

1. Ass, Arabic.
2. Infidel, Arabic.
3. A "nonlethal strike" in the Guantánamo lexicon.

their race, creed, gender, sexual orientation, etc. Even religious fundamentalists are tolerated to a point. Once I was back in my cell I flipped through my Qur'an, looking for a passage about all this—men, equality, something to come back at these animals with, something to say, "Look, you imbeciles. Look what it says so right here in your blessed book!" But I couldn't find an appropriate passage. However, I did find a chapter that mentions homosexuals, and it was a straw man's argument:

Do ye commit lewdness such as no people in creation committed before you?

To that I answer yes. In Western society ye may practice lusts on other men in preference to women, because ye are free to do so, proudly, heroically, and with multiple partners. Someone should drop these men in the Chelsea neighborhood of Manhattan just to teach them a lesson. Would they be shouting, "Hey, foggot wit no slivs!" at everyone who passed? I doubt it. If they did, along would come a moment of reckoning. Perhaps a great big bear named Stephen (a stylist I once knew from Rhode Island) would come along, put down his gym bag, and rip out their awful throats.

To set the record straight once and for all, I am a lover of women! Let there be no mistake. From Marianna DeSantos on, I was in for life. I had many girlfriends too, right up until I left for America. Rachel in Cubao, Marlene in Malate, Elisa in Pasay, Filomena in Makati. I had fallen for each of them completely, but it was always so hard for a man like me to keep relationships together. In fashion, where one is surrounded by so many beautiful women, it is impossible to prevent those inevitable jealousies from occurring in the mind of the one you love. So I found that when I arrived in America, I told myself, no longer would I wear my heart on my sleeve, no longer would I swear by love and openly abuse its name. I didn't want a repeat of the hurt I had felt over my ex-girlfriends, or the hurt I had inflicted upon them. Love had burned before, and it would only burn again, and America was my chance to start anew. I would devote myself to my craft without love getting in the way. Sure, I would need sexual fulfillment of a kind—I wasn't a priest—but it would be different now. I imagined myself as someone older, someone more skilled at moving in and out of bedrooms discreetly, someone who could love as much as he wanted and not be held accountable for his haphazard nature.

But then I fell in love.

It was October, the start of a season known only to me for its brooding colors and warm accessories on the runway. Coming from the tropics, I had never before experienced anything like the fall of the Northeast, with its autumnal color palette and ravishing foliage. The farther north you went the more ravishing, and so many New Yorkers christened the season with an annual drive up the Palisades Parkway. What an exciting time in America! It's all right out of a J. Crew catalog. Everyone returns with bushels of organic apples, miniature pumpkins for their offices, and driving moccasins by Cole Haan. I had delivered Ahmed's two suits, and I didn't expect to have any more contact with the man outside of the occasional hello in the hallway. I had money, but not the kind of money where things came easy. Vivienne Cho rehired me around this time to fill in for a stylist who was down on account of some gallbladder stones. Working closely out of her studio on West Twenty-seventh, we quickly became friends. She was young, brilliant, successful, and willing to help me out whenever the time came for me to launch my clothing line. With a day or two a week devoted to her, and with the money I'd made from Ahmed, I could work on my collection most afternoons and take a Saturday off to frolic.

I made my first autumn excursion away from the city with Olya and her Turkish boyfriend, Erik, a Harvard man, on one such Saturday in mid-October. Erik drove us in his Saab across the George Washington Bridge, and then up the Hudson. We had planned to spend the day at Dia:Beacon, the former Nabisco factory turned museum, and then hit one or two organic fruit stands on the way back. Olya was in a terrible mood, because Erik, her boyfriend of only a few months, was leaving for boot camp in the Turkish army in two days' time. Could you imagine? He was a Harvard graduate and an American citizen, in fact. He even had a semi–Long Island accent. But for him to retain his dual citizenship, he needed to complete the three weeks of boot camp.

(Let the record state that I would be happy to surrender my Philippine passport in order to become a proud U.S. citizen. Not that that means anything, since there are millions of people the world over who would do the same. And I suspect some of them are right here in No Man's Land.)

When Olya wasn't sitting on Erik's lap on a bench in the museum, soaking up every last bit of him, she was brooding to me in an aside over losing him to Turkey.

"Fall in love, and they go off to die for their country," she said. "This is what happens during wartime."

"He's not going to die," I said. "He'll be back in three weeks. It's just boot camp."

She shook her head. We had lost track of Erik over by Richard Serra, where he'd excused himself to the men's room. Olya explained to me that his bladder was very weak, and this was one reason why he would most certainly perish in the Turkish army.

Then I saw her. Michelle. She was alone, walking along an installation of broken glass. Like a fashion editorial out of the 1970s, she seemed so vibrant in a Diane von Furstenberg wrap dress made of green jersey. I wanted a picture of her in front of the shards of glass for my mood board.[4]

"Quick," I said, interrupting Olya. "Let me have your camera phone."

"You can't take pictures in here."

"Who will ever know?"

"I will," a deep voice said. We turned around to where a museum guard, a large man in uniform, was leaning against a column.

I sauntered over to explain my situation. "Excuse me, sir, I wanted to photograph a girl standing there. Not the art work, you understand. Would that be possible? With your permission, of course."

"It would be possible. But then I'd have to confiscate your camera."

"It's just a cell phone."

"It wouldn't be the first."

"I get it," I said. "Doesn't matter."

Michelle had moved on to another installation. I hurried Olya across the factory floor and found Michelle among the gorgeous Bridget Riley paintings, those massive horizontal lines from Riley's *Reminiscence* series.[5]

---

4. An assemblage of photographs, sketches, fabric swatches, magazine clippings, anything incorporating the ideas of a designer's collection.

5. *Reconnaissance*, paintings from the 1960s and 1970s.

I made sure we kept our distance so it wasn't at all obvious that I was staring. Erik rejoined us, and Olya put her arms around him like she wasn't ever going to lose him. She gave him an open-mouthed kiss, and I removed myself by a few steps, hands in pockets. I cleared my throat and felt Michelle turn to notice me. I pretended to be involved in Riley's squiggles before glancing over to her. Ah, that game of notice me, notice you!

I continued to track her, a remote observer. Women were always the apple of my eye, as I have said before. All women too. Tall, short, plump, willowy. I didn't necessarily look at them as any ordinary man, objectifying them as men do. (Although I cannot deny what I am, for in Michelle's case there was a definite attraction.) I saw my subject foremost through the eyes of a designer. I was inspired by her sense of style, her dress, her flats, her hair, her tortoise frames that lent her a certain intelligence. She was a budding New York intellectual but from another time altogether. I watched her stroke her strong Anglo chin as she contemplated each painting in front of her. You see, every notion of style could be obtained just by watching.

I suppose it would have been easy enough to talk to her, seeing as how she was alone. But I didn't. I held back. And then I lost her in the darkness of the basement gallery among the neon lights and video installations, in a maze of shadows and echoes.

Flipping through my Qur'an, the one that belonged to D. Hicks, I've come upon a chapter on women. There's an interesting passage Hicks must have underlined, which seems appropriate now: *"Believers, do not approach your prayers when you are drunk, but wait till you can grasp the meaning of your words."* With Michelle, I would get that chance.

The following week I went hunting for old *Vogue* magazines from the 1970s, the Grace Mirabella[6] years. I bought a stack on Sixth Avenue and flipped through them at my worktable, until I found a black-and-white spread of von Furstenberg herself looking as gorgeous as ever, modeling one of her own wrap dresses. I tore out two pages, one of DVF in the wrap dress and a close-up shot of her with those dark Belgian eyes. I pinned them both to my mood board.

By November an entire wall of my apartment was covered with ideas that had bled well beyond the board. Swatches, paisley scarves, magazine clippings, photos. I was ambitious and productive, sure, but I was lonely as hell. Olya had left to do fashion week in Paris and would be gone for the rest of the year. On my way home one night from Vivienne's studio I decided to wander, to try a different route, to get lost underground in the hopes of discovering a nook of the city I had never known. This was how I found so many of the city's charms. Accidentally. And this was precisely how I found Michelle. Dumb luck. I caught the downtown number 4, and there she was, standing in the middle of a packed train car reading a paperback, among all of the other commuters. She was just as beautiful as she had been that day in the museum. With her book she was shielding part of her face but had the cover tilted in my direction just enough so that I could make out what she was reading. It was a play, *The Dutchman*. The one about the femme fatale who stabs her black love interest in the back with an apple core on the A train. The apple was meant to be symbolic. Death by desire. The other passengers help dump the body off at the next

6. Editor-in-chief of *Vogue*, 1971–1988.

stop, and the femme fatale goes off into another car to pick out her next horn-dog victim of a prevalent ethnic minority.[7]

I once again admired her keen fashion sense. She was wearing a vintage frock, tastefully unbuttoned at the start of her breastbone. My, how she wore it all with such womanly precision. (A woman at twenty-one is so rare!) I noticed how much went into her hair for the first time. Its weighty layers seemed endless—I wanted to get lost in them! I traced her ivory legs from her hemline to her flats, where an out-of-place L.L. Bean backpack with the initials T.W.M. rested against her ankle. I would find out later that the initials belonged to one Todd Wayne Mercer, an ex-boyfriend. He took her virginity; she took his backpack. Fair is fair.

She looked up from her play and I held her gaze. Her hazel eyes, nearly colorless in the light of the subway car, pierced through her big glasses. As I mentioned, from the way she held the paperback tilted in my direction, I suspected she must have already recognized me as the guy who'd followed her from Bridget Riley to Joseph Beuys. Once she smiled at me I knew I'd been given the green light. *Do not approach your prayers when you are drunk but wait till you can grasp the meaning of your words.* To my fellow passengers, I said excuse me and made my way over to where she was standing.

The next stop came. Commuters on and off.

"You've read it?" she said, suddenly. "You're staring at it like you've read it."

---

7. *The Dutchman*, LeRoi Jones, 1964. Most—if not all—of the details recounted here are wrong.

"Yes." I hadn't. *"The Dutchman,"* I said. "The quintessential work out of the Netherlands in the last half century."

"That's funny."

"I haven't read it," I admitted. "But I've seen it."

"You've seen it performed?"

"No, the movie with Louis Gossett Jr."[8]

This made her laugh.

"Anyway, I love the theater," I said. "Broadway and everything."

"I hate Broadway. Yuck. It's nothing but overpriced garbage. Have you ever noticed who goes to the theater these days? Blue hairs and tourists. The theater's dead. I guess that's why I want to be a part of it. I'm drawn to swan songs. What's your name?"

I told her and she laughed again. When I asked her what was so funny she said, "Oh c'mon, the irony. It's like a philosophical comedy. I am girl. You are boy. Hello, Boy. I'm Michelle."

She was on her way to see her grandmother in Brooklyn Heights. Nana owned a townhouse on Henry Street where Michelle would be spending the weekend away from college.

I missed my transfer at Union Square, but I hardly cared.

She told me about her nana, the fall she'd recently taken at her weekly tango lesson, and how Michelle planned to read Frank O'Hara at Nana's bedside. "He was run over by a dune buggy on Fire Island," she said of O'Hara. "Can you believe that?" Nana was a poet herself. Quite accomplished in her day, as I understood it. She published under the name Willomena Proofrock.[9]

"A dune buggy," I repeated, imagining a man sunbathing on

---

8. It was Al Freeman Jr. who starred in the 1966 film adaptation.

9. Spelled Wilhelmina Prufrock (1931–2003).

a towel, and the recreational vehicle plowing over him. "That sucks."

"It's totally ironic."

Michelle had a great passion for irony. To her the world was chaotically doused in the stuff. It was one big *Oedipus Rex*.

"I take it you're an actress?" I said.

"Hardly. I'm a playwright. But I've acted before in plays at school. I'm in the drama conservatory at Sarah Lawrence. Are you Filipino?"

"How did you guess?"

"Our maid growing up had your nose. She spoke Filipino on the phone, long distance. My parents never minded."

"They export them, you know," I said. "OFW's, they're called." I wrote OFW in the air between us. Whenever I was nervous I overused hand gestures. "Overseas Filipino Worker. You know, in some countries the word for maid is Filipina."

"That's so ironic."

The two seats in front of us opened up and we sat down. Michelle tended to slouch a little, with her bottom too far out on the edge, her shoulders and neck folded together. At first I thought she did so to make me feel comfortable about our difference in height, but I would soon realize she always sat like this. In truth, it was the only thing about her that was unwomanly. The rest I found ravishing.

I talked about Manila, my dying city. Cancerous, metastasizing, degenerate. Funny, I never harbored such feelings growing up there. My chief objection then was that it wasn't a major fashion contender like New York, London, or Paris. I couldn't give a crap about what went on in my country politically. Terrorism, the

NPA,[10] government corruption—none of these could make me bat
a lash. Suddenly I was telling Michelle that what Manila needed
was a Giuliani type. "Someone who can keep his hands out of the
cookie jar for a single political term and clean up the poverty."

She, in turn, told me about New York when she was a kid in
the eighties, a time when no one went out on the Lower East Side,
and SoHo didn't even have a Prada store yet.

I complimented her on her vintage frock. "YSL?"

"What are you gay?" she joked.

"No, I'm a designer. The color seems like YSL, late seventies.
But I could be wrong."

"That's my favorite YSL period. But I think this is Dior."

"That would have been my second guess."

"You're a *straight* fashion designer? That is so ironic."

Soon we were off the train, and I was carrying Todd Wayne
Mercer's backpack for her along Joralemon Street. I confessed that
I had seen her before. I described what she had been wearing to
a T that day at the museum, the green DVF wrap dress. Michelle
was not at all taken aback. She was flattered that someone had
paid attention and found her to be something she'd never considered herself to be: memorable. Only much later would she admit
that she remembered me also as the small Filipino guy in tight
jeans with the cute backside.

We walked on. She showed me the Brooklyn promenade, the
waterfront of a tree-lined Everytown, USA. She pointed out where
Arthur Miller, her favorite American playwright, had lived. This

10. New People's Army, an armed wing of the Communist Party of the
Philippines (CPP), deemed a terrorist organization by the United States in
2002.

was a neighborhood so picturesque, so literary, so quaint, so *white*, that on any other day, with anyone else, it would have made me uncomfortable. I felt far more at ease on the corner of McKibbin and Graham among the drug peddlers and Puerto Ricans and blacks and hipsters, right in the heart of Bushwick—all immigrants in some way, encroaching on each other's turf. But on this first foray into Brooklyn Heights with Michelle, I wasn't thinking about any of this. Through the open collar of her frock, I could see her pale skin, the ridges in her chest, and where the plumpness of her small breasts began. Then there was her long freckled neck—a branch. How intoxicating. Her face a ripened piece of fruit! Take a bite, it said. I resisted this compulsion to sexualize her, I swear. Oh, but how I lusted for a body! Still, I knew I needed patience and self-control if I wanted to get together with a girl of Westchester stock. I wasn't going to kiss her yet, I decided, and so in my head I recited a bunch of American clichés: easy does it, early bird gets the worm. "I find you to be fascinating," I told her. At my compliment she smiled and seemed to fold over like a lily whose petals were too heavy. (Why do we go floral when it comes to love?) God, how I remember her at first, so easily swayed by flattery, regardless of how crude and domineering she would become. Michelle was a sledgehammer but could melt in your arms like lead if you said the right things.

From the waterfront we walked back to Henry Street, and then parted at the corner. I found it strange that she didn't want me to walk with her all the way to Nana's door. I suppose she realized that I was still a man she had only just met. After all, it was a city where anything could happen. You could be blindsided by a stranger and wind up on the Brooklyn promenade. I watched

Michelle trail off along a row of oil street lanterns with Todd Wayne Mercer's knapsack slung over one shoulder. I watched his initials fade away.

Everything I did in my studio that fall I did with the intention of impressing Michelle. I sketched her from memory, putting her in dresses I hadn't yet completed. She was both a muse and a curse. I was productive, but I wasn't working for myself. Sometimes there isn't a difference. I make clothes for women, so who cares if I was making clothes for one woman in particular.

A week after our chance meeting on the 4 train, we had our first date at a Polish diner in the East Village, an old-world place, narrow and heavy on the linoleum. We sat at the counter and ordered from a chalkboard of specials. Michelle introduced me to borscht and challah bread. We split a grilled cheese cut from the lofty Jewish loaf that reminded me of the *pandesal* rolls back home. She dropped a teaspoon of sour cream in my borscht and stirred until it became a milky fuchsia, like a thick bowl of Pepto-Bismol, though still quite appetizing. She told me it was her favorite color.

"Your favorite color is borscht?" I teased. She laughed and punched me in the side. Michelle was so strong, with big hands and slender, soft-tipped fingers covered in antique rings. Those hands could grip my whole being and hold me close. I felt safe whenever she put one on me, as she did at the counter while we slurped our borscht. I placed mine on top of hers and we interlaced our fingers. What warmth! That first breach: My hand touching hers, her hand touching mine, my thigh in her hand, her hand on my thigh. The first time two lovers touch intentionally is always more memorable than a first kiss or a first time, at least for me. It's that rare singular jolt that can never be replicated. When the time came to split the grilled cheese, we were forced to let our hands go, and yet we craved that touch like addicts. So we faced each other to eat the sandwich, interlocking our legs under the counter. My knee was gripped by her two thighs, close enough to feel her inner warmth. It was our first date, but in the mirror behind the counter we already looked like a couple who couldn't be separated. When I called for the check, she put her hand on my lower back, just under my shirt, and we waited.

On Division Street in Chinatown we shared a bubble tea and ate sweet rice out of a banana leaf. I confessed that I didn't want her to leave and asked her to spend the night with me in Bushwick. It was a Sunday, and to get to school the next day, she needed to take the train from Grand Central Station back to Bronxville. We hadn't even kissed yet.

"Of course," she said without hesitation. "I hadn't even thought of leaving." And then she gave me a kiss, partly on the mouth, partly on the cheek, but wholly wonderful. I kissed her again. A breeze came and went. I felt the moisture she'd left on my face evaporate. I was a marked man from then on.

Michelle came home with me and we made love, but I'll spare you the details, except for this:

Naked, we bare our souls to each other. There are no pretensions. It is the antifashion. Whenever I show skin in one of my dresses—an open chest in front of the heart, or a slither of exposed back—I feel I am providing a peek at the truth. Michelle's body, naked, was like truth serum. I melted at the sight of her bare shoulders, lightly freckled from a summer spent on Nantucket Island; her breasts, two matured handfuls of pale white flesh, outlined with a bikini tan line. I'd get down on my knees and breathe her in just below the navel until her white stomach fuzz stood on end. American women are so wonderfully hairy. Oh, how I fell apart before everything down there! The scent of young womanhood, so unmistakable! Her ass was tremendous—I still dream about its two halves. And what her buttocks held within its dark shadow was the God's honest truth! It was His work, revealed. Go tell it on the mountain.

Lately I've been thinking about mistakes. That's all I have the chance to do these days. There were times during the course of our two years together when I would ask myself how could I have gotten involved with a girl like this. Looking back now, isn't it obvious? I did it for love.

Bronxville Revisited

By mid-November I was putting in serious time in the top bunks of Sarah Lawrence, with its communal kitchens, RAs, visitor slips, damp halls, pot smoke, cut grass, big oaks, track and fields. I would take the Metro-North to Bronxville to watch Michelle endure the hardships of college life in a pastoral setting with lots of ivy on brick.

On the commute from Grand Central Station each weekend I'd see faces from my neighborhood—poorly dressed hippies, musicians, privileged brats such as myself. I learned that many Sarah Lawrence alums had flocked to Bushwick after graduation to hold on to their American collegiate squalor. They went back on the weekends to see their girlfriends and boyfriends, youth holding on to youth, as if there existed some underground pipeline between the two places. Discovering this made me determined not to be mistaken for one of them, even though one of them was upending all my happiness and fulfillment.

What's that, you ask? How does a young man veer from love to resentment in a matter of weeks? Well, as I've said, I wanted no attachments. And within two months of starting my new life I had found just that: an attachment. But this is a young person's dilemma, not something to waste the precious pages of my confession on when there is so much dirt in the filthy air that needs clearing. The last I will say on the matter is that when one does fall in love, there is always a dose of resentment that comes along with it. They go hand in hand. Things get put on hold when two people fall for each other. I was spending all of my earnings on trips to Westchester and mediocre dinners for two, even though my presence was actually needed at parties and events in the city. Without my presence, the dream could easily slip away. The dream of Bryant Park. New York Fashion Week. You see, whenever I found myself on Forty-second Street I liked to walk over to the square plaza and take in the way the light came through the London plane trees and down upon the stone balustrades and trim lawn. Oh, how this small green enclave would be transformed twice a year into the center of my world! I felt a connection to this space. The bustle that surrounded the park—the offices and revolving doors—made no real impression on me. In the park I was in my zone. It's where I planned to make my splash. To be remembered in the tent during fashion week is to be made immortal.

Michelle, just by being with me, was steering me away from all of this. She was keeping me down and out in Bushwick. Ahmed's three thousand was nearly gone. Between the puffy coat I had to buy for winter and the train fare back and forth each weekend, Williamsburg was being completely squeezed off my horizon. All the hip, artistic people—my people—were thriving in the industrial colony that was Williamsburg without me, foraging their bohemian urban dream out of the lost grounds of SoHo and Greenwich Village before it. Each time I rode past Graham and Lorimer and Bedford on the L train, the neighborhood called to me. Behind every garage door was a sculptor, a painter, a band practice, a recording-in-session, a designer, a fashion shoot, altogether united in the common pursuit of trying to one-up each other in their respective areas of focus.

Where was my label in all of this? Without the proper funding, there was no label. Just a man in a room making women's clothing. How sad. I had all the right friends ready to help—Vivienne Cho, Philip Tang—but what I didn't have were the investors. And so, while doing everything myself—designing, sewing, creating—I was my own headhunter too. My plan had been to finish a small collection, secure a proper studio in Williamsburg, have Vivienne and Philip fall in love with my line, and get them to introduce me to the right people willing to invest, all in the name of high fashion.

The Friday before Thanksgiving, as I was hurrying home to grab my weekender, I realized I was being followed. Outside the Kosciuszko warehouses, where many of the SLC graduates took up residence in packs, I turned to look into the glare of the headlights of an idling car behind me. When I slowed my pace, this car didn't pass, just coasted alongside of me. As anyone with good American street sense can tell you, this meant bad moons were rising.

"Boy!" someone shouted, and I immediately recognized the voice. It was Ahmed. He pulled over to the curb in a small hybrid vehicle, a Toyota Prius. "I thought that was you. I know that walk anywhere. I said to myself, that's the walk of a Filipinni. That ragtag bunch of opportunists! They're everywhere at once. How the hell are you?"

I went over to the car door and shook his hand. He was dressed in one of his new suits. The double-breasted gray plaid. He wore the jacket buttoned without a shirt underneath. His open chest reminded me of the TV actor Philip Michael Thomas, whose style I'd grown up emulating from the show *Miami Vice*.

"Check out my wheels," said Ahmed. "It's a Zipcar."

"What do you mean?"

"It's kind of like a rental, only it's not. This one's a hybreed. You should see the mileage I get on this fucker. Astounding. Get in. I'll take you around the block."

"No thanks. I'm in a hurry."

"All the more reason."

Just then I heard a bottle smash somewhere nearby, and so I scampered around the front of the car and got in.

We rode along Broadway under the overpass of the el. This was Brooklyn's Broadway, a series of replicated blocks on which each shop was named after its service—Hair Braided, Checks Cashed, Jewelry Bought and Sold—and where young men huddled outside of Chinese takeouts, congregating with their dinners in white Styrofoam platters.

"So what's the hurry?" Ahmed asked.

"I'm going to Bronxville tonight. But I need to run home first."

"Bronxville, eh? What the hell is in Bronxville?"

"My girlfriend."

"Your gelfriend? That's a lot of trip for a little pussy. She must be worth it."

"She is," I said. "She's totally hot."

"What's her name? Your gel?"

"Michelle."

"Ah, Michelle. 'Mee-chelle, my belle. Sont des mots qui vont très bien ensemble' . . . It's French for 'these are words that go very well assembled,' or *ensemble*. The Beatles. Nineteen sixty-something. The year rock was born."

Ahmed had an enthusiasm about him, a live-for-the-moment

kind of feeling, which made you overlook the incongruous details. And we were foreigners, remember, speaking a second tongue. In Ahmed's case it was his forth or fifth language. Together we spoke an outsider's English. A language that sometimes incorporated terms from our homelands, words in our hearts that couldn't be translated. Out of our mouths came the world *ensemble*.

"You know where I live, Boy. Why have you insulted me by not coming by? Unless, of course, you've been working. You genius." He tugged at his lapel. Then he reminded me of how we had established a bond of trust, likening it to a California redwood.

"You seem preoccupied. If something's on your mind, out with it. Don't let these things fester. It's no good for the heart, man."

"I'm late, that's all."

"You're late. I'll drive you."

"It's like an hour. Don't be silly."

"Nonsense. I'd be honored. Besides, I have the hybreed for the rest of the night. And I still have to show you the mileage this beby gets highway."

I ran upstairs to grab my weekender—giddy, I admit, over scoring a ride to Bronxville. What good fortune! A girl was waiting to see me. A little money was still in my pocket. Why couldn't I have just been happy?

When I returned, Ahmed was fiddling with a GPS gadget.

"So, Boy, I've been thinking about the dress on that blonde."

"You mean Olya?"

"Olya. How could I forget Olya. Your business is very high-end women's wear, yes? Boy, I have to say. Ever since I started wearing your suits I've felt like a beautiful blonde myself." Ahmed belched. "Excuse me. It's amazing what a primo piece of clothing can do for your confidence. I've been a success in whatever I've chosen to tackle, as you may or may not know. But wearing something like this makes me *feel* like a success. When you get to be my age your successes pile up and nothing seems to surprise you anymore. You need to take losses just to let yourself know you're alive. I don't expect you to understand. But know this: Lately, I've been rejuvenated. With this suit I've been garnering respect and attention wherever I go."

"You see," I said, "this is what fashion can do to you. This is its raison d'être. To make you feel good about yourself. When I hear this I know I've done my job."

"A confession, Boy. I suppose your artistic endeavors have been making me envious. To be so young and talented. You're leading the life that I wanted to lead, once upon a time. The social constrictions of my upbringing prevented me from exploring my true fashionista. I was brought up a Muslim. Allah is great, Muhammad his prophet, *haraam* this, *haraam* that, praise Allah. Look at how the women still go around in hijab, covered up, unable to flaunt their tremendous beauty. What a shame. Possibly the greatest shame of Islam. To be a fashion designer would never have been an option for me where I come from. Especially as a man. I'm not the first to call out the elephant in the room when I say it isn't the most masculine of professions. And now, at my age, would you believe that I'm getting the sudden urge to dress myself up? To be shameless for once!"

We drove through Williamsburg, where I knew I belonged. A safe haven for the artistic mind, where youth and fashion seemed both effortless and destructive. It was precious to me in that way.

"Look at that bitch with the rainbow dreads," Ahmed said,

pointing out a pale, white, quasi-Rasta girl in a parka. "She's tattooed her face!"

"But you see, Ahmed, these are the people who set the trends for a good part of the world—the hipsters, the young, the transients. And that's the edge my collection will exploit. It's not necessarily beautiful. If anything, one might call her a freak. But what attitude! Am I right? She has so much attitude that you felt absolutely compelled to call her out on the street."

"It takes cojones to tattoo your face, I'll give her that."

As we coasted down Metropolitan, an Englishwoman's voice instructed us to turn right and then merge onto the BQE after two hundred yards. I can't explain it, but everything on this night seemed to be happening with such absolute precision.

True to her guidance, we rose onto the BQE.

"I am beginning to see your vision, Boy. You're very persuasive. I like that. As I said, I've been envious lately. Allow me to expand. I've linked this envy to two desires. I am envious of your talent—some of us can only be so lucky. The second is related to the fine suits you have made for me. I was once satisfied, but now I want more. Don't get me wrong, the suits are perfect. But I crave a closet *filled* with suits of the finest quality. This is a very strange feeling for me. It's like your former first lady with the shoes."[1]

"Ahmed, it's nothing to be ashamed of. This is what keeps the industry going, don't you see? We're all hooked. It's insatiable. Nothing is satisfactory, certainly not for the customer."

"Enough, Boy. You don't have to sell anything to me. Our trust is like a beautiful flower. We both need to care for it. Oh, let it

1. Imelda Marcos, aka the Steel Butterfly.

rain! Let our garden grow! You see my enthusiasm. It's unwavering. And from the perspective of an investor, I know of no other industry with a five hundred percent markup on product. Well, besides oil. And we all know the Saudis have that cornered."

I didn't know how to respond to this. "What do you mean?"

"Do I have to spell it out for you? A-B-C-D? I want to be in business, what else? I'm a fabric salesman, but there's no honor in that. There's no art."

Bronxville suddenly seemed as far away as Siberia.

"We have trust, no? Trust is one-on-one. Otherwise it's a cluster fuck." He slammed his fist down on the dash. "I want to invest in your clothing line."

"Ahmed, start-ups are too much for a sole investor to take on." I was thinking on my toes now, trying to stay one step ahead of this dubious benefactor. "First I need to move the operation into Williamsburg. Then I need to find cutters, people who can sew. I need a good publicist."

"Don't bullshit me. What's a start-up? Sixty? Seventy thousand? So there are overheads. I talk to my accountant, Dick Levine. He handles all my finances. And I know landlords in Williamsburg who owe me. Converted warehouses. There's one I already have in mind. A former toothpick factory."

I was beginning to think of Ahmed's lies as just another occupational hazard. Models dieted. Writers drank. Athletes enhanced. And businessmen lied. I lowered my window.

There is a distinct change in the atmosphere along the Major Deegan. A transition from stuffy Bronx air into the more temperate chill of lower Westchester. The wind numbed part of my face. For a flash I saw myself trailing along the Major Deegan, my essence removed from my body, soaring above the Zipcar. I was flying. I let the air fill my lungs.

Then Ahmed swerved the car. "My God, did you *see* that pothole? It was bigger than you."

Maybe securing my financing this way was truly as foolish as I felt deep down at the time. But look at my position. Monday through Thursday I was selling my label to anyone who would listen, and no one was biting. Here was a guy who seemed genuinely excited about fashion. I didn't see Ahmed as a sucker, someone I could dupe into financing my label. I saw him as someone who believed in what I was doing. All of the flattery aside, I thought he had recognized me for what I was, a talented designer. You might be shaking your heads, "Look, look at the nincompoop! Just like a jihadi, swayed by all the virgins he's been promised in heaven." I ask of you once again to put yourself in my size 7 shoes. My life depends on it! The prospect of me being his patsy never even entered my mind. Why would it?

"We'd be in West Nyack if it weren't for this GPS bitch," Ahmed said. "She's one hundred percent accurate. Entering Dodge in two point seven minutes. And look at the fuel gauge. The fucking needle hasn't even moved! Did I tell you this gets great highway or what?"

Once we hit campus, driving slowly along Kimball Avenue, I took in the pleasant offerings of a night in Bronxville. The smell of a wood-burning fire, the *pock* of tennis balls echoing off the courts even in November, the imposing Tudor buildings magnificently lit. Crisp fallen leaves, like cinnamon and dried flower petals, were being crushed under our tires.

I directed Ahmed to drop me off in a faculty parking lot.

"Fancy pantsy," he said as he pulled in. "All this education shit costs a fortune. Your gelfriend, she comes from a rich family?"

"I think so. To tell you the truth I don't know much about them."

He shrugged his shoulders. "Never went to college myself. I started working at thirteen and I never looked back. I'm not a great artist like you, but I could always make money. Maybe that's my talent."

Before I got out, we agreed to meet Monday morning, as soon as I was back in the city. We would further the details of our partnership.

"Boy, know that I'd like to be a silent partner in all this. To be included in your business alone would be enough. I am not after your spotlight. Our trust can be a thing of beauty. Now, let's get out and hug like two men who aren't afraid of how it looks."

The way things have turned out for me here in No Man's Land, it could be said that I used very poor judgment. In fact, maybe this whole confession so far makes me look like a complete dunce. But what is good judgment? Good is too often confused with *morally sound*. In business, morality is a hindrance. I'm just saying. It is at complete odds with the fashion industry. There's no morality to it. Good judgment, in business, equals profit. In fashion, profit translates into fame. For all his contradictions, Ahmed did manage to convince me that he could make a profit. And I wanted to be famous.

Yves Saint Laurent said it best: "I began uniquely for the fame."

Michelle lived in her own handicap room in Titsworth, a Tudor-style building bordering the commons. When I first broached the subject, she said that she'd been lucky: The college had a surplus of these rooms with not enough disabled students to fill them. One of the room's amenities was a private bath with a large tub.

I always thought the blue handicap symbol plastered to the out-side of her bathroom door was typically ironic, a flourish she embellished by referring to it as the loo or the toilet or the powder room. She called all bathrooms everything but the bathroom. It was her way of acting desirable.

She signed me in with the RA, and we retired to her room for a nap. She took off her knit sweater and I undid my shirt. We kissed for a while and then held each other in deep loving embraces on her single mattress.

Lying on my back I told her about what had just transpired between me and Ahmed. "I can't fucking believe it. I have the start-up money."

"You think he's for real?"

"We just hugged on it in the parking lot."

"Uh! You're so weird. I mean, are you sure he's going to come through? It seems like a lot of money."

"With Ahmed, we have a special bond. I made him two suits, remember. This guy flipped over my work. I think I roped him. We're meeting Monday."

"That's so great, baby." But there was hesitation in her voice. In the word "baby."

"What?" I said.

"Nothing. It's great."

"No, what?"

"It just seems like a lot of money to get your hopes up. And this man . . ."

"Ahmed."

"He's your neighbor. He seems so strange. He doesn't seem trustworthy. I mean, he just picked you up and drove you here?

That's so random." This was another famous outlook of Michelle's. According to her, everything seemed to happen at random, or with great irony. We were completely different in this respect, because as I just said, everything about this night had felt precise to me. As if predetermined.

"We're friends. He trusts me."

"And what was this car? He borrowed it. He doesn't even own his own car?"

"I told you, it was a Zipcar. It's like a rental, but not."

"I can't see how a man without a car, who has only met you a couple of times, is just going to hand you seventy thousand dollars. I'm sorry if I'm being a total pessimist, but I'm trying to protect you. This, this, *Ahmed*"— and here she stressed his Arabic name "has something else on his agenda. And it's not to see you succeed. You said yourself, you thought he was a liar."

"He *is* a liar. I know this all sounds so crazy. But he has a compulsive disorder. Like ADD or something."

Michelle slapped me across the face. It was the first of her many violent outbursts. "Uh! Have some sense. Don't you mean OCD? I swear, you have the intelligence of a sixth-grader."

"God, why would you hit me? That fucking hurt. Right, 'OCD.' What the fuck?"

"I'm sorry, I didn't mean it. You were provoking me. I felt under attack." She placed her head into my chest, ashamed. "Let's not do this anymore."

"Hey, it's okay. It didn't even hurt." I started to stroke her hair.

"I'm so embarrassed."

"Baby," I whispered into the back of her neck. I wanted to tell her how I felt about her at that moment. She had just slapped me in the face, her eyes had betrayed me, and for that quick second she wanted to tear me apart, and yet I was seduced by her hot temper. My cheek still stung—I had never been slapped by a woman—and now with her head on my chest, strange, I think I loved her. Only I didn't confess it. Baby, I had said, and left it at that.

After our little tiff, we snapped right back into an enjoyable mood. How easily this can be accomplished when love is so young! The consoling and petting and apologies on the edge of her bed quickly evolved into kissing and embracing and then fellatio.

Later, when we were on our sides facing each other, I again stifled the urge to tell her that I loved her. Like I said before, her naked body demanded honesty. I resisted, however, by looking past her flushed mouth, her open heart, and stared off into a corner of the room. The humidifier was set to a low hum. The engulfing vapor made it seem like we were lying in a cinematic dream. What I felt and what the situation called for was not going to come out of me.

Michelle asked what I was thinking.

Chaos theory, I answered.

Two Whole Minutes

Though our weekly shower usually happens on Sundays, it has become common for them to change the schedule on us, sometimes a day early or a day late. It's barbaric. After forty-eight hours one already begins to stink, so you can only imagine going more than a week without a wash.

The outdoor stalls have been built in pairs. Therefore each of us gets a bathing partner, though we don't shower together. You merely wait in line with your partner for the next available set of stalls.

My bathing partner from yesterday spoke English. He had a thick British accent, very intelligible. "How long have you been here?" he asked. Since the rules prohibit us from talking to each other, I was surprised that my bathing partner's guard acted as if nothing had been said. I looked to the man guarding me, and he was not about to reprimand my bathing partner either. Both were ignoring us completely while we waited for the showers.

"I am Riad. I'm a British citizen," my bathing partner continued. "What's your name?"

I looked to my guard once again. Still, nothing.

"Boy," I said. "I've been here three months."

Riad nodded.

"How long have you been here?" I asked.

"Two years."

I thought I had misheard. "How long?" I said again.

"Two years. Well, over that now. My daughter was three when I was sent here. She is now five. She's already started school." He noted this as a matter of fact. "But I was in Bagram for one year before this."

Three years in captivity! How terrible it is that I can now imagine just how a man can survive such an ordeal. And I have only been here a fraction of that time. When I arrived I thought surely I was done for. *Finito.* The steel cot, the thin mattress no thicker than a yoga mat, a towel for my head—what kind of conditions were these? At home I had been sleeping on a platform bed from West Elm and a $150 Swedish pillow that adapted to the contours of one's neck. My first morning in No Man's Land, when I heard the call to prayer start up at sunrise, I thought I'd been dropped in the pit of hell. But soon enough I found that my surroundings could be tolerated. I was able to endure. I don't know how. I have been able to survive on the tasteless rations I am fed through the slot in my door. I am able to be still for days on end without going mad. Being still was never something I could do. Yet, once I was confined to my little box, I discovered it could be done. What choice did I have?

I said to Riad: "Have you had your tribunal?"

"All right, move," said my guard. "You two on deck."

We were pressed forward to the showers, then separated so that we each could enter our designated stall.

There is no roof over the stalls. Just open sky, bright, hot. At this hour the late-summer sun is directly overhead. Once we're inside the gate is locked behind each of us, and then we turn around so that our hands and feet can be unlatched through the lower slot of the stall doors. We undress, quickly, handing our uniforms through the center slot, because at this point one only has two minutes to wash. Two whole minutes are given to do something so basic. The guard hands over the soap and a packet of shampoo. Then a towel. Some of us are permitted little plastic razors to shave, depending on whether or not we've been deemed compliant. Another tactic of punishment dressed as kindness. There simply isn't enough time to shave in a shower, and the blades are too dull and painful anyway.

Cold water in the showers.

Even though it is so unbearably hot in No Man's Land, the water is too cold to get comfortable. Your breath quickens as your body tries to adapt to the temperature, and it feels, for a moment, like you are being suffocated. Anyone who has jumped into a frigid lake knows the sensation. The two minutes of bathing cannot be perfected either, because each shower is different. At times the water will be cut short while you are still working up a lather. "Time's up!" the guards will say, even though there's still time remaining. And what can you do? Complain all you want, you're getting out.

I begin each shower the same, by quickly soaping my underarms, then my chest, my genitals, my anus, and finally the rest of my body—my back, sides, legs. I don't bother washing my face, because this can be done in my cell. Same with my feet. Last, I wash my hair with the packet of pink shampoo. It is most common for the water to be cut off at this stage, so I would much rather have shampoo in my hair than soap still on my body. The hair, too, can be finished in one's cell. I fantasize about the untimed shower, in which you have all the minutes in the world. Oh, to wash behind your ears! To lather between the cracks of your toes! What luxury!

"Where are you from?" said my bathing partner over the dividing wall.

I turned around to look at my guard, who was facing the opposite direction, his arms on his hips.

"Are you American?" my bathing partner asked.

"I live there," I said.

"I've been to Miami and Fort Lauderdale. Also San Diego, and Virginia."

"When?"

"Years ago. I was on foreign exchange to the University of Miami. I was in San Diego on spring break. I was in Virginia—"

"No talking," said Riad's guard. But then he added, "Keep it low."

"I was in Virginia to see a girl. I forgot the name of the place already. I've even forgotten the name of the girl."

I began to laugh. Miami, San Diego, Virginia! I couldn't believe what this man was telling me. He was a prisoner! He looked just like every other prisoner here. Skull cap, black beard, dark skin, dark eyes. While we were waiting in line I half expected him to spit in my face, but here he was, talking to me.

"I can't believe it," I said. "What are you doing here?"

The water was shut off. That was the end of our shower. I still had suds under my arms and shampoo in my hair. Riad didn't answer my question, though I realized it was not something that could be answered in the span of two minutes. I toweled off quickly as my guard waited with a clean uniform to hand me through the slot.

"Ah, I remember now," said Riad over the wall. "Rachel. The girl from Virginia was named Rachel."

Of course I couldn't put a face to this Rachel from Virginia.

When I asked Riad over the divider what she looked like, we were told to be quiet for the last time and whisked off separately back to our cells.

The mention of my bathing partner's love interest had me once again reminiscing about Michelle, the trips to see her in Bronxville, etc. I was embarrassed to discuss my failed relationship so indulgently with Spyro, but at the very mention of Michelle and Sarah Lawrence College my Greek acted intrigued. "Tell me more," his eyes seemed to say. I shouldn't have been so surprised. He's very familiar with the five boroughs and all the outlying districts, correcting me on locations and so forth. I'm almost sure he lives in Manhattan. Maybe, when this is all said and done, I will run into him on the street. In New York one always seems to bump into someone from the past, strolling along the avenue. Even if that person lives on the other side of the world, there they will appear, as if they had been there all along.

"You spent a lot of time with the girl," Spyro said.

"We were together two years."

"So it was pretty serious."

"It was very complicated. Michelle could be giving in her own way. She loved me. But I was holding back. Soon it became routine. We were together for that long out of comfort. There were others. I saw other women. Of course, this doesn't leave here."

"Go on," he said. "It's just you and me. Talking."

"You and me and whoever's behind that glass."

"Who? Behind this glass? There's no one." He knocked on the two-way mirror. "See?"

"I'll take your word for it. Just remember," I said. "I'm not stupid."

"Did I say that? You're a college graduate. Okay, there's a camera behind the glass, recording our meetings, but that's so we have documentation. It's mainly for your safety."

"And the camera's operator?"

"Listen, we can sit here and argue all day about whether there's someone back there or not, but the fact of the matter is, you'll never really know. Because you'll never get to see what's back there. So what's the difference? You're in here. And don't you forget it."

"How could I?" I brought my hands up from beneath the table so that he would be reminded of the chains around my wrists.

"Now, as you were saying."

"What was I saying?" I asked.

"For someone who's not stupid you're readily forgetful."

"Selective significance, like you said once."

"Did I say that?"

"Maybe it was a Russian."

"Let's get back to that weekend with the girl. Michelle. Qureshi drove you to Bronxville to see her. That was on Friday. What happened on Saturday?"

"Michelle and I went to see a play."

"And?"

Why did Spyro insist on hearing this? He wanted to know who I met. Who I talked to. Even the name of the play we saw. It was called *Goodbye, Agamemnon*. Written, produced, directed by, and starring Guatemala, one of Michelle's close friends. The play was an avant-garde piece with full-frontal nudity and dialogue without language. Actors crawled around onstage in diapers, moaning and wailing. They tore off each other's diapers with their teeth, ripping

Velcro from the poly fabric in attacklike formation. As the play went on, everyone became doused with all-purpose flour, their magnificent faces powder white. Guatemala, in character, rose to her feet, center stage, her black bush covered in white flake, and as she splayed her hands in the air the other actors began to crowd around her, pawing up at her body. She was a god reaching into the heavens, an extraterrestrial returning to the mother ship. She was Clytemnestra[1] about to kill her babies. In the denouement of voice and breath, with the life taken out of them, the actors collapsed into a pile, a mountain of bodies covered in lye. Guatemala was last among them. She fell onto her back, her armpit hair erect like two ashen flames.

What could this possibly have to do with my special agent's investigation?

The performance is significant to me only because it gave me an idea for my first New York collection. My models would march down the runway in whiteface, à la Comme des Garçons. Only not in a goth fashion, but in a clean, almost empty way. A blank, lifeless face captured so much—death, purity, sorrow. All of this would be apparent in the models' look, and it would still be faithful to my initial plans for the collection vis-à-vis hipster Williamsburg, with its youth and destructive beauty.

After the performance was the after party held at one of the dorms just a short walk from the theater. We mingled with the cast and crew, got drunk off red wine that came in cardboard boxes. The air was thick and damp with pot smoke. I met many of Michelle's

1. Medea.

friends, and we talked about the show—its open-ended meaning, plotless structure, nudity, artistic merit:

"Remember the pileup at the end? I was at the bottom left. Stage left."

"Our right."

"I remember."

"Next to Jack."

"You remember Jack. He was the one with the great cock."

"Ah yes! Of course, Jack. How could I forget? Forgive me. I didn't recognize you. I was too busy staring at his great cock."

"He's kidding. That's his sense of humor. He's Filipino. It's so random."

"That he's Filipino or that he has a strange sense of humor?"

"That he has a strange sense of humor."

"Though both are equally random."

An actress, Poppy, continued to talk to me, but I was too drunk and high simply from the air in the room, and soon I wasn't listening to her at all. I found a bowl of wasabi seaweed crackers on a chair and became involved in the sound my mouth was making as I attempted to devour the entire lot of them. The clarity brought on by the wasabi was immense. The bowl fell out of my hands and the crackers spilled onto the floor. Poppy said I was making a mess. But when I looked down I saw a pattern. Little rice crackers wrapped in dark seaweed against a black hard tile. The scales on the seaweed were natural sequins reflecting the light in the room. I arranged some of the crackers into a figure and took some pictures with my camera phone for my mood board. Poppy asked what I was doing. I ignored her. When Michelle found me I was still on the ground. Poppy told her that I had spilled the crackers.

"He's normally not like this."

That night I made love with the sour taint of beer on my lips. Michelle's skin gave off the odor of a girl intoxicated, but it was also warm and wet. Our bodies generated suction. Afterward we smoked in bed. Then we slept for a while. I woke up with her rough bristles tickling up my leg and then over my penis. I let her pin me to the mattress. Lying there, under her, I once again thought of the floured bodies in the play. The dangling cocks and Guatemala's armpit hair, the powdered faces moaning for dear life, Poppy plowing into Jack, Jack clawing up at Guatemala. I imagined Michelle blowing Jack's great cock. I pictured Guatemala naked and all white, the folds of her flesh. The images began to overwhelm me, and I lost my erection. Michelle continued her thrusting until she finished and quickly passed out on top of me. I remained awake for the rest of the night ruminating about my career and the prospect that awaited me. Ahmed as the sole investor in my clothing line.

My arrival into Grand Central Station Monday morning was always my favorite part of the trip. Commuters crisscrossing like mad under an aquamarine cathedral ceiling, their heels clicking across the marble floor, everyone out of time. They are like cattle being herded toward the slaughter. I liked to walk against the flow of traffic, to paddle against the current, and to observe the tense look on people's faces as they rushed to their offices.

I had breakfast—a café au lait and a croissant—at a coffee stand on the northwest corner of Bryant Park. I bummed a cigarette off an old Italian gentleman in suspenders and smoked while I finished my coffee. My ass was wet from the morning dew on the chairs. I remember this so clearly. It was November and it was humid, the start of a new week, the week that would have the greatest impact on my career in fashion.

That morning, back in Bushwick, Ahmed and I went over the details in his living room. Details that seemed fluid and flexible. Perhaps working this way was just easier for me because of my naïveté in business.

"If our courtship is going to blossom into fruit, and our trust grow into a stern oak, we must give it all of our fluids," Ahmed said. "By fluids, I mean water. And water is what sustains life, Boy. Life is energy. You see what I'm getting at? I'm in it all the way. Tackling a new business is like farming. Today we will plow the soil. Tomorrow we plant the seed. Come."

We took a drive—our second together. It was as if the open road was his meeting room. The Zipcar his conference table. It was all very American to me.

"I spoke to my accountant, Dick Levine. He's a Jew, good with numbers. The funds are all in place. The numbers we talked about, seventy-five K. Yes? But you understand I can't hand you the total amount. And this has nothing to do with trust! No, we're cuffed together, you and me. Dick will handle the finances, but the money is ready when you need it. When you get back to the apartment Yuksel will give you an envelope containing your first ten thousand. Well, nine thousand five. Dick feels it's best that I give it to you in these increments, for tax purposes. You understand, of course. And as expenses arise, as I said, the funds will be available to you."

He drove us over to Williamsburg so we could check out twenty-two hundred square feet of available space in the toothpick factory. The old brick building boasted giant bay windows—elliptical arches of steel and glass. It was right on the waterfront on Kent Avenue.

The loft was a dream. It was completely open, with a high cast-iron ceiling and a tremendous view of the East River. The bay windowpanes were cloudy and stained. Some were even cracked and had been taped many times over. A piece of New York history, as I saw it. My own piece. And in the whole time I lived at 113 Kent, I never had them replaced. Not even for the spanking clean view that I would have attained. Besides, at night one could make out the city skyline as if one were viewing it through a stained-glass mural. There was the sprawling Williamsburg Bridge reaching out to the Lower East Side, the towers of light downtown. The arched windows reminded me that in its original form this was once a factory of workers. And that is what I would be. A worker. Sure, I was an artist, but I had a whole first collection needing to be worked on. For all of my high-minded intentions, I knew what I needed. A dose of practicality. A blue collar around my privileged neck.

If there was one oddity about the space, it was the cage. The only freestanding structure left behind from the old factory days, the cage was a storage area under lock and key, tucked away in the darkest corner of the loft. I entertained converting it into a bedroom. It wasn't that much smaller than my studio in Bushwick, and it would give me something of a division between my sleep and work spaces. I went ahead and told Ahmed my idea. He opened the grated door, lowered himself beneath its six-foot ceiling, and ascertained that it was indeed big enough for a queen mattress, but little else. "It'll be your very own sleeper cell," he said, amused. We went on for a time referring to it as my sleeper cell. (This type of humor would be used against me prior to the Overwhelming Event, courtesy of Herizon Wireless.)[2] But in the end I determined the space too small and used it for storage.

"So, Boy, what do you think? Is it what you need?"

I was so enamored of the space—industrial concrete columns holding the turn-of-the-century ceiling aloft, newly finished hardwood floors that squeaked and cracked beneath my Nikes, natural light from the bay windows illuminating nearly every square inch, a remodeled bathroom with checkered tiles, and a modern kitchen. What a far cry from my apartment on Evergreen Avenue!

"It's perfect," I said.

---

2. Responsible for handing over Boy's phone records and transcripts of text messages in compliance with the USA PATRIOT Act of 2001.

Philip Tang 2.0

Launch me from the cannon! Boom! I say I was a bomb ready to go off on the entire industry. My collection in the works was growing, sprouting in new and unforeseen directions. Its antennae grappled for everything around me. And I stole like a bandit. For color I looked to Catherine Malandrino. For textures I turned to Comme des Garçons. For pure bravado, Galliano and McQueen. Andrew Saks once said of Coco Chanel that she was like a general, obsessed by the desire to win.[1] Nothing could better describe where my head was at this moment in time. The new pieces would draw from all of my heroes but with the added chutzpah of my own acutely developed style. And what was that style? I had been asking myself this question my whole life, but only now was it becoming clear to me. It seems that my place in New York, particularly Williamsburg, was the final piece in the maturity of this style.

The neighborhood proved to be most productive not only for my state of mind but for my state of multiple affairs (big pun coming).

Williamsburg! The name alone rang out with history and made

1. It was Maurice Sachs, the French writer, who said this. Not Andrew Saks, founder of Saks Fifth Avenue.

me think of other exotic cities that also donned the authoritative "burg": Johannesburg, St. Petersburg. It conjured great men who belonged to even greater cities, like Johan Lindeberg[2] of Stockholm, Sweden. Williamsburg was not just a place; it was a heightened state of mind. Though like any good thing—white Ferragamos, uncorked vino, mama's breast milk—it couldn't be preserved forever. I hadn't been settled into the toothpick factory for long before I noticed button-down nincompoops landing on our main strip. One could catch a glimpse of these finance types, the kind known to wear their work shirts untucked on the weekends, speaking into their clunky BlackBerrys, defaming our neighborhood by branding it "Billyburg."

With a little help from Ahmed, I had been grandfathered into my building ("grandfathered" being a term Ahmed liked to use for the way things got done in the city), and like a true New Yorker I was possessive of my own 'hood.

At those khaki financiers, I scoffed.

My disdain for these impostors swelled to outrage as winter descended. The snowfall, which looked so fresh and clean from inside, created nothing but black puddles of slush that one stepped in when not paying attention. And then the salt that the shopkeepers laid down to defeat the ice ate its way into even the best leather boots. By four o'clock the sun already began its retreat. Darkness by five. Wall Street wankers with their wrinkled shirttails along Bedford Avenue by six.

Could it be that I missed the humidity of the tropics, that muggy weather I had despised all my life? Was I, in fact, a little

2. Founder of J. Lindeberg.

homesick for a thin jersey T, a short plane ride to Palawan, a skinny-dip in a salty lukewarm bay, a cigarette in the hot sun? My very first winter in New York and I was contracting what Americans call "seasonal depression." It is because of their hard winters that so many of them require Zoloft.

What saved me from this pharmaceutical was my new studio in the toothpick factory, which by January 2003 was fully operational. Ahmed had proved true to his word. I had a sturdy drafting table, a workstation for cutting and sewing, dress forms, racks of new dresses. It was now time to tend to my neglected living quarters, marked by a mere mattress on the floor and a few bar stools. Between traveling up to Bronxville and working, I hadn't found much time to furnish. Michelle never came down because of her classes and a new play that she was writing for an independent study. When she finally did stay over one gloomy February weekend, the loft was too cold, dry, and sparse for us to get comfortable. So that Sunday after a morning brunch with her nana in Carroll Gardens we boarded a shuttle bus to New Jersey bound for exit 13A, the site of the Swedish furniture warehouse.

A strong flag has always struck me as the reason for a nation's prosperity. Look to Japan's red sun, Korea's yin yang, America's red and white bars, Israel's Jewish hexagram, Russia's hammer and sickle.[3] These are symbols of power. Color coordination, balance in design, distinguished composition. Compare those to the suffering nations. Moons, stars, evergreens—things that can be seen only through total darkness or which cast tall shadows. Put those

3. The flag of the Soviet Union ("hammer and sickle") was last used in 1991 at the time of the communist state's collapse. Russia's flag once again uses three colored stripes: red, white, blue.

symbols on palettes of blacks and reds and yellows and whites and you can almost guarantee a disaster. As colors clash, nations clash. The Philippines, Malaysia, Lebanon, Pakistan, Afghanistan—these have flags that will never fly above flourishing nations. They'll always come in dead last. You think when Francis Scott Key or whoever unveiled that season's Old Glory, the president turned to him and said, I love it but does it come in Third World?

Sir, no sir!

Perhaps these are the ramblings of a simple man taking a stab at world affairs, but when our shuttle bus pulled up to the grand furniture warehouse draped with the Swedish flag, I was overcome with a feeling of solidarity for that powerful symbol of economic prowess.

Unfortunately, this titanic pride went flaccid when we began to pace the living rooms and bedrooms and bathrooms of Swedish modernity. Sad couples took turns trying out love seats and faux rockers in a maze of domesticity. All of it—the thin walls sliced in half, the strategically lit scenes—a stage! We were walking through sets like actors in one giant play, pretending! Michelle and I, we were pretending too. Could it be that my reluctance to tend to my living area in the toothpick factory loft had stemmed from this fact, buried deep in my subconscious? We were *pretend* lovers.

Turning one of the corners, Michelle and I came upon a day care area. A child was bent over, being spanked by his mother. The child whined. Other parents and couples stood around, wondering if they should say anything. But it was the winter, a season of inaction. Everyone watched the young child get his and continued to do nothing. Perhaps it didn't matter. He was wearing a snowsuit, so I can't imagine he felt much of anything.

Nor did I as I let Michelle fill our pushcart with random marketplace articles. A colander, French press, glass jars, rice-paper lamp, bath mat, throw rug, plants, various other knickknacks. At checkout I again saw the child trailing his mother, his tears gone, and he gripped a hot dog in his hand without any sort of bun. How could he have forgotten what had just transpired? Could a little piece of beef frank make everything in his world better?

I turned to Michelle, who had a vacant look on her face. Under these lights she was no longer beautiful to me. I didn't want to be playacting anymore. But I was helpless to resist the entropy of our love. At the time I blamed the winter, but another full year would pass before I would manage to put my liberation in motion.

These were still, after all, my salad days, a time of green judgments, if I may borrow one of Michelle's stock phrases. (She was always quoting Stanislavski.)[4] In 2003 my actions addressed nothing—not Michelle, not my bed frame, which I'd have to order from West Elm. I was not concerned with the world outside of the shiny couture bubble that is the Fashion Industry—capital F, capital I.

Deep inhale now.

The industry bubble, first inflated in New York City, stretches out across the Atlantic to Paris, London, then Milan, until it goes

4. Shakespeare: "My salad days, / When I was green in judgment." From *Antony and Cleopatra*, Act 1, Scene 5.

pop at the end of a given season. That's when the designers, investors, publicists, stylists, and models look up as the profits rain down. But once the bubble is dispersed, and before you can catch your breath, there's already another bubble, a second, being inflated back in New York. Look, there it is, stretching out over Seventh Avenue. Look at all the hot air it's taking in!

Now, after months of slaving over my new line, I still wasn't one of the mouths fattening that bubble up. Who was but Philip Tang, my friend and former classmate. For all the help he'd given me when I first arrived in the city—the equipment, the connections—I was still envious of him. He had been in New York only a few years more than me and was already flirting with the top echelon of the industry. He certainly had his mouth on the bubble, and with his clothing line Philip Tang 2.0, he was giving it all he had.

Philip, the enfant terrible, was a Taiwanese immigrant who at age six had come to Manila with his family. His parents quickly made a small fortune with their store chain, Lucky Dry Clean Non-Toxic. Lucky? Try blessed. By age nine Philip was sketching couture and could operate a sewing machine all by his lonesome. At eleven he was making dresses for his two older sisters, sending them off to middle school dances like divas. By fifteen he had been admitted into FIM as the youngest student in the college's history.

It feels like yesterday that I was watching Philip work in our collective studio. My table was directly behind his. Our dress forms were side by side, outfitted with whatever we were assigned in a given week.

I sometimes called him over for his opinion in those days, but only when I had come upon something really magnificent. Once I remember finishing a short cocktail dress, what I considered the best piece I had whipped up that semester. I was proud of it, and I wanted his approval. More than anything, I wanted him to tell me I was great too.

"What do you think?" I asked him.

At first he said nothing. Just rubbed that famous mole of his, lodged in the cleft of his chin.

"I don't know," he said. "I mean, there's nothing too new here, is there? I see a tired bow where I should see something simpler. Like a belt. Here," he said, turning the dress form around. "Try this." He unraveled my ruffled bow, the piece of cloth that gave the dress its shape, and began to iron it flat on my worktable. "Look," he said with a pin in his mouth, wrapping the improvised belt around the dress. "What if it was like this? Get a buckle and make it into a belt. It's stronger. What do you think?" He pinned it into place and stood back.

"I don't know. I thought what I had was sort of Dior."

"Dior? What you had was totally conventional."

"I like conventional."

"You don't know what you like. That's why you asked me. Avoid convention at all costs. You want to end up doing bridal wear for the rest of your life? I didn't think so."

He was right. My problem as a student was that I relied too heavily on the expected. If I had a space that needed filling, I put a bow around it and called it ready-to-wear. I tried my damnedest to be as cutting-edge as Philip, but I always stopped just short of innovation. What Tang created spoke. He was in a dialogue with fashion history. I, on the other hand, merely took things from here and there, borrowed, stole, recycled. Even worse, I was unable to tell my good stuff from my bad. Isn't that the hardest obstacle we artists have to cope with? Admitting to ourselves when something isn't any good. Only during the final fashion show of that year, the dreaded contest for a scholarship to Central Saint Martins, London, did I realize what growing up I had to do. The competition for a seat at the famous art college that had spawned John Galliano and Alexander McQueen wasn't a competition at all but a Philip Tang showcase.

Models went up and down the runway before a committee of experienced judges: FIM president Gloria Sanchez; our dean of textiles, Romel Reyes; Cecily Cuaron of *Pinoy Big Brother* (season one); and Leslie T. Wasper, director of international admissions at Central Saint Martins. The judges watched Philip's collection crush the other competitors, me included, and I had a front-row seat to my own mediocrity.

When they announced the winner, Cecily C. of *Big Brother* handed Philip a bouquet of flowers. Not too long after that, he galloped off to England.

He left a big gap in our program. Draping Proficiency, Apparel Design, Corsetry, Paris versus Milan—none of our classes were the same without Tang leading us, without Tang telling me what I was doing wrong. His vacant work space in our studio was a constant reminder of his absence. His dress form remained just as he had left it, in front of my worktable, naked and alone. One night, slaving away late, I turned the form's back to me as a reminder of what I was chasing. When I cut myself accidentally with an X-acto knife, I lost it, crawling over my table and stabbing the damn dress form in its neck. It wouldn't take the first time, so I held the thing down on Philip's table and stabbed it until it did. What had I become?

Shame on me.

We stayed in touch off and on. He interned for Alexander McQueen at the same time I secretly took a job in bridal wear, though I never told him. I often thought fondly of my friend in England, but still, feelings of jealousy would arise. How I wished him to the bottom of the Thames on so many occasions—though even in these fantasies he'd rise to the top, belly up. I couldn't kill him off. I'm no murderer. As I've said, I could never hurt another soul. Not even in my dreams.

By the time our paths crossed again in New York, anybody who was anything had made their way through his studio at some point or another. It was Philip who put me in touch with Vivienne Cho my first fashion week. And as you will soon see, it was Philip who introduced me to my publicist, Ben Laden (no relation). Even my career-making involvement with Chloë, the actress-singer-songwriter, I owe partly to Philip.

Still, the snippety charm on top of his flair for the extravagant could only be taken in small doses. I had built up a tolerance for Philip long ago, but I suspected Michelle would never warm up to him.

And she didn't. She said of Philip once, "I can't see why you put up with him. He's so artificial. After listening to him go on about marketability and the state of couture, I don't know how you don't slug him right then and there. And did you notice that he always has to have the last word. Plus, he thinks he knows every-thing."

"Yes, but he's a genius," I said.

"He's not a genius."

She simply didn't need him like I did.

Philips's studio was in the old superglue factory on Grand Street, just a few short blocks from my new loft on Kent. Michelle and I had recently finished furnishing my living room with a set of pröntö chairs and a low coffee table, a mere half-shin's length above a lamb's wool throw rug. Scandinavian modern. After giving up one of her precious Saturdays to help me assemble it all, she made me promise to take her to Philip's, for she was a fan of his clothes. I'd put off their inevitable personality clash for long enough. I must also confess that a part of me wanted Philip to meet my Michelle. Although he was very gay, I thought I could still make him jealous over her, because she was an affluent American and white.

"I'm so glad you're in New York," Philip announced the moment we walked in the door. "Come here." We kissed hello. "Do you two want champagne?"

"This early?" I said. It was ten in the morning in the middle of February. Hardly the conditions for bubbly. And yet how could I know this was the day it would all really begin for me?

"We're celebrating. I haven't told you? I finally sold out. I took a Gap campaign. It's just a thing on the side. They want me to reenvision the little black dress. The Gap is trying to revamp their image. Bring a little glamour into suburbia. Infect the malls with a little Philip Tang. Doo Ri Chung[5] did it last year. The money is insane. I'm buying everyone turquoise Vespas."

5. Proprietor of the label Doo.Ri.

Philip called to the other end of the studio, where a few of his assistants were crowded around a fit model, taking Polaroids. "Rudy, bring the champagne from the minifridge. And come meet my friends."

Rudy Cohn, a beautiful black Jewess, was a dear friend of Philip's from their London days interning with Alexander McQueen. She often hung around his studio because he cherished her opinion the way I valued Olya's, scarce as she'd become since Michelle entered the picture. Now Rudy dabbled as a freelance stylist to the stars in both America and Europe. Of particular relevance to my state of affairs: She was Chloë's stylist. The actress-singer-songwriter was on track to become the next Madonna faster than the world needed one, and it was Rudy's job to put her in the right clothes. Chloë wasn't too big yet. Her second album, *Blueballer*, the one that garnered a Grammy nod, hadn't yet "dropped," as they say. And so her famous ass could still fit into something by an obscure designer such as myself.

Rudy arrived with the champagne and plastic cups. I was hopelessly attracted to her working-class Manchester accent, complemented this wintry morning by a blouse that showed a tasteful amount of cleavage, just enough for one's imagination to get lost in the gap between her two mocha breasts. Her fragrance was something by Serge Lutens. Cèdre or Ambre Sultan. No, I remember, it was Sa Majesté la Rose.

"It's crazy around here," Philip said. "I'm working a thousand hours a day. You know, I'm doing the Gap thing, but then I'm pushing forward on this new fall line."

"Mustn't forget Chloë," said Rudy.

"Oh, right. And Chloë is coming by later this afternoon."

Who doesn't get starstruck? The mere mention of Chloë drove me up the wall with jealousy. She was coming to Philip's studio to see Philip. I had to be there. This was an opportunity not to be squandered. "Really?" I squeaked.

"The pop star?" Michelle added, with just the slightest detectable touch of sarcasm.

"Well, she's going to be more than a pop star in a few months," Rudy answered. "Her acting has gotten a lot better."

Philip poured my glass. "Actually, Boy, maybe you and Rudy could have a word?" He turned to her: "Boy's got a great collection in the works. You should put Chloë in something of his." Then he said to me: "You need a publicist to make things happen, Boy. Give my friend Ben Laden a call. He's the shit." He waltzed over to a side table and returned with Ben's card. "I'm so sorry," he said to Michelle. "I'm all ADD today. A gazillion things are happening at once. How are you?"

She smiled at Philip's enthusiasm, but it was a manufactured smile, I could tell. She despised him already.

We took a seat on the sofa, away from the flash of Polaroids, and sipped our champagne. Philip stood up. "We forgot to toast."

"My God, Philip. We've been toasting all morning."

"Well, we're celebrating."

"We're always celebrating," Rudy said.

"What can I say? To Boy and Michelle. You're so cute together. Aren't they so fucking cute?"

Rudy blushed.

Philip sat down again next to Rudy and placed his little shaved head on her shoulder with a lover's intimacy. Rudy looked at me, but I tried to ignore whatever was happening between us for

Michelle's benefit. Michelle was very perceptive, however. Picking up on this flirtation, she studied me. I felt the pressure of her gaze, even after I'd turned my attention to the skylight in the ceiling. "This studio gets wonderful light during the day," I said.

"When else would it get light?" Michelle said.

"I suppose you're right."

"Michelle," said Philip, "did you know that Boy was all the rage back in the Philippines? You should see the blogs during last year's Philippine Fashion Week. It was all about Boy."

"I didn't even know they had a Philippine Fashion Week," she said.

"Neither did I."

"Boy's just being modest. Michelle, you want to see the hype around this guy, go to Bryan Boy dot com. Bryan Boy is this brilliant blogger whose site gets like a jazillion hits a day. I was telling Marc about him last week. He may name a bag after him."[6]

Bryan Boy had featured my clothes one day on his blog shortly before I left Manila. It was the only coverage I'd gotten in my career.

One of Philip's assistants called over with a question. Julia, I believe, who worked on textiles. As this Julia distracted Philip and Rudy, Michelle looked at me wide-eyed and mouthed: "Let's go." She mimed hanging herself with a noose. I gave her a face that begged for a few more minutes, and she in turn tugged the

6. Marc Jacobs did name a bag after Bryan Boy. The BB by Marc Jacobs, $2,199, Fall '06.

rope even harder, tightening the imaginary noose, gagging herself.

"You all right?" Rudy asked.

"I'm fine. It's champagne. It makes me gag."

"Ha," I said.

In later encounters with fashion types like Philip, Michelle would often put an imaginary gun in her mouth, slit her throat with her index finger, or mime sticking her head in an oven. I asked her once how she could be so turned off by my crowd when she was so fashionable. One of the things I found incredibly alluring about her, remember, was her sense of style. She told me: "I love clothes. I just don't see the need to suck up to those people like you do. They're hideous, egocentric . . . *hyenas!*"

But Philip really had produced an ungodly amount of work in a period of only a few months. And nearly all of it was brilliant. He had twenty to thirty new looks completed. To give you an idea of where I was in comparison, my first collection had ten to twelve.

"I'm really into baggy right now," he said.

"Well, it's not baggy, is it?" Rudy said.

"No, I suppose not. Not baggy but loosey."

"Yeah, more loose than baggy."

"What's the difference?" Michelle interrupted.

"Baggy, I think big jeans worn below the waist, yeah? Hip-hop is baggy," said Rudy. "Baggy is deliberate, in'it? This is loose."

"And puffy," I added.

"Right," said Philip. "Puffy."

"Well," Michelle concluded, as if the whole thing made no sense whatsoever.

Philip went through most of the dresses. They were knee-length and sleeveless, made from exquisite wools. He took a few off the rack and held them up to the light, one by one. I'd admired him when we were students, but now he was a fully formed artist, I stood in awe. How different each look was from anything I had seen, even from him! This new line was much darker than the collections he had done before. It brooded and slouched. It was sorrow and anguish and jealousy. I saw myself. In the greatest art we see ourselves reflected back at us, do we not? *Guernica*, *The Scream*. For me to witness an artist of such caliber at the height of his capabilities was a gift! Even Michelle, responding to the dresses, couldn't deny Tang his due. She despised him, it was true, but she could never say anything bad about the clothes.

And oh, how he could weave beauty! There was one dress in particular that I still remember. I could pull it out of a lineup to this day. It was a black, sleeveless evening dress made from recycled hosiery. Going green got you noticed. The skirt was ruffled, layer upon layer, like a blossoming flower. "Puffy" and "loose" were the wrong words to describe it. It was flowing and movable even though it was composed of highly constricting material. Its hem was laced with black floral knots. It was a dress that was completely unwearable, yet you knew it would be the centerpiece of the collection. I believe it's the very dress that got the CFDA[7] doing cartwheels. They gave Philip Best New Designer 2003. Within eight months it was on display at the Tate Modern. Joseph Beuys, Marlene Dumas, Pollock, Tang 2.0.

7. Council of Fashion Designers of America.

Damn him, he was that good.

Michelle pulled us out of there before I had the chance to meet Chloë. As soon as we were on the street she launched straight into her bad review of the day. "Abhorrent. Flimsy. Those people are lost beyond repair. And did you see how your friend Philip offered me those sample sizes knowing very well that none of them would fit me? And I had to go over and act all interested. And that Rudy! Ugh. I'm sorry, I know they're your friends, but they're just not my kind of people."

But these same abhorrent, flimsy people were how I met Ben Laden, my soon-to-be publicist and good friend. If it hadn't been for Philip, perhaps I would be sewing bridal wear in some backroom in the garment district of Manhattan. Then again, perhaps sewing bridal wear would ultimately have been a fate preferable to mine.

Thinking about this moment in my life makes me wonder about fate. For most of my life I believed I was bound to a certain destiny, a purpose to exist. I believed that good things were in store if only I believed in myself. But look at what happened to me. For that matter, look at what happened to Ben. What did he do? An American native, Irish Catholic in fact. You'd think he'd have luck on his side. But because of some phonetic coincidence with the world's most wanted man, Ben ended up losing most of his clients. He took a hit because of some other guy's mess. Makes me suspect there is no such thing as fate. Only coincidence. Life is a series of coincidences. It was a coincidence that Rudy Cohn, Chloë's stylist, happened to be at Philip's studio that day, and that Philip had pitched my work to her, triggering a series of events that would lead Chloë to make a red carpet appearance in my inside-out dress at the

Grammys two years later (but for the performance of her hit single, "Chas-titty," that same night, it would be Philip Tang 2.0 that she'd change into). My rise as a hot new designer was precipitated by Ben Laden's loss of clientele after 9/11, coincidentally, and so I was given a dedicated publicist willing to promote me to the world. What great coincidences. So many random connections! And far too many mythical explanations for them!

I ask you, is it fate that I am in here and you are out there?

The Story of My Bathing Partner

I shall devote today's installment to the story of my bathing partner. I cannot, in good conscience, keep it to myself any longer. (I trust my special agent will know what to do with this information.) You see, over the last few weeks I have gotten to know this man, my bathing partner, and from what I have learned about his situation, I believe a mistake has been made. Just as a mistake has been made with me. I do not mean to abuse my writing privileges by indulging in what the officials here may deem a cryptic tangent, and so I will respectfully curtail this digression.

Riad S—, my bathing partner, had trained as a civil engineer but left his discipline for something nobler in his eyes. He became a bookseller, opening his own specialty bookshop with the small amount of money he had inherited from a distant uncle in Pakistan. The shop was in Birmingham, England. The uncle was a real loner, as I understand it, and so he left everything to Riad, his favorite nephew, the boy who was already so well traveled—Europe, the United States, the Middle East, Asia. It wasn't as if the uncle didn't have any other descendants. Riad came from a big family. But the uncle knew that by giving the money to Riad he was ensuring that it would not be squandered. And good for the uncle, because he was right. Riad opened his own business, the only bookshop of its kind in this working-class section of Birmingham.

Unfortunately, the shop was not much of a success, and Riad had to close its doors within a year. There were really too many factors to say why the shop failed. Now a failed bookseller, Riad gathered his very pregnant wife, packed their bags, and moved the whole family to Pakistan, a place he often mythologized. Why? Several reasons. For one, this is where his family was from. The S—'s of Islamabad. And Riad felt he could do some good in Pakistan, perhaps by returning to his career as an engineer. The decision was also one of faith. Riad, a practicing Muslim, wanted his unborn daughter to grow up in a country where she would be surrounded by other little Muslim children. And there was no shortage of those in Pakistan. As we all know, childhood can be such a cruel stint, and Riad felt it best that his daughter not grow up in a place consumed by fear. This was the age of fear, remember. Riad saw Pakistan as a second chance, a new way of life for his family, one where they could live comfortably numb. His wife could have a maid to help with the baby. And when the baby got older, she could attend a Muslim school with other little Muslims just like her. Life would be sweet in Pakistan.

And so the young couple moved to Islamabad, where the wife, we'll call her Manal, did get her own maid. Riad was able to find work as an engineer, for the government. And the baby, born by a reputable doctor, was healthy and fat. And then there were three, plus the maid. But Riad had a weak spot. His empathy. After all his good fortune in his new country, he just wasn't satisfied. Even as his boss at the government office, aware of Riad's talents, showered him with promotion after promotion, would you believe that Riad still wanted more? Not more, I should say, but *less*. Riad longed to help the lesser off, the poor. Call it a hobby. We all have

those. There were plenty of corners in Pakistan for Riad to practice his new hobby. Which led him to travel outside of Islamabad,
where the lesser off seemed to proliferate. He traveled to the
southern provinces of Sindh and Balochistan and to the western
towns bordering Afghanistan (a horrible place at the time, and
even more horrible today, as I understand it).

What can be said? Riad had a soft spot for the poor. He was,
in the classic sense of the term, a real "do-gooder." Eventually his
empathy led him away from his career. He began to take more and
more time off to travel to these impoverished areas, where he
brought along, among other things, books. Literature. He still had
a passion for books. He never gave up on them. (His words.) He
frequented bookshops all over the country. Books were cheap in
Pakistan, and he bought them in bulk, as he once had as a bookseller. Then he distributed the literature to these impoverished
towns, where the people could barely write their own names.
Though Riad claims never to have stepped foot in Afghanistan,
his charity brought him into tribal-run areas in the north where
the border between the two countries is somewhat blurry—where
Riad may as well have stepped across the border. "What's the
difference?" his interrogators would say to him anyway.

And yet Riad wasn't arrested in one of the poor districts or the
dangerous tribal areas. Riad S—, of Birmingham, was in no way
connected with weapons or jihad; in fact, he was promoting just
the opposite—the word. Not just God's word but poetry and
literature—Islamic, sure, but also translations of English clas-
sics, like Charles Dickens. And he had help. Friends, translators,
others involved in his cause. A whole caravan of book peddlers.
No matter. You see, the man we perceive as a do-gooder was to

others an antagonist. Throughout his travels he got on many people's nerves. One such nerve belonged to a mullah who was up for reelection in some poor, shitty district. This mullah saw Riad as someone trying to undermine his campaign, administering foreign literature to eligible voters who couldn't even read. The mullah had ties in the government, a cousin's cousin or what have you, and it might have been as simple as placing a call, speaking Riad's name into a receiver to so-and-so, who gave the name to so-and-so, and on up the chain of command. Well, what happened next wasn't so pleasant, and it is the only part of Riad's story that mirrors mine.

The knock on the door in the middle of the night.

My Name Is (B)oy

So very much is in a name. Ralph Lifshitz and Donna Ivy Faske are nobodies, but Ralph Lauren and Donna Karan are gods. A name can bring happiness, fame, fortune, but it can also destroy you. Such was the case for my publicist, Ben Laden.

Ben was an architect of fame. He could build names into brands, and he operated with panache. He had everything to do with getting my own name exposure. Ben had been an established name himself in New York in the late nineties, representing all of the hot ethnic designers, mostly Asians. Doo Ri Chung, Derek Lam, Pho[2], Yellow Bastard, and later Philip and Vivienne. But after 9/11 Ben felt the hurt, personally and professionally. His brother, Patrick Laden, a police officer twice decorated, was in the north tower when it fell. Then, without a minute's notice, more than half of Ben's clientele dropped out—most of the aforementioned, with the exception of Vivienne and Philip. All because of a name. When I finally worked up the courage to ring him, Ben was willing to take on even the smallest unknown designers. Though he would have taken me on Philip's word alone.

We first met over dinner at Freeman's. We were drunk by the time the appetizers were served. One Manhattan after the next, we talked about fashion, art, and all the latest gossip: which sell-outs had an eyewear or fragrance deal in the works, who was banging whom. By the time I dug into my pork chop it had gone cold. At the end of the night, out came the Macallan, and Ben couldn't contain himself.

"Boy," he started in, "you think I give a lick about what people think of me? Do I look like an Osama to you? I'm a gay Irishman from Queens. The youngest of four. Our name used to be McLaden, but my grandpappy dropped the Mc because he didn't like being called Mac everywhere he went. In his day it was derogatory. He took an offense. This was at a time when an Irishman couldn't get a cab in this city, let alone a decent job. My, how everything comes back around. So he changed the family name, and I'll be damned if I'm going to change it back because some jihadi thinks himself Allah's messenger. Disgrace my grandpappy? I've lived lies for most of my life, but when I came out to my parents in 1987, I said, 'That's it. No more.'" Ben took a swig. "Honest to God. That's all we can be."

"True that."

"There isn't a lot of loyalty in this business. Believe me, I've borne the brunt of it. But I'm a goddamn patriot first and foremost. I'll be the first in line to wring al-Qaeda around the neck. We'll skip trial, verdict, what have you. And my brother, the hero . . . After all this, would you believe the FBI has been to my house? Do you know that I was detained trying to fly out of JFK. I missed London Fashion Week altogether. I never made it past check-in. The clerk looked at me like I was putting him on. This is the age we're living in. My job will be to shield you from all of this nonsense. The world as it is will not be your world. With me you won't have to worry about a goddamn thing. Now where's that rugged waiter? I'm running on empty." Ben snapped his fingers and the waiter appeared.

"We'll get the check," I said, trying to inspire our exit. I didn't want Ben to become any redder in the face. I'd soon learn that the scotch whiskey only came out when he talked about his namesake.

"Nonsense, we'll have two more," he told the waiter. He turned to me. "They made us wait forty-five minutes for a table, now they can wait on us forty-five minutes more. It's an eye for an eye where I come from."

"You come from Queens," I said.

"I mean America, Boy. America."

He was hungry like I was. His clients were still dropping out by the fistful, only he used that betrayal as fuel to salvage his reputation. He was a stand-up, all-around, cutthroat guy's guy. He had grit, guts, and gusto—the three Gs as he called them. His rough, leathery face had seen one too many hours in the tanning bed, and written in the lines around his eyes was the story of a man who wouldn't be defeated.

Christ, Ben was born into this world just as we all are—with no say in his damned name. And he would help me make mine.

Philip opened his own boutique in the summer of 2003 at the intersection of Howard and Crosby—the crossroads of Chinatown and downtown chic. Opening Ceremony, Rogan, Chinese teashop, bad dim sum, and then Philip Tang 2.0. Philip had just been awarded best new designer in women's wear by the CFDA, beating out Zac Posen, who came in second. They gave Philip one hundred thousand dollars for his promise. Me, a familiar face from Manila and a close personal friend, I got to share in Philip's success. I spent the rest of that year helping him with his seminal fall/winter and spring '04 collections. I sat front row at the shows with Ben, Vivienne, Rudy Cohn, and even Chloë. I was introduced to editors and buyers alike as Ben toted me around on his arm like a trophy lay, displaying me throughout the tents in Bryant Park, the after parties at Hiro and Masquerade. It had been a year since my stroll down Forty-second Street had brought me face-to-face with menu man, my doppelgänger, in front of the Sovereign Diner. How it could have gone that way for me! I owe all I owe to myself, because I was not going to let it happen. I was not going to be a walking menu! And now I had Ben and a whole crew of important people who would shepherd me away from all that darkness.

I was also consistently working on my line in preparation for the (B)oy launch scheduled for the following winter. We were planning a small runway show for February during fashion week. Ben would make sure all of the right people showed, and after, depending on whether anything sold (which was unlikely for a first collection, even I knew that), I'd adapt whatever worked best into a line of knitwear that I could sell out of consignment shops. There was indeed a market for handmade clothing by new designers on a small scale. One couldn't make a living off of it, but it was a way to get some notice. And if an editor was putting together a story on rising New York designers, particularly Brooklyn designers, Ben would make sure I got in.

Throughout the year Ahmed stopped by the studio intermittently to check in on his investment, or his "garden," as he put it. "Look at all of these clothes! How our garden does grow! Didn't I pin the tack on the camel's ass? You and me together will take over the world!"

But more often than not he would disappear for long periods of time, sometimes weeks. I never really knew where he went off to. One day he'd stop by for a look at the collection; the next he'd

be in Moscow or Marrakesh. Yes, it's true. Michelle always hassled me about whether I thought I could trust him. But she hassled
me about everything, and I honestly didn't think I was in a position to question Ahmed's trust. I mean, he was funding my label
entirely. He had set me up in Williamsburg in the toothpick factory. It was Ahmed who should have been worried about trusting
me. I could have run off with his investment.

Plus, it wasn't like I'd been completely relying on Ahmed's
payments, anyway. I had plenty of money coming in from my work
on Philip's line, combined with filling in some days at his new
boutique on Howard, as well as the odd job for Vivienne Cho.

But as 2004 approached, and Ben and I started scouting locations for our first runway show, I was suddenly in need of capital
I didn't have. And of course the one time I desperately needed
Ahmed, he decided to take off for an entire month, only to reap-
pear at my doorstep one January morning straight from JFK.

"Where have you been?" I said. "I've been trying to get ahold
of you."

"Russia. Scouting mission with modern-day Cossacks. It's
another business venture. I'll tell you all about it if and when it
pans out."

"We need to put a large down payment on a space for the
fashion show," I told him. "Somewhere near Seventh Avenue."

"Talk to Dick. What's the problem?"

"I did talk to Dick. He has me on a spending freeze."

"Why?"

"You tell me. This is a crucial point in our business. If we don't
have a show we have nothing. We have a collection that doesn't
get seen. Tell me, what good is that?"

"Boy, not a problem. We call Dick now. We figure it out. And stop giving me that look."

"What look?"

"Like you need to crap."

Immediately, we got Dick Levine, CPA, on speaker. It was over my cell phone, so the speaker volume was a little weak. Ahmed and I had to lean into each other, our heads turned at a most uncomfortable angle.

"Dick?" said Ahmed. "It's Ami, beby. I'm here with Boy Hernandez, our designer."

"Don't beby me," said Dick. "I knew this was coming. You ratted me out, huh *Boychik?* You little snake. As if this is all my fault."

"Easy, Dick. What's the problem with the account?"

"What's the problem? I'll tell you the problem. It's dry. We've run dry. Boy has been spending like it's going out of style. No pun intended."

This was a gross exaggeration.

Ahmed turned to me. "Boy, is this true? What Dick says—"

"I had to hire a publicist. A good one. Ben Laden."

"Who?"

"Christ O mighty," said Dick.

"Ben Laden. There's no relation. He's the best publicist in town. We're getting all sorts of good press because of him."

"Dick, you heard Boy. He had to hire a publicist. This Bin Laden."

"I heard. Way to go. Bin Laden. We'll all end up in federal prison by mere association. I can see it now. Dolce, Gabanna, and Levine indicted on tax fraud and conspiring to commit acts of terror. Listen, I'm just telling you two how it is. We've run out of money."

"How?" I pressed him.

"How? He asks *how*. How should I know? You don't keep receipts. We've been an all-cash operation so far, so who's keeping track of where the money's going. Not me. Boy, I've said it before. You have to be vigilant about keeping receipts. *Vigilant*."

"Vigilant, Boy," repeated Ahmed, who had once called receipts *reeshmeets* just to mock me.

"Okay," I said. "But both of you have been giving me mixed signals."

Dick continued: "You're my only two clients—who may or may not be legal residents—schlepping pricey product in a very public sphere. Before you two Versaces steer us through the fog into that very big iceberg up ahead, I'm putting a cap on all spending."

"Ah, so there is money left. You see Boy, he's good at what he does."

"Oh no, we're definitely in the red," said Dick. "I wasn't kidding about that."

"Hmm, Boy here says we need to put a down payment on a space for the fashion show."

"Somewhere downtown," I added.

"Well then, we'll need a loan. I can do the paperwork if that's what you want to do."

"Hold on that, Dick. Let me talk to Hajji first. I think I can get one without going through the banks."

This was the first mention of Hajji, a man who would come to plague me in my final days before the Overwhelming Event. Had I known what I was getting into then, maybe things could have worked out differently. Damn these known unknowns.

"Ahmed, let me say this. If I don't know where the money is

coming from, we'll be entering some very scary territory," Dick said. And he was right. I suddenly thought of my auntie Baby, the moneylender, who was murdered in her hotel room at the Shangri-la.

"It's Hajji, beby. You know Hajji."

"The Indian gangster?"

"He's a businessman."

"God help us. Just call me back when you figure out what you want me to do. Maybe the less I know the better. They can't flip me if I don't know anything."

"Beby, cool your jets. It'll all work out. If it doesn't we'll think of something."

"Like one-way tickets to Venezuela."

"He's such a kidder this guy. You're such a kidder, Dick. Ciao, huh."

Expecting a reprimand, I quickly tried to explain myself to Ahmed. But he wouldn't hear me out. "Zip! 'Am I my brother's keeper?' as Cain once said to Abel.[1] Money shan't ever come between us. This is why we have Dick, accountant nonpareil. We're a legitimate business company now, Boyo. I'll talk to Hajji."

"This Indian gangster?"

"Listen, I was borrowing money from Hajji when you were still feeding from Mama's teat."

Without fail Ahmed always got the last word, dropping such bestial metaphors from philosophical heights. He could go from French jargon and biblical tales to tits and ass in two seconds flat. Tolerating him was at times incredibly difficult. Though it would be nothing in

1. It was Cain who asked this of God after Cain murdered Abel.

comparison to what I've had to tolerate here in No Man's Land. I've never spent so much time with other men, and it becomes increasingly testing. Tolerance? Ha! I knew nothing about what I could or couldn't tolerate. Which leads me to mention that my circumstances here grow more absurd and inhumane by the day.

For instance, yesterday—Columbus Day, in fact—they took away our plastic water bottles. We each get a plastic water bottle in No Man's Land, and as punishment, they were taken away from us. All because one of the men on the block tried to eat his during the night. The man crumpled the bottle up and then began to chew. Of course, it's a piece of plastic, so he didn't get anywhere by chewing alone. Assisted swallowing is what the guards are calling it, I believe. Meaning once the man determined he couldn't swallow the bottle by means of chewing, he used his hands to force it down the hatch. Though he didn't manage to eat all of it. It was early morning when we were woken up by the medics and guards rushing to his cell. He was taken out before the morning prayer. I caught a glimpse of him convulsing on the stretcher as they took him out, the bottle already removed from his mouth. Blood spatter covered his shirt and face. So much that it looked as if he had slit his own throat.

Because of yesterday's incident with the water bottle, everyone on the block suffers. No more plastic. They've switched us to Styrofoam cups, which Win tells me is what they used in No Man's Land at the beginning.

Me, I couldn't care one way or the other what I drink my water out of. But the others reacted very badly to the Styrofoam. Today, as the guards administered the new cups, one per cell, the prisoners started up a protest by cursing and spitting. It was a synchronized protest, everyone at once. I am used to their outbursts by now. I have been its target in the prison yard, remember. But this time, when the guards told them to quiet down, they resisted, and continued to act like a bunch of animals. Each prisoner did a fine job of contributing to the overall chaos, banging his cell door, kicking and screaming, throwing piss at the guards with the new Styrofoam cups. I could make out Riad's voice at the other end of the block. He was carrying on just like the others. Cursing, not in his British voice but in the voice he used when he spoke Arabic. The guards put on face protectors to shield themselves from the urine being hurled into the corridor. I tell you, it was madness. There was a brief second when I thought the prisoners were really going to take control of the cell block, that somehow they had the power to get out of their cells and overtake the guards.

What happens to the animals in their cages when they become unruly?

The SMERF[2] squad is called in to sedate them. The SMERF squad is composed of four guards in black riot gear, and they come marching through the corridor, one behind the other, at a slow, intimidating pace. One, two, three, four. The first soldier carries a shield, and the others have various contraptions: shackles, cuffs, clubs, pepper spray, etc. They tell each prisoner individually to stand down. The prisoner does not listen, of course. In fact, at the sight of the SMERF squad most everyone goes ape shit. So the SMERFs proceed to enter the cell while the prisoner stands at the back of his cage. First he gets doused with pepper spray. Then he is rammed with the shield. All the SMERFs hold

2. Secure Military Emergency Reaction Force.

him down while he is shackled, and if the prisoner resists he is
met with a series of non-injurious acts (clubs, fists, boot heels,
etc.). Once the SMERFs have the prisoner sedated, they drag him
out by his feet, sometimes facedown. It is a most violent display
of authority, but completely necessary, especially when the prisoners carry on as they have been today.

Oh, if I could only transport myself back to my first show in
New York, moments before curtain! February 10, 2004, a Tuesday. Each model backstage standing at attention, perched in
dress. Olya, Anya, Dasha, Kasha, Masha, Vajda, Marijka, Irina,
Katrina, etc. Anya in silk organza, Vajda in a lilac taffeta, and
Olya, dear Olya, running around topless with sequin pasties! To
see this again would give me the most fulfillment. All of my girls
did the show for free as a favor to me, though I made sure I paid
them in trade after the trunk show. Always return a favor. Ahmed
taught me that. When the loan came through from Hajji, Ahmed
shipped him a case of scotch, Black Label.

My first collection, Transparent Things, was composed of a
modest twelve looks. Striped evening dress in black and gray-
asparagus. Ultrashort bloomer skirt in gray silk organza. White
tucked schoolmarm blouse. Sequin cocktail dress in seaweed with
matching mittens and skullcap. Transparent black lace burka over
sparkling G-string and matching pasties. Black silk crêpe cocktail dress with velvet turban. Unstructured pantsuit in floral black
lace atop silk blouse. Bias-cut dress in black lace with embroi-
dered web overlay. Bustier sheath dress in lilac taffeta. White
A-line skirt in thick nylon sailcloth. Stretchy gabardine skirt,
dyed seaweed. Evening dress, double-layered pink organza. I
used the faintest splash of color when I could, an occasional pink

or yellow atop a controversial black or antiseptic white. Because fashion, as Chanel once said, is both caterpillar and butterfly.

In the audience were a few minor editors low on the totem pole; Binky Pakrow for Neiman Marcus and Chester Pittman for Barneys were the only two buyers maybe worth naming. Chester was a Telly Savalas look-alike, a real fatso with a penchant for handsome young boys. He once tried to bed me after a lunch meeting at the Thompson Hotel, promising a room he'd booked upstairs with a bottle of Dom Pérignon on ice. Getting my clothes into Barneys could have been that easy, but I wasn't willing to whore myself beneath the folds of Chester Pittman.[3]

In the front row was Gil Johannessen for *Women's Wear Daily*. He was sandwiched between Natalie Portman and one of the members of The Strokes.[4]

Ben was there, of course. So were Philip, Rudy Cohn, Dreama Van der Sheek, Ester Braum of Pho$^{(2)}$. Most of my friends from Williamsburg came to fill out the seats and support the label. Musicians and artists and models. I had rented a dance studio, and the mirrors on both sides gave the show a crowded importance. The guys from the design-build collective at the toothpick factory cut me a deal and built us a runway.

Michelle came, all alone, since I had been preparing for most of the day. She looked adorable in a Jill Stuart dress I had given her on her birthday. I sat her up front next to Ben, away from Rudy, with whom I had begun a working relationship filled with

3. A spokesperson for Barneys has publicly denied this allegation.
4. Natalie Portman wasn't there. According to my notes, I was seated in the second row between Kelly LeBrock and Scary Spice of the disbanded girl group the Spice Girls.

not-so-innocent flirtations. I knew it would only be a matter of time before we became lovers. Our advancements in friendship, the constant making of plans so as not to leave our next run-in to chance, confirmed my suspicions. After being in Rudy's presence, off I would go, my hyperactive imagination working. I dreamed of kissing her flagrant lips and then having them wrapped around my anaconda while I moved on to kissing her other fragrant lips.

Ahmed turned up backstage to wish me luck on his way out of town.

"Cover up, gels," he said. "Grandpa coming through. Boy, there you are! Look at these clothes! We're really making waves in the garment business. Anywho, as this is our first fashion show together, I wanted to wish you much success with tonight's big event. As they say in our adopted country: break a leg. Break 'em both. It just so happens I have business tonight out by the airport and I won't be staying. But I see that you have everything under control."

"But Ahmed?"

"I know, I know. I'll make it up to you, Boy. Ciao, huh?"

"I can't even be mad right now I'm so nervous."

Olya came over and kissed Ahmed hello. She was wearing only the sequin pasties over her nipples and a matching G-string. Both were to be visible through the transparent burka.

"Darling, you are beautiful as the day is long."

"Ahmed, why don't you call me like I ask?" she pouted.

"My dear, I wouldn't last a minute with you. You know that. You'll kill me in a heartbeat." He tapped his chest.

"Olya, where is your top? And why aren't you in makeup?"

"Boy, I'm wearing a burka with a veil over my face. God, *ree-lax*. I go to makeup now."

"Yeah relax, Boy." Ahmed winked. "I will see that Olya finds her top. Come, dear. Show me."

She took his arm and Ahmed escorted her over to makeup where most of the girls were getting their faces powdered stark white.

I peeked through the curtain and the house was filling up. But there were still more people backstage than there were out front. I had called on all of my friends to help with the show, and the downside of this was that my friends invited their friends, and so everyone was hanging out backstage. Sure, it was festive and exciting but we were running thirty minutes behind.

"Listen," I announced, "if you're not working get the fuck out of here! I'm sorry to be an ass, it's just too confusing. Ahmed? Where is he? Ahmed?"

The line manager began the curtain call. "Dasha, Kasha, Masha . . ."

"Where is Ahmed?"

"Anya, Olya . . . Olya . . ."

"What? I'm coming," she said, running to the curtain in the burka and a light veil over her face, deep red lipstick perfect and visible. The girls lined up in order. "Vajda, Marijka, Irina, Katrina . . ." The room began to clear. Olya parted her veil, leaned over, and gave me a big kiss. I looked around again but there was no sign of Ahmed. He had vanished. In his place: a panoply of (B)oy-clad nymphs and goddesses.

From then on everything began to move so fast.

Nothing from the shows sold, but I was able to adapt those twelve looks into a knitwear line that could be produced by two Chinese cousins out in Sunset Park. Ming and Lei. Strong seamstresses who followed directions. Ahmed found them for us. The knitwear we were able to place in consignment shops downtown and around Brooklyn. Some boutiques in Los Angeles got onboard too, and before you knew it, things were selling out. The shops and boutiques were finally asking for more.

Unfortunately, with each new stride my line made, the heavy drag-ass feeling I'd been suffering with Michelle only worsened. Your work takes all of your soul, proving it difficult to come up with another energy reserve, that which is needed to sustain a serious relationship. Now that my label was a full-time job, being asked to travel out to Sarah Lawrence was nothing but a hassle. I don't want to cheapen her feelings for me, but it seemed like I was under pressure to carry two loads, my label and Michelle's mental state. In fact, I was beginning to suspect that Michelle suffered from manic depression. The occasional staring off, the tears after sex, the unmarked bottle of pills in her YSL handbag, the obscenities that came out of her when we fought, like a seasonal Turrets[5]—"faggot," "gay bastard," "twat." She had some mouth on her. It was all related. I came from a family of doctors, remember. She had to be bipolar.

These bouts took a severe turn around the time of her beloved nana's death. The old bugger had made it to ninety-one, nearly a full century of toil. And Michelle didn't think Nana had been given a fair chance. I was by her side during the wake for two full days at the Montauk Club on Eighth Avenue in Brooklyn, forced to come up to the casket with her to view the body. "She had just begun a new chapbook of poems," Michelle said. "She was so

---

5. Tourette syndrome.

happy writing again, looking back on her life. Why now? Why couldn't it happen after she finished them?"

"Maybe you can finish them for her?" I said. "Like a collaboration."

"Not while I'm grieving. Let me grieve, you miserable twat. Just hold me."

Ahmed tried to help me through the small crisis of guilt I was having in wanting to leave Michelle. "Go, have this fling. It's a cure-all," he swore. "How do you think I got over my second wife so quickly?"

"I thought you were only married once."

"That was Sheela. I was married again for six weeks to a dancer in Lahore. Yasmin. She ran off to Bollywood and I never knew what became of her. I like to imagine she contracted some horrible skin disease and had to have one of her legs amputated. What beautiful legs too! I know—cruel and unusual, but that's love. Anyhow, it was a blonde with big tits who got my mind off of her. A *prostituta*. Go out and get your ramrod sucked, and don't feel like you owe anybody anything."

"That's not exactly what I wanted to hear at the foot of temptation."

"Consider this. During both my marriages I remained completely faithful. It's true. Now I've told you some stories about my adventures in the sheets, but it's time to come clean. The truth is, I never strayed. Not a slipup. This was at a time when I was dining with the world's upper classes. Lady Di, the Prince of Wales, Boutros Boutros-Ghali. These were the circles that your Ahmed ran in, beby. And I grappled with temptations on more than one occasion. Real propositions, Boy. These weren't the models you're so

The Enemy at Home

As of this morning's reservation it has come to my attention that my ex, Michelle Brewbaker, the whore of Bronxville, has written a play about me. This play, conveniently titled *The Enemy at Home or: How I Fell for a Terrorist*, is causing quite a stir—as reported in the *New York Post* dated September 15 (over one month ago). Special Agent Spyro was kind enough to save me the article with a few redacted details regarding the play's location. Due to the fact that I am neither an enemy nor a terrorist—soon to be proven at my tribunal—I'm hopeful that this little Off-Broadway romp[1] will indeed go gently into that good night. According to the article *The Enemy at Home*, then in rehearsal, was set to open on the thirtieth of September, which means it is already a few weeks in the running.

"I would like a copy of the play, if possible," I said to Spyro.

"I'll see what I can do. As you know, getting you things to read can be quite difficult. They have to pass all sorts of clearances. You see what's happened with this article. It's from September. We're now in the middle of October."

"Please try," I said.

"I'll see what I can do."

---

1. The play would premiere at the Eugene O'Neill Theater—on Broadway.

Oh, isn't this the ultimate betrayal! Even more conniving than the time Michelle cheated on me with her ex-boyfriend, Todd Wayne Mercer. (She met him for "a drink" that turned into too many Hoegaardens, but since I was already sleeping with Rudy Cohn, it made no difference to me what Michelle did with Todd Wayne.) How could she turn her back on me when I am in here? She is the only one on the outside who knows the truth. For she was there on the night of the Overwhelming Event! And why should I have to pay for a failed love affair when I'm already paying for everything else? Why can't I be spared just this once? Maybe it is like the Qur'an says: I was placed on this Earth to be tried with afflictions.

All I've done is love America. Isn't that the way it goes: Love somebody with all your might, and what do you get but a heartless backstabbing.

Onstage I am being portrayed by the actor Lou Diamond Philips of *Stand and Deliver* and *La Bamba*. According to the article, Lou Diamond plays Guy, the fashion terrorist, who turns gay for pay.

What a blatant attack on my sexuality! As I said before, I am a lover of women! My lovers back home I can plot out in my head, visualize them on a map of New York and metro Manila as needles, little pinheads, all of them, stabbed into my brain. Some still puncture the nerve to my heart. Isn't that one of love's prisons? To walk alone with a stabbing migraine of heartbreak. Oh sure, the hurt may lessen, but never does it completely cease. It's only a matter of time before you see her dining across from you with some Chinese guy who works in finance. And then the excruciating text exchange later that night:

—Stop texting me DRUNK

—Who is he?

—A friend

—Fuck u. I fucking luvd u

—U nvr sed it

—Yes I did U bitch

—Whn???

—Dat time on fire island, member?

—U nvr sed it

I nvr sed it. Oh, the salt on the wound! I did say it, to so many lovers, countless times. But to Michelle I never did. I withheld that intimate bond, those three one-syllable words. (I lied to her about Fire Island, in fact. See above.) Is this why I'm paying for all my sins?

In the lead role of Freedom is the abominable actress-singer-songwriter Chloë. Where's the justice? This is the same actress-singer-songwriter responsible for putting me on the fucking map. The young starlet who just last year walked down the red carpet at the Grammys in one of my dresses. I watched the whole thing on VH1. When asked about her dress—a deadly evening gown—Chloë looked right into the camera and said, "This is by *Boy*." My God, I thought, I've made it.

I can only deduce that Chloë has taken the role of Freedom to repair her image. After all, being connected to me now via the Grammys probably hasn't done much for her career. And what better way for Chloë to repair her image than to star in Michelle's copious opus, *The Enemy at Home*? For an artist of Chloë's stature ("Don't you want my chas-titty? / Don't you need my chas-titty?"), a debut on the New York stage Off Broadway[2] seems far below her level of celebrity. But in the war on terror, a girl's got to do what a girl's got to do. In this political climate, better to be a patriot first, a legitimate actress second, and a pop star third, in that order.

Chloë. Thou who made me! I toast the day she ends up in *Us Weekly*, photographed poolside with stretch marks!

I'm beginning to think that Michelle's view of humanity— constantly deeming everything "so ironic"—was spot-on. We are drowning in irony. Every last one of us! You, me, even Lou Diamond, because after my tribunal comes around, and this play is unveiled as the farce it truly is, Lou Diamond will go right back into obscurity.[3]

My greatest fear to come of this recent development is that Michelle might actually have the influence to sway public opinion. That is the power of entertainment. Sure, when the government spins a story like mine, you will always have your believers, those dumb enough disciples who follow their leader no matter how much of a stuttering fool he is; but you can also count on a good many doubters, those citizens who question what is being force-fed to them through the media test tube. And it is this group that I am worried about. For no one is immune to the force of good art when it is disseminated through the mass media. I know this better than anyone, for it is this foundational essence of the human condition to which I owe all of my own success.

Many more runway shows followed my debut. Again we set up catwalks in dance studios and art spaces. But even as my own

2. Broadway.

3. According to IMDb, Lou Diamond Philips will be starring as Yasser Esam Hamdi in *Hamdi vs. Rumsfeld*, currently in production.

work began to sell on consignment, it would take two more seasons of hawking my collections before Chloë would appear at the Grammys in my dress just last year.

Yes, Philip and Vivienne were integral to my mounting success. In fact, Vivienne and I had an unsuccessful love affair in 2004 that grew out of her efforts on my behalf.[4] Vivienne was a spark plug, a woman of influence, with a boutique on Mercer Street down the block from Marc Jacobs and, before I went away, two more stores planned for Los Angeles and Hong Kong. Without Vivienne and Philip, my label would have become (B)oy *bridal* for sure.

But it was Ben Laden who took me to the proverbial next level. Only when Ben got *Vogue, Elle,* and even *Glamour* to sprinkle my clothes in their "what's new" spreads did celebrity stylists come knocking. Rudy Cohn, who I continued to see on and off, had introduced me to Chloë, but the actress-singer-songwriter wouldn't touch me until my line got play in the media. It was no coincidence that she showed up at the Grammys in my inside-out dress after it had popped up in the Trends sidebar of *Harper's Bazaar.* And that's when the custom orders started rolling in. Most notably from one junior senator's wife. (Think of a state bordering Wisconsin and Lake Michigan, rhymes with Hanoi.[5]) But I never delivered on that dress. I was captured in the Overwhelming Event before the sketches could be approved.

At the start of 2006, (B)oy finally had enough buzz to make it into the fashion week tents for the New Designers' Showcase. It was my Bryant Park debut. My Strange Fruit collection, that

4. Vivienne Cho has publicly denied this allegation.
5. There is no evidence that a dress was ever commissioned on behalf of Michelle Obama.

bildungsroman, was sandwiched between Jeffrey Milk and Pro-
enza Schouler, the meat between two slices of white bread. I got
to hire all of my favorite models in New York: Olya, Dasha, Kasha,
Vajda, etc. The clothes were more ambitious than ever, and yet
they were tremendously simplistic. The style I had been aggres-
sively molding all my life had finally taken a leap into the next
realm.

And yet for all of our hard-earned good fortune, the label still
wasn't turning a profit.

(B)oy was in its fourth season, and I was under immense pressure from everyone to produce a hit, something to take the label
out of the red and into the black. Most labels fold if they can't get
the funding. The loan Ahmed had taken from Hajji, the so-called
Indian gangster, had supplemented my consignment sales for
more than two years, and for my debut in Bryant Park I received
a grant from 7th on Sixth.[6] However, that one night in the tent
ended up costing us seventy thousand. Ten thousand we spent on
models' shoes alone.

Once again Ben came to my rescue. The coverage he got for
my show ensured several buyers in attendance, and who should I
hit it off with but Lena Frank, Barneys' artistic director. She fell
madly in love with my clothes and expressed a deep interest in
collaborating in the future. She offered me a large advance for
several modified looks from my Strange Fruit collection, a sum
that would cover production costs, show Ahmed a small return on

6. Organization owned by IMG that produces Mercedes-Benz Fashion
Week.

his investment, and take care of my living expenses for another year. Then, armed with such a red-hot new deal, Ben was able to get me a profile in *W* magazine.

For all of the press and buzz, however, (B)oy was coming apart at the seams. Dick, our accountant, was impossible to please. The Barneys advance went over modestly at best, despite the fact that it would cover every expense I needed to claim. Any time I made a decision on my own that would cost us more money I was met with resistance, no matter how much I was bringing in.

Dick Levine: "There isn't any room in the budget for an assistant, are you crazy? How much are you planning to pay this person?"

"Twelve an hour," I said.

"That's too much. I'll send you a girl for six."

"The girl you're gonna send me won't have the right look. I need someone fashionable. Great with clients. Maybe she has a bob."

"Well, well, look at you. Thinks I'm going to send him Chanah from Crown Heights. I'll overlook your anti-Semitism just this once to remind you that until your Barneys advance is in the bank, we still haven't made a profit."

"Be nice," I said. "It's a miracle I've come this far without an assistant. She'll be part-time. Just someone to manage my calendar."

"Fine. When does my opinion matter anyway. When she sues us for benefits, I'll tell Ahmed it was your fault."

"Where is Ahmed?"

"Moscow? Madrid? Tupelo, Mississippi? I can't keep it straight anymore. I don't think he can either."

"What do you mean?"

"Nothing. Just stay out of the cookie jar for a while."

"I never know what you mean."

"I let you have your assistant, now leave me be. Listen, I gotta go."

"When you hear from Ahmed tell him to call me."

Maybe I had suspected that Ahmed was using me in some way. But they were suspicions of what merit? That he believed in the label and in me as a designer? That he wasn't around enough? I dismissed any suspicions I had as erroneous. The accounts were in the name of my business, and after my debut in Bryant Park, the whole world knew all about (B)oy—well, the only world that I cared about. The little fame I was acquiring would be my safety net. If I fell, the industry would catch me, I was sure of it.

Clothes were real. Suspicions were an invention of the mind.

I found a textile major at Parsons willing to work for free in exchange for clothes and four credits toward an internship. Ecstatic about saving the business some money, I called Dick right away to gloat.

"I beat your six dollars an hour. Try nothing. Ha!"

"Tell me," he said.

"I got an intern. She has a bob and everything."

"Congratulations. Now go make me a dress and don't call me back until it's absolutely perfect."

Marcela came in a few days a week to take appointments and assist with clients. She reminded me of Michelle in a way. They both grew up in Westchester and wore a lot of vintage DVF. This resemblance had an unfortunate effect on me. I became confused and regretful, suddenly missing the Sundays Michelle and I'd had together. Those lazy sun-filled hours spent in her handicap dorm room with alcohol emanating from our bodies, mixing with the odor of morning sex. Most of these longings about our past together resurfaced only when Marcela started showing up.

It pains me dearly to know that Michelle has taken it upon herself to dramatize our relationship for the stage. All of these true feelings and recollections I'd had after I dumped her are suddenly tainted. But who is the real dupe, I ask? The one who has been wrongly imprisoned in this cell? Or the one who has fallen into the giant publicity trap set out by the current administration—that I am the fashion terrorist?

One Friday night in May 2006, after a long, busy week, I met Rudy for dinner at DuMont in Brooklyn. Who do I see there but Michelle, now a college graduate, five pounds lighter and wearing a new pixie haircut. Her fantastic black eye shadow brought out a dangerous quality I had never known her to possess. Femme fatale meets Twiggy. Little did I know how prominent this dark side of her would become. She was dining across from this Chinese guy who looked like he had just gotten off work from Procter & Gamble, the human resources department. There was no avoiding them. The two were seated up front in the window, and it was obvious Michelle had spotted me the moment I popped in the door. So I worked up some courage and went over to their table.

"Hello," I said. I was being chirpy, which meant I was taking it badly.

Michelle matched my chirpiness: "Boy? Hi. What are you doing here?" Then she released an apologetic glance at her date, which pissed me off royally.

"Same as you. Dinner." I turned to the Asian American and introduced myself: "Boy Hernandez." Then I pivoted back to Michelle.

"Well, I just thought I should say hello," I said to her.

"You thought you should say hello? So you felt obligated."

"Let's not do this. How are you?"

"I'm great. I caught your profile in *W* last month. You came off like I thought you would."

"How's that?"

"Like someone else entirely."

The waitress creeping up behind me with their dinner proved a good opportunity for an exit, just shy of making Michelle lose her appetite completely. "Well, you two enjoy your entrées. I'll call you sometime," I said.

"Please don't."

"Nice meeting you, guy."

I was incapable of enjoying a meal here while my ex devoured a half chicken on a date with a guy who had hints of Hoboken, New Jersey, wrinkled into his dress shirt. I found Rudy seated outside in the backyard garden, kissed her on both cheeks, and told her we were leaving, just as the breadbasket hit the table.

"But why?" she said. "It's so lovely out here."

"I don't know," I said, and quickly made something up. "I'm refluxing. Let's get Japanese."

"I had Japanese for lunch."

"Then let's get Thai. Who gives a shit?"

"Okay, we'll go."

"Only do me a favor," I said. "Walk with me through the front room and hold my hand."

"I see now, yeah?" I could always count on Rudy, even when I wasn't being fair to her. She gave me a big kiss on the mouth, and we left, holding hands, skirting Michelle's table. Rudy's four-inch heels delivered superbly on their effect as we patiently walked out of the restaurant.

That night, drunk out of my head on a bottle of cheap rosé, I sent Michelle several regrettable text messages. After reviewing the transcript of our fight that had been stored in my phone, I called her the next day to apologize. To my surprise, she accepted. I learned she was living in Brooklyn now. Her nana's town house still hadn't sold, so Michelle would be staying there until it was off the market. We met for coffee and had dinner. Both of us, it seemed, felt the same: incredibly alone. As our postrelationship by nature ruled out the prospect of love, we gave in to love without love. Lust. We started to see each other again but with unspoken ground rules. It was understood, I presumed, that we were having a casual affair. The sex was not loud or angry, like I had expected, but carried a certain music to it, something soft I couldn't name. It wasn't perfect, but it was right.

Knowing what I know now about the play she has written about me, do I regret carrying on with her? I can't answer that. How can we predict what others are capable of doing? How can we even suspect where we will be tomorrow, or the day after?

Even in prison, I don't know what will happen, because nothing is certain. Nothing has been decided yet. And nothing that has been promised to me over the past four and a half months can be relied upon. Though I trust my special agent and appreciate our talks together, he's beginning to seem more and more powerless as time goes by. Because nothing changes about my situation. The more we discuss, the more it seems that we go nowhere. And the only certainty, I'm beginning to believe, is that tomorrow I will still be here.

THE FALL OF (B)OY

by GIL JOHANNESSEN

From *W*, March 2006, Vol. 3, Issue #23

IT'S THE END of New York Fashion Week, boys and girls, and what have we learned? That the young, budding designer has finally secured a place among the established. At least in New York, where out of the 200-plus designers who showed collections for the fall 2006 season, nearly half of them have come along within the past five years. In an industry whose survival depends on new talent ("industry," hell, way of life), it's been damn near impossible for the young and restless to penetrate Bryant Park canvas. It used to be that if your name wasn't Miuccia and inscribed on Italian leather handbags, you couldn't get a cab on Seventh Avenue, let alone a spot in the tent.

But look up, budding designer. You now have a foothold in New York, and you don't need a fragrance deal with LVMH. It's called the New Designers' Showcase. Among those unknown were the American labels Plaque, Urbane, Jeffrey Milk, and, most notably, the Brooklyn-based (B)oy, brainchild of the designer Boy Hernandez.

I caught up with Hernandez recently at his studio in Williamsburg along the waterfront. Some buyers have already braved the L train for an appointment at the (B)oy showcase. Just so you know, Couture devotee, leaving the island of Manhattan for a showcase was entirely unheard-of a year ago.

A native of Manila, Hernandez came of age in fashion school with Philip Tang. Legend has it, the two designers were separated at birth. Tang transferred to Central Saint Martins in London before jumping the Atlantic for New York City, landing a job as a pattern maker for Marc Jacobs. Hernandez stayed behind with lesser ambitions, fine-tuning his craft in Makati City by dabbling in bridal wear before working up enough nerve (and pesos) to come to New York, his home since 2002.

"I literally had one suitcase, a dress form, and a Singer when I started out in Bushwick," he recalls. "I made a work desk out of a steel door that looked like it had been kicked in by the cops."

The (B)oy operation is based out of Hernandez's large live-in studio located in a former toothpick factory. When I arrive, Hernandez greets me in tight whitewashed jeans and a jersey A.P.C. hoodie that he's appropriated by cutting off the sleeves, wearing it like an open waistcoat over an old, paint-spattered T-shirt. The spatter recalls Jackson Pollock's *Autumn Rhythm*.

Though his hyperexuberance suggests a certain towering grandeur, he is strikingly petite. He stomps around the beat-up factory floors in a pair of all-white Nike high-tops that look certifiably orthopedic.

(B)oy wasn't the toast of fashion week. Diane von Furstenberg slayed all with her animal furs in fox, goat, and Mongolian lamb. Vivienne Cho, whom Hernandez has worked for in the past, took apart structured conventions and rebuilt them with her power suits for the millennium. In the New Designers' Showcase, however, the standout was (B)oy.

For the past two years, the label's knitwear line has been offered out of consignment shops like INA and Tokyo 7. "Before you knew it, I was getting calls for more," Hernandez explained. The knitwear line could also be manufactured close to home in Brooklyn, where

all of (B)oy is currently made. The *B* in (B)oy, closed off in paren-
theses, stands for Brooklyn, a little-known fact.

The label has no boutique, and to date has only been sold at boutiques and consignment shops in Williamsburg, SoHo, the Lower
East Side, and Los Angeles. All of that is about to change with the
recent acquisition by Barneys. Next fall women will be able to find
(B)oy alongside Rag & Bone and Thakoon, as well as a most familiar
name for Hernandez, Philip Tang 2.0.

"It's amazing, really, to be acquired by Barneys. If you were to
tell me when I was in fashion school that this is where I'd be in five
years, I would have asked you:

'What are YOU retarded or something?' "

Hernandez isn't the most eloquent designer on the block, but he
might be the most sincere. It's a quality women seek out in their clothes,
and one that can easily be derived from (B)oy. From his silhouetted
evening gowns with just a splash of color to his baggy wool sweaters,
comfort never seems to be lost in the mix, and neither does glamour.

"I found every article in the (B)oy collection to be honest," said
Lena Frank, Barneys' artistic director.

"I've always thought of fashion as my gift to women, even when
I was a kid," Hernandez attests. "I wanted to do something for them
in the only way that I knew how. Every designer will tell you they
were first trying to win over a woman's heart. You know, get the girl.
I don't care how gay they are now . . .

It's ALL about WOMEN."

When asked how the label has changed since the beginning,

Hernandez explains that Williamsburg has inspired significant transformations in the (B)oy style. No longer is every article cloaked in moody black or sallow white. "That was Bushwick's influence, initially. Like I said, I designed for the people around me. Marginal hipsters are moody. They stick to dark and neutral.

"But I've become much more interested in color since really getting into the films of Wong Kar Wai. Have you ever seen *Happy Together*? It's black and white, but then there are a few scenes in brilliant color. That film is also about passion. 'How's passion expressed?' I asked myself. Saint Laurent was great at capturing passion in his clothes, so I looked at a lot of old YSL from the early seventies."

With the convergence of all of these influences, Hernandez found a niche that would prove the cornerstone of Strange Fruit, his fall collection featured in the New Designers' Showcase.

Strange Fruit takes its name from the song most famously performed by Billie Holiday—a song with a very political message about American racism.

"I thought a POLITICAL MESSAGE in the collection would be appropriate since we're LIVING IN such A POLITICAL TIME with the WAR ON TERROR and everything.

"Sure it's the designer's job to predict the future a season or two ahead of time. But we also need to capture the moment, am I wrong?"

By no means. And that's what makes (B)oy so relevant. For his first collection in 2004, Hernandez included a black burka that was completely transparent. The model, tastefully visible underneath, wore a sequined G-string and matching pasties. I happened to be at that first show. The patch of sequins down below shimmered like diamonds in the ruff. But at the time, no one quite knew what to think.

Political statement or sign of the times, Hernandez was playing with the possibilities of the silhouette, subverting our image of sexy, and calling attention to those parts of the world where women lack the most basic freedoms. The see-through burka added a context to a collection that was otherwise off everyone's map.

"I closed the show with that burka, not to start controversy, but because a friend of mine at the time was wearing a lot of dishdashas, you know, those Muslim gowns. By putting the burka out front on the runway, I was exploring our collective fears about Islam. Although I don't think I was as self-aware of its political impact as I would be now."

Boy is a designer of circumstance. He matches floral patterns with dark silhouettes. He rips passion out of thread, maintaining comfort in chic ready-to-wear even as he makes a bildungsroman with its style. If this is his gift to women, let us hope it's one that will keep on giving. Season after season.

Pieces from the (B)oy fall collection are soon to be available at Barneys.

News to Me . . .

I now have a lawyer. The lawyer I've been asking for since I got here. Not the measly personal representative they keep telling me about (and who I have yet to meet), but a civilian lawyer from New York. Ted Catallano, of Catallano & Catallano & Associates. Apparently Ted's been my lawyer all along; I just didn't know it. The letter I've received from him is postmarked July 23 (over three months ago) and bears the return address of 35 West Twenty-fourth Street. It goes without saying, the letter came to me already opened, with some phrases redacted. My, the censorship that goes on here! I consistently fail to see the relevance in what they choose to black out.

I shall paraphrase the letter. My attorney informs me that he was hired by my publicist, Ben Laden, on behalf of my parents "who remain alive and well." Ted has gone ahead and filed a writ of ▮▮▮▮▮▮ ▮▮▮▮▮▮[1] (and here the words have been redacted). He has petitioned that I be returned to the United States and charged

1. Habeas corpus, the writ by which detainees may seek relief from illegal imprisonment. This would challenge the legality of Boy's detention, though the Military Commissions Act (MCA), signed into law by the president on October 17, 2006, suspended habeas corpus for any alien determined to be an unlawful enemy combatant. Since Boy was awaiting determination of his own status, his habeas corpus petition was denied. In June 2008, the United States Supreme Court found the MCA's suspension of habeas corpus unconstitutional.

with a crime or released at once. It is a short letter but very effective. Sound logic in the last bit: *released at once.* Since I have not committed any crime whatsoever, I remain confident that I shall be returned to America, where I plan to resume my life, the one I had before I became Detainee No. 227.

Ted writes that he is going through procedures in order to meet with me, and that as he drafts this letter he is awaiting clearance from the Pentagon to fly to No Man's Land. "See you soon," he concludes. His closing salutation has been redacted.

I strain to understand what crime Ted imagines I'll be charged with. Knowing? Maybe that was my only crime. But knowing what? I'm a patsy, have I made that clear? A flunky, a pawn. Pawns are always the first ones to go. Soon, when you look up "patsy" in any reputable encyclopedia you'll have your picture of Oswald holding his rifle and me, Boy Hernandez, cross-referenced with "fashion terrorist," "world-class lackey," and "failure." Oh, the shame I've brought upon my family! I can only imagine their reactions to the headlines. COUTERROR PLOT THWARTED! BOY HERNANDEZ, FASHION TERRORIST! If my father's dementia hasn't completely taken over (he was very sick last we spoke), then hopefully his idea of his only son hasn't changed. Papa, believe that I am a patsy in all this; believe that, like you always thought, I'm too dim-witted to have pulled off whatever CLASSIFIED offense they're saying I've committed.

Papa, *mahal mo pa ba ako?* Do you still love me? Even after the shame I've brought on our name?

Don't buy into the term they've created for my current state ("detained"). I am within the walls of a prison that sits on the gulf of nowhere behind rows and rows of concertina wire. Mines, left over from a faded conflict with the *communistas*, litter the grounds outside the prison. Even in the bay, I'm told, there are mines. There is no way in or out of here but to be taken into custody, escorted to and fro, as far as I know. So if it is true that I am a prisoner here, then I must have been arrested! Otherwise, how did I get here? Even prisoners of war must be placed under arrest. And if my captors will not admit to my arrest, then I shall increase my charge against them to, simply put, kidnapping! And kidnapping, even where I'm from, is no small offense.

Sure, it began with the knock on the door in the middle of the night, but a kidnapping is a kidnapping is a kidnapping.

I am willing to give my captors the benefit of the doubt—they're Americans, after all, they deserve it. Let's say that I have been arrested and that the crucial parts that come after the arrest (arraignment, trial by jury, etc.) were mistakenly skipped because of some loophole in the system.[2] They must have their reasons, we have to assume.

Just as I must continue to assume that my reservations with Special Agent Spyro exist simply to determine what I know about Ahmed Qureshi, aka Punjab Ami, alleged arms dealer and broker of my dreams.

And what do I know?

I know that the small operation in Sunset Park that had put together all of our samples for the Strange Fruit collection would never have been able to handle the Barneys order. And that the

---

2. Most notably the Detainee Treatment Act of 2005, forbidding prisoners to challenge their detention in federal district court. Also see the Military Commissions Act of 2006.

manufacturing costs on Fashion Avenue were too expensive to be covered by the advance, generous as it was.

To further complicate matters, in April Ben got word that Neiman Marcus was now interested in acquiring my collection. They had passed on me during fashion week, but because of my profile in *W*, things were suddenly spinning out of control.

Ahmed, once again, was nowhere to be found.

"I'm not cut out for this shit on my own," I told Ben.

"You're right. You have to hire more people."

"I just got an intern."

"So get three more. Will you listen to yourself? If Neiman Marcus wants a taste, that means Bergdorf Goodman too. We're gonna make *una milione*! Just keep your head out of the oven."

Sound advice.

By then I had begun popping Xanax by the fistful to fend off spells of anxiety. Now that I was a known designer, the little purple pills were the only things that could get me through a day.

Armed with the Neiman news, I tried to reach Ahmed on his cell phone again and again with no such luck. In the beginning, having a partner who was never around had felt like a blessing. Be careful what you wish for. A fashion label is a company in the end, and a company can't be run by one person, me especially. I needed Ahmed to step up more than ever. Not just to keep us afloat with funds, but to handle the manufacturing aspect with his wily head for business. Not knowing where to find him, I grew desperate. Then, an act of serendipity: Herizon delivered a stack of phone books to my building. Those big biblical books were normally an annual nuisance that littered the foyer until someone eventually employed the good sense to toss them on behalf of all the other tenants. I only noticed them this time because, on my way out one morning, the guys from the design-build collective were using one of them as a doorstop in the foyer while they loaded their van with custom-built sets. Putting my foot in its place, I tore the book open, and there, would you believe it, was Ahmed Qureshi, listed next to my old address on Evergreen Avenue. It was a 718 area code, a landline. I tore the page from the book as they do in the movies and threw it back down where I had found it.

I ran up to the roof of the toothpick factory, dialing the number. What was I doing up there? I have no idea. Only that it would somehow feel more dramatic to make a phone call from the roof. Perhaps I thought a cell phone calling an ancient landline needed the best reception possible.

Yuksel, Ahmed's houseboy, picked up.

"Yuksel, it's Boy. Where's Ahmed? It's urgent."

"I ays so sorry, sir. He ays busy."

"Too busy to talk, eh?"

"Very busy, sir."

"Devil take you! I need to speak to him at once."

The dimwit hung up on me as soon as I became irate. I pictured him glowering on the other end, that permanent smile of his plastered above his weak chin. Redialing brought on a sound I had thought extinct. A goddamn busy signal! The stupid imp had left the phone off the hook. I could have killed him. "Arrrgh!" I yelled out over the city.

What choice was I left with?

I hopped the train to Bushwick.

The neighborhood hadn't changed. It was just as depressed as it had been when I'd left it more than three years earlier. Broken bottles and butts, newspaper coupons from the local pennysaver scattered along the sidewalks. A new crop of recent college graduates had filtered into the Kosciuszko homes—I could tell by the different tags along the buildings. Crypdick and Smock and ART-JOY, the writers of my day, had been replaced by G.W. S8tan, Viet911, FUCK BUSH, and BITCHES NOT BOMBS. Everything had taken on a political slant. A little Hispanic kid across the street from the Kosciuszko homes called out to me: "Go back to China, faggot!" The tiny bugger actually got to me. Had it been that long since I'd been openly harassed? I looked down at my red jeans and my patent leather Nikes and my Marc carryall, and I felt ashamed.

So I reacted with something I'd thought myself incapable of. I gave the child the finger. If the child had been any older I wouldn't have dared! But seeing as how he had acted alone, I felt he deserved his own lesson in humility.

"Oh, no you di'n't! No you di'n't!" he shouted.

But oh yes, I most certainly did.

Now pumped with adrenaline, I walked up my old front stoop on Evergreen Avenue and rang the bell. The shades were drawn at Ahmed's. I stepped back to have a look at my old apartment on the second floor. The air conditioner Ahmed had helped me install back then was still in the window. It was leaning out, tilted at an unsafe angle. A pigeon landed on top of it and shat.

I was buzzed in.

"Where the hell have you been? I've been calling and calling. All I get is busy, busy, busy."

Ahmed took me by the arm and led me into the apartment. He peered out into the hall after me. "Were you followed?"

"What?"

"It's a fair question."

"Why would I be followed?"

He closed the door and bolted the locks.

I turned around and walked right into a large bureau in the foyer.

"Give me a hand, will you?" He directed me to help him move the bureau against the front door as a barricade.

"What's going on?"

"Just push."

"Yuksel!" I called. "Where is that devil when you need him?"

"I sent him out for supplies."

"Supplies? What supplies?"

"Bottled water, tea, scotch, liver pâté. Supplies!"

"What's going on?"

"Come," said Ahmed, leading me toward the kitchen. The storage room was packed to the brim with sacks of fertilizer covered with blue tarp. Now, from the perspective of an innocent man—my perspective—there was nothing too unusual about this. Ahmed always had things in bulk coming and going.

"I'm in the midst of a huge deal," he said. "This is the big time, Boy. It could mean my early retirement."

"Have you completely forgotten about our business?" I lashed out at him. "You remember, our fashion label. I need you, man. Where have you been? We have orders now. Barneys. Maybe Neiman Marcus. Bergdorf Goodman. I can't possibly fill these on my own. Have you gotten my messages?"

"Messages? How are you still leaving bloody messages? I had that number disconnected. Don't leave any messages, Boy. That line is probably under surveillance."

"Surveillance? What are you talking about? Who has you under surveillance?"

"*Who*? What do you mean, *who*? It's nothing. The ASPCA. I had a horse deal go horribly wrong. We lost some in transit. Did you hear about the freighter collision up north? No? What a mess. Hooves and manes everywhere. You remember I told you about my connections in Saratoga? Anyway, not to worry. This ASPCA, they have no real authority. They're a nonprofit."

"That sounds like a lot of shit."

"Okay, okay. Don't I know it. But it's for your own good that I leave you out of it."

"All you ever talk about is trust, yet you can't even tell me the truth. And why are we barricaded in here like it's World War Three?"

"Okay, I can't fool you. It's not the animal nonprofit. And I'm not moving any horses. It's fertilizer."

"Manure?"

"That's what I said. Manure. 'Cow shit?' I asked them. But no. Not that kind of fertilizer. It's for a group of Somalis who need it by the ton. And they've come to me to get it. I swear, I'm back, beby. These Somalis mean business too. After this the sky's the limit with these guys. And they're really called the ASPCA, I wasn't lying about that.[3] Boy, if I tell you only half-truths it's for your own safety."

"Fuck that. I can't believe a single thing you say anymore. My only concern now is for the label. It may be ours together, but it's my reputation that's at stake."

---

3. This is true. The Armed Somali People's Coalition of Autonomy is a terrorist organization that has been linked to the 1998 bombing of the U.S. embassy in Nigeria.

Where was my judgment? My moral compass? My common sense? Sometimes I think I never had any. I see now that I was blinded by my own pride. Let me propose for a moment a hypothetical. If, in my desperate state, I had to choose between finding the location of a deadly time bomb and saving my fashion label from complete demise, I would choose my label—my dream, my work, my livelihood.[4] That's how self-absorbed I was. But I'm still innocent, I swear it, despite my disposition at the time.

"Let's visit the task at hand," said Ahmed. "Now, what is it that has your panties in a bunch?"

"I don't know where to turn to fill this Barneys order. And Ben is saying that Neiman might be interested. We need to start mass-producing this shit. This is your end, motherfucker."

"One thing at a time, Boy. As you will see, this is no matter. I make a phone call, it's not a problem."

"Then do it. Make a phone call. But here's my concern. Can we get a large order done in New York? Cost-effectively?"

"Not possible. Unless we visit the child-labor option. But that's a high-risk game none of us want to play. We'll have to go overseas."

"First, can we just try to think of a way to manufacture the clothes locally? That's one of the selling points of the label. Made in New York. Here in Brooklyn. People respond to that shit. Look at American Apparel. Christ, I was just featured in *W* bragging about this very thing. I'll come off looking like a complete idiot."

"You're being unreasonable."

"I'm unreasonable because I don't want to look like a liar."

4. The ticking time bomb scenario is normally used by those who would permit the use of torture in exceptional circumstances. It was a concept first introduced in the novel *Les Centurions* by Jean Lartéguy (1960).

"We're way past that now, aren't we?"

"What does that mean?"

"You're the one who made promises you can't keep. You're selling garments made in a place where they can't be made."

"Is that a threat?"

"Of course not. Because ours is a thing of trust."

Michelle had been right from the start. Ahmed couldn't be trusted: I realized that, finally. I'd mistaken her opinion as an attempt to hold me back. How blind I had been! How stubborn! Why couldn't I just see it? "I was put on this earth so that I could be tried with afflictions." But I swear: I only imagined Ahmed was screwing *me*. It never crossed my mind that he could be capable of harming others.

"We'll have to go overseas, Boy. I've been saying this from day one."

"Okay, but if we go overseas I need assurances that we don't employ sweatshops."

"You're one to talk, Mister Nike Airman."

"Listen, this is high-end fashion I'm doing. The reputation of how we manufacture is as important as the garments themselves."

"I can get it together overseas. This is what I do, Boy. But you're not bloody trusting me."

"I want everything done legitimately!"

"Beby, I swear on my children."

"You don't have any."

"Doubter. Fine, my unborn children. May Allah have me shoot blanks between the cracks of our mother's—"

"I get it. You swear. Just make it happen."

"Glad to know my word is still good around here."

I felt like a pinball machine, my head ringing with plans bouncing back and forth.

"Come, have something to eat," he said. "I make you panini."

"I'm not hungry."

"Then what?"

"Last I checked you said you were going to make a call."

"I will, I will. But not from here, are you crazy? Haven't I told you I've been under surveillance? I'm trying to keep all calls to a minimum."

"So send an e-mail."

"E-mail? E-mail is a written record. No. No e-mail."

"So use my phone. Wait, I'm already over my fucking minutes. Great. You're really putting me through the wringer here, Ahmed. Get me some water, will you? I need to take a pill."

"Look in the mirror, Boy. You're gaunt like a fish." He puckered his cheeks at me, the bastard. "Look at me. I take vitamins. And when something is bothering me I tackle it head-on. I don't let it fester. That's what's rotting away inside you."

"I don't let things fester. That's why I'm here. *You're* what's bothering me."

"Oh, come off it! Okay, I know. I haven't been there for you and you're hurt. But consider what's in that room there." Ahmed took me by the shoulder and pointed over the sea of blue camping tarp. "What I got going is going to make me a fortune. And this here is just the tip. Once I give these Somalis their taste, then we'll see some real money. Hell, enough to produce your clothes for ten seasons!"

The price of success was something I had been weighing in my mind in those days. Every penny we'd started with came from

Ahmed. He was the wizard pulling the strings. My rent, my salary—
I owed it all to him. I can't believe I could have overlooked what was
now staring me right in the face. I hadn't stumbled upon a venture
capitalist, eager to break into fashion. I had found a schemer, a liar,
a cheat. He was up to something, I can see that clearly now. Only I
was too blinded by my own greed, or too dumb, to have suspected
it then. I should have known that the money he was funneling
through my label was as dirty as the fertilizer in the next room, that
there must have been other motives behind Ahmed's generosity.

Was I that deluded to think I had a fairy godmother?

Maybe it's as Hicks underlined in my Qur'an, and I deserve
what I got.

*When that which is coming comes, some shall be abased and
others exalted.*

No Man's Land

I have known fear and the
terrors of solitude.

—Yves Saint Laurent

Boyet R. Hernandez, Plaintiff

How long have I been in No Man's Land? Shall I count the days? It has been more than five months since the Overwhelming Event, the snatch and grab that rendered me here. Another sweltering New York summer has passed, and now fall is darkening toward winter back in the city. See the foliage in the parks, like feathers on a turkey! See the wet raindrops dancing off the sides of cab windows! All of this, I can only imagine. To think the collection Gil Johannessen called a "bildungsroman" was composed for this very season, and I am not in New York to see it worn! Bildungsroman! Such a phallic term! I have completely forgotten its meaning, can you believe it? That's what five months in No Man's Land will do to you. Your mind becomes so clouded with dirty thoughts, bloody thoughts, that you begin to lose sight of what once seemed so important.

In here they make every effort to keep those bloody thoughts away by doctoring their own lexicon. A No Man's Land lingua franca. Did you know that in No Man's Land we have a hundred words for suicide? It's true. Self-injurious behavior (SIB), hanging gesture, asymmetric warfare, self-harm (attempted suicide), induced cardiac failure, checkout pact (hunger strike), life circumvention, personal extinction, grooming incision (cut while shaving), the list goes on and on. But never will you hear anyone mention suicide. It is completely forbidden! And you won't hear any of us called prisoners either. That's forbidden too. We are detainees. It is all very clever on their part. Because we are not called prisoners, they don't have to charge us with a crime.

I no longer see Riad, my bathing partner. I heard from Cunningham that he had stopped eating. It was in protest, no longer about the plastic water bottles being taken away, but about the bigger picture: No Man's Land. And just like that, Riad disappeared from the block. They moved him to the infirmary, where, I hear, he is force-fed through a tube via his right nostril. "He's a vegetable," said Cunningham. "The man is lost. The man is a vegetable. Who gives a fuck."

Earlier today I received a letter from the president, dated this very day, November 3, 2006. An MP I had never seen before brought it directly to me, bypassing the hands of my day guard, Win. The envelope bore the official seal of the executive office: a bald eagle dressed in a shield, holding in its talons an olive branch and arrows. The seal actually says SEAL OF THE PRESIDENT OF THE UNITED STATES. I always assumed it said something else; "life, liberty, the pursuit of happiness," something like that. Anyway, at the sight of the president's seal, my heart bounced. It was the first piece of mail I had received since the letter from my lawyer. An apology, I thought, from the president himself. Only it was no such thing. The letter informed me of my upcoming tribunal. *The President of the United States v. Boyet R. Hernandez, plaintiff.* It went on to explain that the proceedings would determine my status as an enemy combatant or "no longer enemy combatant."[1] It

1. Also known as NLEC.

mentioned who would be present at the tribunal (a judge, a prosecutor, and my personal representative, no jury), and stated that I would be meeting with my personal representative in due time. *In due time!* With my tribunal closing in on me (just two weeks from the day, said the letter), they still haven't made it clear just *when* I would be meeting this elusive phantom, the man who is to defend my life! And not a mention of my lawyer in New York being present at the tribunal.

The letter had a return address:

1600 Pennsylvania Avenue

Washington, DC 20006

My special agent has read everything I have written up to now. All of it he consumed directly in front of me during our latest reservation. To keep me busy during the hours it took him to read my confession, he brought me a review of Michelle's play from the *Daily News* (again severely outdated, again with certain details redacted). He also brought me the October issue of *Vogue* and a carton of doughnuts. It is as if Spyro anticipates my needs before I myself know them, and I find that he brings the only consistency to my life here in No Man's Land. His willingness to please reminds me of, well . . . me. I was once willing to please everyone in my path, and I found out soon enough that it always got me what I wanted. But don't misunderstand me. Spyro doesn't just tell me what I want to hear. I never did such a thing either. No, I'm finding him to be completely genuine in his intent to extract the truth. And it is because of his genuine nature that I want nothing more than to please him. To give him the facts straight, to remember those things that I may think insignificant but which he deems very useful.

"You're quite the toast of Broadway," he said when he handed me the article.

"Off Broadway," I corrected him.

"It's only an expression. Don't get bent out of shape," Spyro said. And he let me read the review. Which I did.

Try to picture your life adapted into a performance. Things are twisted for the benefit of the audience's enjoyment. You see, it is more entertaining for all if I am the fashion terrorist. Michelle is more sympathetic as the victim. Motives make more sense once they are overly simplified. It's all part of the entertainment. Events *need* to be fabricated in order to resolve the third act. That's theater. Sure, everyone knows a play is a work of fiction. But out of that fiction the audience is forever searching for the one or two nuggets of truth. Which may they be? Maybe this one, maybe that one, they're guessing. But who really knows? What you have is an audience of reasonable intelligence swayed by a bunch of actors telling lies. That's what fiction is. Lies. Spyro of all people should know this, considering it was his Greeks who banned storytellers for their mental poisoning.[2] Perhaps he was indeed asking himself as he read my own document: What can I believe? Is this true confession a flawless rendering of the facts? One must take into consideration the extreme circumstances under which I must compose my confession. I'm alone in my cell. I'm surrounded by a bunch of no-good terrorists. I am under twenty-four-hour watch. While my little pen scratches this yellow pad, I practically have a gun to my head. (So to speak. Spyro would never do such a thing. Nor would Win or Cunningham. They're all unarmed.) I haven't

2. See Plato, *The Republic*.

the time to make a mistake. There are no rehearsals in No Man's Land. Here it's do or die . . . and shame on you if you tell a lie.

I was so disgusted with what I was reading in the review of *The Enemy at Home* that I had to stop myself several times in order to consume one of the doughnuts Spyro had brought along. Lou Diamond Philips's performance as Guy the Fashion Terrorist was called "heroic in light of such a dark tragedy." And Chloë, who apparently "bares all" as Freedom, made "a debut of the highest order." And would you believe, there is not a mention of me or my situation in the review. It is as if I've been completely forgotten. The play revolves around a fashion designer, loosely based on my life, and there's not a nod in my direction. "In light of such a dark tragedy . . ." Yet no mention of what is so tragic. Not since Andrew Koonanan's[3] shooting spree, which ended with the tragic death of Gianni Versace (and thankfully one less Koonanan, who did his own honor) has a cloud this dark been cast over the industry, and already I've been forgotten.

Anyway, after such a traumatizing experience, I really had no interest in reading *Vogue*. I flipped through the magazine merely to please my special agent, because he had brought it all this way. Its contents seemed irrelevant to anything in my life. I'm beginning to realize that as time progresses my career, my friends, my love affairs, each aspect of self so carefully detailed in my confession is growing less and less important to me. It's as if by writing about them I am willing to let them go.

Have I really suppressed something, like my interrogator suggests? Something so despicable I can't even recall it?

3. The correct spelling is *Cunanan*.

After a short while of feigning interest in the magazine, I put it down and ate the rest of the doughnuts.

Spyro read through my legal pads with a steady determination, flipping through pages at a much quicker pace than I would have expected. No one should have to be put through a thing like this—sitting across from their most important critic while he scrutinizes the given work. It was my life, the truth, written down for him to judge. (The letter from the president has reminded me that it is my life on trial. I sometimes forget that. What an incomprehensible notion, being on trial for one's life. It is almost impossible to fathom.) I would liken the experience of having my confession read like this to that of a fashion show, where editors and buyers make notes while viewing one's collection. But at least as a designer one gets to wait backstage and isn't subjected to their scrutiny head-on. Spyro, however, remained a complete professional as always and rarely broke from his stern reading face: crinkled brow, pursed lips, etc. Only when he released a spurt of air through his nostrils did I relax. For I realized he was holding back a laugh. He found something in my confession funny. This placed me at ease. And he continued to read on.

Where was I on May 25, 2006? Spyro wanted to know as he turned the final page of my confession.

The significance of the date had escaped me, although I knew we were getting closer to the Overwhelming Event.

"It was the day Ahmed was arrested," he clarified. "Do you remember where you were?"

"I can't say that I do," I said.

"See if this will help you remember. You were at the Hotel

Gansevoort. You had a meeting with Habib Naseer, or Hajji, as you know him."

Spyro was revealing to me for the first time that he knew much more than he'd let on. I recalled the period he was speaking of. Yes, I remembered. It was Fleet Week. The city was full of handsome sailors in their pressed whites, real men on R&R walking up and down Seventh and Eighth avenues and haunting those hideous Bleecker Street bars for Joanie and Chachi.[4] This was a most stressful time for me. I was still trying to put the plans in motion for the overseas manufacturer to fulfill the Barneys order. The argument I'd had with Ahmed nearly a month prior had resolved nothing. I hadn't heard from him since. And so I was a tad sour about the whole ordeal and grateful for the diversions New York's annual seamen's surge offered.

Fleet Week in a lot of ways reminded me of the Manila of my youth, when my mother would take me on errands in the Malate district. From the window of our Mazda I'd often see tall, handsome Americans in khaki officer uniforms walking around the city with shopping bags, flirting on street corners with the college girls along Taft Avenue. Odd, but I remember wanting to be one of those girls, giggling at the attention they were getting from the Americans. For a young *pinoy*, soaking in the attention of Americans was something to be desired.

4. Women and cocaine, presumably. Lifted from the title of the 1982 series *Joanie Loves Chachi*, a spin-off of *Happy Days*. Although *Joanie Loves Chachi* didn't connect with viewers in the United States and was canceled after two seasons, it was actually a big hit in the Philippines, where it still runs in syndication.

I was, in fact, at the Hotel Gansevoort on the night of May 25 (I take my special agent's word on the date), but I wasn't there to see the man I knew as Hajji. I was there for a party, the launch of Philip Tang's new shoe line, Size 2.0. Beforehand, I'd dined with Vivienne Cho at the Spotted Pig on raw oysters and a glazed pork belly. Nothing to report. On the way to the Gansevoort we went for a walk along the West Side Highway, then out to one of the piers to get a look at the ships parked in the Hudson, the massive vessels that transported the heroes back and forth from the war with the Iraqis.

Watching the sailors walk along an adjacent pier in the distance, Vivienne said to me, "I don't think I could love a man in uniform."

"Neither could I," I said.

"I'm being serious. A man who's away at war. A soldier. To love one would drive me crazy with worry."

"You can't love a man who's around all the time either."

"With my record, you're right. But at least I'd be getting laid daily."

"Sounds so penciled in. Sex is supposed to be spontaneous, an urge that comes over you, not a recurring event in your Black-Berry. Imagine the sex you'd have with one of these sailors home on leave."

"Honeymoon sex. It would be righteous. I'd be doing my country a righteous thing."

"Glorious patriotism. You've inspired me. I'm going to find myself a girl sailor tonight."

"They're all lesbians."

"They are not. It'd be the perfect match. I would relish the fact that she'd be away at sea for most of the year. I would write to her every week, sometimes twice if I felt compelled. And when she came back I would worship the ground beneath her feet. That's how I could make a relationship work. To be left in waiting for six-month intervals."

"The many upsides to dating a sailor. Look. Now's our chance." Vivienne pointed to two sailors on the pier who were out for an evening stroll. A man and a woman, timeless, as if Ralph Lauren had magically willed them into existence. "We should invite them to Philip's party," she said.

"It's Fleet Week themed. They'll fit right in."

"Perfect."

Vivienne approached the two officers and invited them, only they declined.

"They say they're not to stray far from base." She indicated their ship, the USS *Katharine Hepburn*.[5] "Isn't that darling?"

"Did you mention it was open bar? Did you mention models both male and female?"

"They're married to the sea, I guess."

What is it about a great body of water that gets me so sentimental? Standing at the edge of the pier, before those giant ships lit up like Christmas, I once again thought of my first day in America, when the Statue of Liberty was veiled in her mournful state, an image I refuse to allow my memory to relinquish to this place. On that day, among all of the mixed emotions stirring deep in my groin, I'd felt very much like a free man. To be truly and utterly free is very hard for me to conceptualize from the confines of this cell. But I do believe I felt it on that first day—real freedom. The kind people all over the world seek out in America. You

---

5. No such vessel. Most likely it was the USS *Katherine Walker*.

see, real freedom is something tangible—it's the American birthright—but it is also something that can be taken away without a moment's notice.

At approximately 9:00 P.M., Vivienne and I arrived at Philip's party on the roof of the Hotel Gansevoort. Models in tight sailor whites strutted around in Philip's heels, lace-ups, and zippered ankle boots. The waiters wore those old vintage deck uniforms with sailor gob caps. The pool was lit up, turquoise and clear. It felt as if we were on the deck of a cruise ship, floating above the rooftops of the meatpacking district.

"Looks like we'll have our sailors in the end," said Vivienne.

Philip came over to us cradling two models in officer uniforms, one on each arm. "Happy Fleet Week," he said.

Vivienne gave Philip a lapse greeting, a kiss without contact. They hadn't been getting along over something that didn't concern me, and this created a staleness in the air.

"You look great," I told him.

"Me. I look like shit. I'm overworked. I'm just glad the shoes made it to the party. They were stuck in *Milano*."

"*Milano*," I said, shaking my head.

The girls released themselves from his arms and walked alongside the pool, modeling the shoes.

"Black velvet with an open toe," said Philip. "The other's a patent leather burgundy boot with a two-inch heel. It comes in black, navy, platinum, and bone."

The girl in the velvet heels returned and introduced herself. "I'm Jeppa," she said.

Jeppa stood still, with her hands on her hips, one leg partly open to the side, her foot at a perpendicular angle.

"Hi, Jeppa. I'm Boy."

Vivienne turned and waved to someone at the other end of the party. Philip was pulled away by a photographer who wanted a shot of him on a chaise lounge.

"I know who you are," Jeppa said.

"We've met before," I said.

"I casted for one of your shows in February."

"Of course you did. How could I forget? Jeppa. What's your last name?"

"Jensen. Jeppa Jensen. But my agency makes me go by Jeppa only."

"The Iman theory," said Vivienne.

"How's that working out?" I said.

"You didn't hire me."

"You're kidding. I'll fire my casting director."

"I don't take it personally."

"Where are you from, Jeppa Jensen?" I always felt that using a woman's full name created a playful intimacy, regardless of the formality.

"Sweden," she said. Her accent lilted with that pleasant lisp European women use when they speak English. French and Swedes and Germans all do this.

"I remember now," I said.

"He doesn't remember you," said Vivienne. "Your uniform is getting his dick to move. Beware of straight designers who prowl rooftops in the night. You may get pounced. Stand away from the pool. I need a drink. Anyone?"

"Ignore her," I said. "Come, let's all grab a drink."

A male model sailor served us three glasses of champagne off a tray. We moved to the bar to lean. I ordered us three ginger-flavored vodkas. Vivienne said into my ear, her breath hot, "You can thank me later."

"For what?"

"I mentioned you were *straight*. How else would she have known?"

"She's working. I don't expect anything."

"You expect plenty."

Vivienne turned to say hello to Carl Islip, a famous stylist.

Jeppa pulled out a pack of Gitanes and turned to Steve Tromontozzi, a friend of mine. She asked for a light. She must have heard Vivienne's petty attack on my masculinity, though she acted unaware. I used the opportunity to observe the outline of Jeppa's bra under her arms and around her back, its black straps visible through the white cotton of her officer's blouse. Steve lit her cigarette and she exhaled a plume of smoke into the night air. Jeppa was like some teenage dream. Platinum blond, fair complexion, hazel eyes. And I love Scandinavian noses, so unlike my own flattened olive. This Swede had the power to entrance! By my second drink I was ready for her spell.

"Cigarette?" she offered.

"Please," I said.

She took one more small puff off of hers and handed it to me. The fibrous filter was still moist where her lips had just been. She lit another off of Steve Tromontozzi, and I gave him a nod. I turned back to Vivienne, but she had gone. She was by the pool again talking to Leslie St. John and Rudy Cohn. I should go say hello, I thought. My affair with Rudy had long since cooled, but we still remained good friends. I turned back to Jeppa, who lightly kissed the edge of her Gitanes, then adoringly twisted her neck away from me to blow her smoke. I was about to suggest going over to join Vivienne when I felt Jeppa's open toe graze my ankle. She had engaged me in a game of touch. I smiled at her. She played the innocent, oblivious to what she had started.

Then my phone buzzed in my pocket.

I looked down to see that I had already missed two calls from an unidentified number: 555. A movie number. I placed the phone back into my pocket, but then it buzzed again. Same number. I excused myself and answered it. The voice on the other end was unfamiliar.

"What's the big idea?" he said. "You don't pick up?"

"Who is this?"

"What's the big idea?"

"Excuse me? I think you have me confused with someone else."

"He told me you were testy, but this . . ."

"Okay. I'm hanging up now."

"Meet me in the lobby."

"I'm sorry?"

"The lobby, Tenderfoot."

"Who is this?"

"You can call me Horseradish. No names on the phone. Get it? I'll wait in the lobby for two minutes, and then I'm splitsies."

"You're in the hotel? Wait, how did you get this number?"

He hung up.

I apologized to Jeppa, excusing myself, and then took the elevator down to the lobby. It wasn't hard to spot the man who had just called. He still held his cell phone in hand. And he was wearing one of Ahmed's suits, the double-breasted gray plaid I had made custom. It was much too big for him. When he saw me, he spread out his arms, as if expecting a hug.

"Who are you?" I said.

"I told you, call me Horseradish." He turned a full circle. "What do you think?"

"I think that's not your suit."

"Come with me to my room. We talk there."

"I'm not coming with you. I don't even know who you are."

"The suit. You know it. So you know I'm good people."

"Yes, but it is not yours. It is my business partner's suit. What have you done with him?"

"Keep your voice down. He give me the suit. I'm here to help you with your manufacturing difficulties. I'm Hajji," he whispered. "You know me?"

"You're here for this *now*? How did you find me?"

"I followed you."

"You followed me?"

"What, is there an echo?"

"Why didn't you just call? And where is Ahmed?"

"He left town on business. Come upstairs. I got a room just so we can talk."

"I have a party to attend."

"Then let's talk at the party. But I got a room because I figured you wouldn't want to introduce me to all your fancy friends just yet."

"Okay, I see now. Let's go."

I followed Hajji. In the hallway we passed a man I knew but couldn't place. He was coming out of a room with a young model.

There was lipstick smeared on his shirt collar. He was probably a friend of Philip's. I nodded to him but he didn't catch it.

Once in Hajji's room I got to thinking about my auntie Baby, the moneylender of Cebu City, who met her end in a setting very similar to the one I found myself in now. No one ever knew how it went down exactly, but since there were no signs of a struggle or break-in, police suspected that the murderer was an acquaintance, someone she had dealings with. Someone she knew.

I looked around, paranoid, trying to convince myself that nothing bad could happen to me in the Gansevoort. It was a fortress of luxury and hedonism at the gate of the meatpacking district. According to the celebrity blogs, Kate Moss had celebrated her birthday here just a few weeks earlier. I took solace in that piece of gossip. And Hajji and I had been seen in the lobby together. But then maybe my aunt had similar thoughts running through her mind, just before some son of a bitch came up behind her and put a bag over her head.

"You want a glass of water?" asked Hajji.

"No, I want to get back to my party. What are we here to discuss?"

"You get right to the point, Tenderfoot. I like that."

"Do you even know my name?"

Hajji opened his jacket to the label I had sewn onto the inside breast pocket.

(B)OY.

"You're this guy," he said. "I know all about you. Question is, Do you know about me?"

"Ahmed mentioned you, yes."

"So you know my reputation. And you're comfortable with this?"

"What are we even talking about?"

"Working together."

"Excuse me?"

"Sit down. Relax."

"I'm still wondering why you're wearing that suit?"

"I told you already. Ahmed give it to me. I couldn't take my eyes off of it. I said, 'Where did you get such a magnificent suit?' The sheen. The pattern. The cut. I had to have one. 'It's truly magnificent,' I said. He said, 'You can't get it anywhere. It's one of a kind.' I said, 'Impossible!' Then we wrestled for it. He took off the suit, of course, not to get it messed up in the stable."

"The stable?"

"The stable where we go to talk. Anyway, once I had his arm pinned behind his back, he told me you were the one who made it. Custom."

"Yes, but I still don't see why you're wearing it tonight."

"He give it to me. I said I would take a percentage off the vig. He give me the suit. Happy now, Tenderfoot?"

I was wasting time. It was a feeling I got around people like Hajji, a melancholic fog that draped over me whenever I was in the company of someone below my level of intelligence. This feeling took the place of my paranoia.

"On second thought," I said, "I'll have a glass of water."

He turned on a light over the sink and kept an eye on me through the mirror while he filled a glass. Hajji had deep pockmarks in his face. His hair was dyed a cheap black, and under the light I could see the violet base in the color.

He brought over the water.

"Thank you." I sat on the edge of the bed and took a purple pill.

"That stuff will kill you," he said.

"They're prescription."

"Me, I don't take pills."

"Surprising."

"So, Ahmed tells me you have a manufacturing problem. I'm here to tell you it is a problem no more, my friend. I can have your clothes manufactured overseas in India. It can be done quickly. We send them dresses, they send us the samples, and back and forth until we've reached our agreement. Ami explained to me that you had problems about going overseas. That you want everything manufactured in New York. I don't blame you. Everybody wants American. People pay big bucks for quality. It's a simple matter of switching the labels once the garments make it past customs. We send the shipment to a factory in Brooklyn and have all the labels switched there. Wallah."

"Bait and switch. That's your plan, huh?" I put my water down on the nightstand and stood up, frustrated. "I'm sorry. This is what you followed me here for? We couldn't discuss this over the phone? Listen, you have my number. Call me on Monday and we'll talk."

He took me in his hands and pushed me back down on the bed.

"Now you listen, Tenderfoot. I'm not here to waste my time. Ahmed said you needed to have clothes manufactured; now I'm offering you my services. I don't offer this sort of deal to every-body. And with the kind of money he owes me, you're lucky I don't just take my share of your business. You think I don't know who you are? I read!"

"Are you threatening me?"

"Not at all. I'm only trying to explain to you how it is. The clothes we make together, people will wear, goddamnit. And, I must say, ever since I saw Ahmed wearing this suit, I've been envious of his new friend, the tailor. I think we should be in business. Someone who can make a suit like this . . . one of a kind. No question. It's truly magnificent."

I knew I had to get out of his room as quickly as possible, even if it meant telling Hajji whatever he wanted to hear. "Okay," I said. "It sounds fine. You're a friend of Ahmed's. And I trust him. So let's talk Monday. Call me and you can come by my studio."

I stood up and was met with the same hostility. He pushed me back down on the bed.

"We're not finished yet! This suit still needs to be taken in. And you are the one who's gonna do it."

"Now? Are you out of your mind? I have people waiting for me. They're going to get suspicious if I'm gone too long."

He stepped over to the bedside table and grabbed a plastic CVS bag, which he then threw at me. I looked inside. He was serious. He'd bought a needle and thread, a small travel kit. The receipt was still in the bag.

"I can't do this now. I need a sewing machine. And where are the scissors? We'll ruin it. Listen, make an appointment and come by my studio. I'll have it done then."

"I want this suit—" Just then, his phone went off. His ring tone was an Arabic pop song, exotic chants over a fast dance beat. He took the call and stuck out his finger, placing me on hold. He spoke a language I would later learn to recognize as Urdu.

I waited on the bed for a few seconds before realizing that this was my opportune moment to make for the door. Hajji was at the desk fumbling with the hotel stationery. I got moving. He ended his call abruptly just as I was turning the door handle. Suddenly he was so preoccupied he didn't seem to care that I was on my way out. I should say good-bye, I thought. Keep it friendly but quick. "Ciao," I said. "See you next week sometime."

"I'll call you about the suit."

"You know you can take it to any tailor. They'd do a better job. I can recommend one."

"Only I want you to do it."

"Okay, fine. No problemo." I was dealing with a maniac. "Call me Monday and make an appointment. I'm busy, but it won't be a problem."

I ran out of there and took the stairs back up to the roof. I called Ahmed's house from the top of the stairwell.

"Yuksel, it's Boy. Is he there?"

"Eh?"

"I want you to take a message. You ready? Good. Tell Ahmed that I don't like being followed. Tell him that I've just been black-mailed by his friend Hajji. The Indian gangster with purple hair. Tell him if I ever see this Hajji again, our business together is through! You hear me? Make sure he gets it. And Yuksel?"

"Sir?"

"Read it back to me."

It took us several more tries before Yuksel was able to capture the spirit of the message. Then I returned to the party.

My special agent has informed me that Ahmed was taken into custody that same night at approximately 9:00 P.M., just as Vivienne and I were stepping into the Gansevoort for Philip's Fleet

Week party. It's strange to think about what happens simultaneously at the most insignificant times. Never for a moment did my mind wander outside of the industry bubble.

You see, it never did occur to me that a higher authority would come knocking on my door.

Camp Delta Blues

Yesterday, I witnessed a grooming incision. It is very hard for me to gather the right words for such an act of brutality, and so I must use their term. A grooming incision. A cut on the wrist by a dull razor.

Khush, which is what I heard him called in the prison yard once, was not a likable man by any means. He was unwell. How, you ask, could I tell this when he didn't speak a word of English? Isn't it true that we can detect illness much like the way we can sense an attraction? Khush reminded me of a rabid dog. He looked fine from afar, but once you got closer you caught the glisten in his eye and the foam around his jaw. This is the replacement I was administered when my first bathing partner, my friend Riad, decided to turn himself into a vegetable through a diet of air.

We were together on deck, Khush and me, waiting for the showers. I didn't even look at him.

Once they became available, our numbers were called.

We moved swiftly in our shackles, entering our respective stalls. Khush to the left, me to the right. The metal grate slammed behind us and the guards locked the dead bolts. We turned around and moved forward, placing our hands through the opening of the shower door. Our shackles were removed. We undressed and handed our clothes to the guards through the slot. We were given our small bar of soap and other amenities. Khush, like me, had also been deemed compliant, and so we were both given the option of the plastic razor. A very dull razor.

Cold water from the nozzle. Two minutes.

Looking down at my feet I watched the streams from both our showers converge into the single drain between the two stalls. I was able to see my bathing partner's feet. The water pooled together before it went down the drain. This time I didn't muster the will to lather myself with the bar of soap, or even shampoo my hair. Instead, like a child, I opened my eyes to the sun overhead and let the rays blind me. I remember doing this as a kid in the outdoor shower at my parents' beach house on Samar. I'd rinse the salt off my little body and the sand out of my scalp under a trickle of water.

One learns to tell time without clocks in prison, automatically counting the seconds in one's head. And so I knew when our two minutes were almost up. I looked down at my feet and my eyes were not yet adjusted to the light. They were subjected to that distortion of tone one gets after peering directly into the sun. Everything was tinged red. So, you see, I expected the puddle at my feet to be the color it was.

I suppose it should have been no surprise what happened. As I said, this Khush was not right in the head.

"*Medic! Medic!*" a guard yelled. The water was cut off. My sight began to return to normal. I had to squint in order to see that it was indeed blood at my feet. I stood back against the shower gate. I crept onto the balls of my feet, but there was no escaping it. The blood had seeped underneath and filled my stall entirely. Khush must have hit an artery, because once all the water had drained, the blood just kept coming.

"Let me out," I said, but no one did.

I asked Spyro about the incident during our reservation this morning. We've been meeting more and more frequently now that he's read my confession.

"It was a suicide," I said.

"I haven't heard about it. Let's get back to Ahmed and your relationship with Hajji."

"That can wait," I said. "A man cut himself while we were in the shower. I want to know if he is alive or dead."

"It's that important to you? You want me to stop. You want me to stop our progress so we can find out what happened to this guy. You barely knew him. Why the sudden interest? Why are you stalling?"

"His blood was on me. I would like to know if he's alive."

"So you got a little blood on you. So what?"

My interrogator took out a pen from his inner breast pocket.

"Do you have a name?" he said.

"Khush," I said. "I don't know his last name."

He wrote it down. "Do you know his number?"

"I only know my number," I said.

I could hear him breathing through his nostrils. He was like a bull at times, my interrogator. He stood up, took the scrap of paper, turned to me once more in frustration, then left the room.

I don't know why I wanted to know whether Khush was still alive. I'd never said a word to him. With the amount of blood I'd watched him lose it would be a miracle if he was still breathing. But what did I know? I needed closure on the matter of this grooming incision, this *suicide*, you see. Otherwise, it would remain uncertain, just like everything else in No Man's Land.

My special agent returned and sat down at our table.

"Your friend . . . Khush. You'll be happy to know he's alive. He hurt himself. Badly. That's all. He's in the infirmary in critical condition. They say he wasn't right upstairs. He was depressed. On all sorts of medication. But he's alive. According to the CO it wasn't too serious. Happy now?"

"Am I happy? A man tried to kill himself next to me. He should be dead! But only he'd be too lucky!"

"All right, will you calm down? It was self-harm. A cry for help."

"Bullshit."

"What is?"

"Everything. This place. This room. This is all bullshit. I've had enough."

"Now just calm down. You haven't had enough of anything. We're just getting started, you and me. Now, focus. I told you what you wanted to know. Now I want to know what I want to know."

"Which is what? The same thing over and over."

"I want you to stop delaying and tell me the truth."

"*Delaying*?"

"Yes, delaying. Delaying."

"A man tried to take his own life!"

"But he didn't, did he? He's alive!"

Perhaps I'd hoped my disposition would return to the way it had been before the incident, so long as I knew Khush was alive. But nothing changed. I felt no relief. It was the act alone that haunted me, not the condition he was in now. Spyro was right: It didn't matter one way or the other.

"I'm going insane in this place," I said, placing my head in my hands. I couldn't continue with our reservation. I wanted to go back to my cell and curl up under my blanket.

"This is a natural reaction to violence, Boy. You saw something that's hard to understand. You're traumatized. I know how you feel. Don't act like I don't. I've seen it happen too. I've seen people get killed. I've seen innocent people get killed."

"He wasn't innocent? Who's to say?"

"He was in here, wasn't he? There was a reason he was in here. Just like there's a reason you're in here."

"I'm in here because a mistake has been made. A grave mistake."

"You're in here because you associate with terrorist scumbags. And I want to know who and when."

I stood up.

"Sit down. We're moving on."

"But we go nowhere. We're not moving. It's the same thing over and over with you."

"Sit down, I said."

I did as I was told.

"I'll recommend that you see the psych tech. ASAP. Happy?"

ASAP. Everything here is promised to you ASAP.

"When will I get out of here?" I said.

"When you tell me everything I need to know."

I continued on. I continue on because the man in the cell next to mine, a Yemeni, is so old that I can smell his dying. Because dying has a particular smell. Because I know that if I do not continue on with my confession, I could end up just like him. He doesn't speak a lick of English, this Yemeni. I think he's too old. At some point the brain is too stubborn to learn anything new. Not to mention, he looks as if he couldn't hijack a bicycle. But whether he is an enemy or not doesn't concern me. I've thought a lot about what my special agent said to me regarding each prisoner, how each of us has a valid reason to be here, though some of us don't deserve to know why. I hardly care anymore. I've been asking the wrong question all along. *Why* is of no use to me. I am here. There is no why. There is only this. Therefore, I shall focus the rest of my energy on getting out.

The old man will soon die. I don't feel the least bit bad about saying so. He's letting it happen to himself. He's given up. Maybe he's reasoned that in here he can get an operation from the Americans, where in his homeland he'd already have expired. Maybe he's thinking, "What would I do out there but die anyway?" Who knows. As I said, he doesn't speak English. He's lost his will to live, that much is clear to me.

I must soldier on and finish my confession. Onward, I say, I am ready. I will not fall through the cracks of history a war criminal, when really, as I've been saying over and over, I'm just a designer of women's clothes. I am innocent! That is the only constant that keeps pushing its way forth into my impossible equation. An innocent man should have nothing to fear. If it is the truth that my special agent wants, then it is the truth that will free me from this cell.

It is true that I heard about Ahmed's arrest the day after it happened. May 26. Ben told me over a Mexican lunch at El Baño. We took the secret entrance through the back alley, because many of the restaurants in the city at this time built secret entrances for the in-the-know regulars. You had to walk through the bathroom in order to get to the main seating area. It was a coed bathroom.

We were expecting a good table, but what we got was so close to the actual bathroom that anyone taking a whiz could hear our conversation.

"This restaurant has lost its je ne sais quoi."

"Maybe we should have taken the front entrance and waited," Ben said. "Why use a secret entrance if we're going to be treated like a bunch of amateurs? So much for this place."

"I only hope the *carnitas* is still good."

"I'll have the plantains," he told the waitress. "Tap water. A coffee, black."

"*Carnitas* enchilada and a café con leche," I said. "You're not eating?"

"New development."

"With Neiman Marcus?"

"No, something else has come up. You know how I have old friends over at the *Post*. Well, this morning I spoke with George Lipnicki, who used to cover fashion and entertainment a million years ago. Now his beat is everything Homeland Security. Counterterrorism. If a terror suspect is under surveillance and so much as farts in the tristate area, George catches wind of it. Anyway, I overheard a name familiar to us. Your backer friend, Ahmed. George mentioned 'Qureshi.' It was in passing. 'How was your day?' 'Shitty, this Qureshi thing.' I said, 'Hold it, not *Ahmed Qureshi?*' He said, 'Yeah, that sounds like the guy. How'd you guess?' Ahmed was picked up in Newark last night. The feds have him."

"What? Get the fuck out of here. For what?"

Someone flushed and exited the bathroom. The man practically had to step over our table on his way out.

"Relax, keep your voice down. George is still looking into it.

There could be some mistake, you know with the feds. I was detained in 2002 on a goddamn typo. And all these Muslim names run together—Ahmed al-Mohammed-Sheik-bin-Barack-Hussein. George thinks that it was an arms deal. Weapons. A fertilizer bomb, maybe. It was a sting operation of the highest degree."

"I'm sorry, a what bomb?"

"A fertilizer bomb. But none of this is confirmed. You need to take steps to distance yourself—"

"That's a real bomb?"

"Yeah, made from fertilizer. But it takes tons of the stuff. You remember the psycho who got picked up coming in from Canada with a truckload of fertilizer. It wasn't manure but the kind that can go boom. And what's his name . . . the Oklahoma City scumbag. He used a similar thing."

"Fertilizer."

"Timothy McVeigh. He's dead now. Why can we never forget the names of these madmen? They don't deserve such places in our heads. Manson, Ted Kaczynski, Khalid Sheikh Mohammed."

"Oh Christ. How was I supposed to know?"

"These fucks always find a way to hurt us. Outlaw fertilizer, they'll figure out how to blow up laundry detergent. Tide bomb, with bleach alternative. I'm surprised they haven't thought of it."

The waiter brought over our lunch. I tried to remain calm, but I couldn't help shifting in my seat. I fumbled for my purple pills.

"C'mon, eat," said Ben.

"Listen, I tell you this not because you're my publicist but because you're my friend. You're my friend, right?"

"Of course I'm your friend. You can tell me anything."

"Okay. I've been to Ahmed's apartment recently. I think I saw what could have been sacks of fertilizer. Piles of fertilizer, like in a nursery. I didn't ask for what. He always has shit coming and going. I mean, a fertilizer bomb? How was I supposed to know? It sounds made up."

"Easy, Boy. Take it easy. Okay, you saw something. A lot of something. But to your knowledge, it's not an illegal substance. And who knows what he was going to do with it."

"Jesus. What do you think is going to happen?"

"Well, let me be honest. There's an investigation. I'd say you're going to be picked up and questioned. Seeing as you two have had plenty of contact, they'll want to know what about—which they probably know already—and you will tell them the truth."

"The truth?"

"He was an investor."

"He was!"

"Take it easy, don't get excited. What's the worst that could happen? They take you in for a day, two hours, maybe they ask you to come back for another meeting. You've done nothing wrong."

"I can't believe this. Fuck! I'll be deported. I can't go back, Ben."

"Easy, Boy. You won't be deported. Questioned, that's all. To confirm what they probably already know. In this day, it's standard procedure. According to our current shit-eating administration, we all have to make sacrifices. Even if it means missing London Fashion Week because of some bureau clown's fuckup— true story. I was detained because of 'homophonic similarities,' let me remind you. Treated like some two-bit criminal. But not you. Don't you worry about a thing."

"You're starting to sound like Ahmed."

"What's the worst that could happen? You're an up-and-coming designer."

"I took money."

"What else? He was an investor! That's the nature of the thing. There's an old saying. Goes, 'Ours is not to wonder why . . .' Ever hear it? You take money from investors; who's to ask how they got it? You're in the clear, Boy. What have I been saying? I come with information so you can be prepared. In *case*. Now c'mon, let's eat."

"I can't. I'm going to be sick."

I excused myself and dry-gagged over a heated toilet seat, a TOTO, desperate for every vile thing within to come spewing out and then get flushed automatically while I ran my filthy mouth through its built-in bidet. But I was empty inside. I laid my head on the warm seat and stared into the depth of the bowl. Oval, like the inside of an egg. Head still on toilet, I got fetal. I reached into my right jacket pocket for my purple pills. I managed to break open the child safety cap on the bottle with my thumb, only this caused many of them to spill onto the floor. I caught two in my palm and brought them to my mouth, chewing them into a dry rocky powder. I swallowed.

Ben must have come in to check on me, because the next thing I knew he had kicked open the stall door, which I hadn't locked. "Dear God, kid, how many did you take?"

"Two. I spilled the rest."

"You're kidding. I thought you tried to off yourself. Here, get up." He grabbed me under the arms and got me onto my feet. "Now, brush yourself off. There. Can you stand?" He gave me a couple of loving slaps on the cheek. "Go clean up. Otherwise who's gonna kiss that handsome face of yours."

I went to the sink and threw some cold water on my face.

"Here," Ben said, handing me a towel. "Dry off. I didn't mean to freak you out. You're going to be okay. Worse comes to worst, I know a good lawyer."

"Worse comes to worst . . . Where does that expression come from?"

"It's just a saying. I don't investigate where things come from, Boy. I was brought up Irish Catholic."

We discussed the possibility of turning myself in, though Ben suggested not to worry about that yet, to go on with my life, and if and when the FBI needed my help, they would get in touch with me. And so I did just that. I went on with my life, unsuspecting. If the time came for my adopted country to call on me, I would tell them what they needed to know.

In the Qur'an, particularly a chapter titled "Sad," there is much about the day of judgment, when that which is coming comes, when all of us will be divided. Believers on one side, nonbelievers on the other, a line in the sand between us. Hypocrites versus the righteous. And each group thinks the other ones are the hypocrites. Who's to say which side is right? There's no guidance in this life but your own conscience. That's what I say. If your conscience is telling you to do harm to others, so much for you, you're finished in this world. No one likes a madman. Only begets more madmen. My own version of the truth doesn't include an afterlife. There's just this one, and if you make the best of it, be true to yourself, treat others with reasonable respect, drop your spare change in a coffee cup once or twice a week, etc., I happen to think you can be very happy. Worry about what comes around next and you're likely to go crazy and override what your conscience is telling you.

I just read: "*Those who deny the life to come, the heavens and all its splendor, shall be sternly punished in the hereafter.*"

This is where I disagree with the glorious book. I haven't studied it intensely, like the rest of my cohorts here. Each one of them has devoted his life to it much like the way I devoted mine to fashion, and that's fine by me. I'm not trying to be social critic number one. People get fatwas for that kind of thing. *Those who deny the life to come* . . . That means me. By the book I'm damned. A *kafir*. The infidel. The unbeliever. Well, now, by the looks of it, I'm already serving my sentence along with these other guys. Judgment day is upon us. What does that tell me? I can't extract much meaning or hope from what it says in the glorious book, but for these other sorry individuals, I'm starting to see why they put all their eggs into Allah's basket. They've come from nothing, fallen into paths of more nothing, and have been put through a lot of shit, so they think: How can things be this bad forever? Logically, if there is no god but God, it can't. Their glorious book confirms that they're onto something special just the way the September issue tells me knit jersey is in. And so, they have their afterlife and I have New York. I got my heaven the first time around. These poor bastards are still waiting.

Apropos of the Fertilizer

I have never been a depressed person. That was my father's disposition, not mine. Me, I thought I could handle anything, which has proved true for the most part. Look at how far I've come. I made it all the way to New York City, a little *pinoy* from Marlboro Street. And look at where I am now—the edge of the world, the rim around America's rectum, and I haven't fallen in yet.

This morning, as Spyro promised, a visit from the psych tech. She had blond hair tied back into a bun. No makeup. Her accent was familiar, the Northeast. Massachusetts or Rhode Island. We talked through the mesh grate of my cell. She made notations on her clipboard each time I answered a question.

"Do you know who you are?"

"Two-two-seven."

"I mean your name. What's your name?"

"Boy."

"What's your full name?"

"Boyet Hernandez."

"What's your mother's maiden name?"

"Reyes."

"What's her mother's maiden name?"

"Araneta."

"What do you do, Boy?"

"What do you mean, what do I do? I'm a prisoner. I do nothing."

"You're not a prisoner. You're being held here indefinitely until we can establish whether you are an enemy or a nonenemy. This is not to be looked at as the end, Boy. This is only a stop at the beginning of a long journey."

"That's bullshit."

"Can I ask you a few more questions. Is that okay?"

"Do what you must."

"Are you eating?"

"If you call this food, then I am eating."

"Are you sleeping?"

"Hardly."

"Are you?"

"It's impossible to sleep more than an hour here. There's always commotion on the block. I hear noises."

She stopped writing on her clipboard. "And these noises—what do you hear?"

"Are you asking me if I hear noises in my head like some psychotic? These are real, believe me. Go ask the others. There are noises that keep us up at night. The guards. And the men being taken from their cells. And bombs. You can hear bombs being set off in the night."

"Bombs."

"Yes, bombs. Explosions."

"Do you have nightmares, Boy?"

"If I can sleep, I dream nightmares."

"Are you feeling despair?"

I started to laugh. It was a nervous laughter that I knew would produce tears. After a few breaths I couldn't hold it in. I began to sob. I turned away from the psych tech. And wouldn't you know it, she continued to ask me questions, even though it was obvious I was too broken to answer. And when I didn't answer, she waited just a short moment before moving on to her next question. She was in a hurry! It was quite obvious she was working from a script. She didn't even ask about the incident with Khush.

"Do you want to harm anyone, including yourself?"

How can a man be expected to answer that from in here? Yes, I'd like to kill you and your entire family, if I could. And then I'd love to do myself, but only under the condition that I am still in here.

Then the young woman from Rhode Island or someplace like it explained to me the benefit of image therapy. "Picture," she said, "your happiest moment. Close your eyes and begin to breathe deeply. In through your nostrils and out through the mouth. In. Out. Take a second to look around in this happiest of moments. Who's there? Why are they there? Why are you so happy? What is it about this moment in your life that makes you want to go back to it?"

I closed my eyes and pictured my white tent in Bryant Park. The catwalk, the collections, my bildungsroman. Backstage. Olya, Dasha, Kasha, Vajda. Thongs, asses, hair, makeup. Oh, but it was no use! What happened to my white tent during this silly exercise? I saw a spatter of red across its canvas surface. Khush's vein carved open with a dull plastic Bic.

I could not lift the razor's edge from my thoughts.

The psych tech took pity and placed me on antidepressants, to be administered daily. Small comfort. The meds don't kick in for weeks, and I don't have weeks. My November 17 tribunal is just ten days away, according to the president's letter.

After she left, I was fed my lunch and then taken away for another reservation with Special Agent Spyro. He had transcripts of my phone conversations in the days that followed Ahmed's arrest, courtesy of those turncoats at Herizon Wireless. Privacy, my ass. There's no such thing as a private phone call these days. He knew the times the calls were made, what was said. I ask you, who would not look bad when listened in on? I'm almost certain that if the circumstances were reversed, and the American people got to snoop on the calls made between the president and his vice commandant, there would be riots on Pennsylvania Avenue. A coup d'état. My point is that when things are spoken behind closed doors they are said with the belief that no one, with the exception of the parties involved, will hear them. Here's a little piece of truth about human nature: Sometimes, we just don't think about what we say before we say it. Once in bed, I called Michelle a whore after she pulled my pubis. "You whore," I said. Of course there was no exchange of currency, though I did end up paying for it in the proverbial sense, with her fucking play.

Apropos of my teletranscripts, those bums at Herizon have taken all of the humor and inflection out of my phone conversations. What we are left with is language without voice. Just words on a page. Even I had difficulty deciphering these words during today's reservation. However, Spyro has allowed me to keep the transcripts, and so I have gone ahead and reestablished the tone of the calls, using Herizon's documents as an aide-mémoire.

Here is what was said between me and the various parties on May 27, 2006.

At 0900 I received an incoming call from Ben Laden.

"Page two of today's *Post*. Do you have it?"

I did. Alarmed by the urgency in his voice, I ran to get the paper, no questions asked. I turned to George Lipnicki's article on page two. I read over the phone: "'Ahmed Qureshi, a former fabric salesman, was arrested on Friday at the Sheraton Hotel near Newark International Airport. . . . According to the criminal complaint, Qureshi has been accused of selling and transporting ammonium nitrate fertilizer, a key ingredient in homemade explosives. . . . The Canadian salesman . . .' Huh . . . he's really Canadian. I wondered. 'The Canadian salesman was caught red-handed in an FBI sting operation where Qureshi allegedly praised Osama bin Laden to an FBI informant.'"

"He praised Osama bin Laden," Ben said. "Can you believe that?"

I read on: "'He's a great man, bin Laden. He did a good thing. . . .'" These were not my words. You see, I was reading the article from the paper. Words taken out of context can go over very badly, especially if they are to be used as evidence in one's tribunal.

"My namesake is back in the paper," said Ben. "Just when I thought I was in the clear. *Allah akhbar* my ass."

"This is bad, Ben."

"When I talked to George he had no idea about Ahmed's connections with the label. And I didn't tell him. I don't think anything will lead back to you. All the information he has is from the feds. He won't be doing any snooping when a story like this gets dropped in his lap. It looks like they got their man, and everybody's happy. The new story is justice—what happens to Ahmed now? That sort. What can I say? I think we dodged the bullet."

"This is crazy. I don't understand."

"He was a psycho. You can't understand psychos. Why try? They're fucked in the head."

"Yes, but I don't believe he would want to hurt anybody. I know him, Ben. He's not capable."

"Do me a favor: Go on with your life. There's nothing you can do until you're called in for questioning. And that's not a definite. You may never hear of this again."

After I spoke to Ben, I made some breakfast. A strange thing to do after receiving such news, considering my reaction on the day prior in the restroom of El Baño. But I would challenge you to name one man who has shown consistency in the face of surprise. Again, I must invoke the president himself in my analogy. Two out of three of the most shocking events of his term thus far brought the same reaction: paralysis and denial. Very consistent. However, consider how he handled the news when his own right-wingman[1] gunned down a fellow septuagenarian, mistaking him for a quail: "I am satisfied," said the president with such outward calm. And what composure! But I am sure that inside the president's own soul he was deeply shocked and disturbed when he uttered those words.[2] Inwardly, I admit, I was a basket case, while outwardly I soft-boiled two eggs for five minutes. Then I ate at my worktable in order to go over some sketches. I cracked the little tops of the shells, salted the eggs, and opened their soft outer whites with a teaspoon. When I was no longer hungry, for I rarely finished two eggs, I turned my attention to the blank page and began to sketch a silk dress, crêpe de chine with sequined details.

1. Vice President Dick Cheney
2. "I thought the vice president handled the issue just fine, and I thought his explanation yesterday was a powerful explanation. . . . I'm satisfied." — President George W. Bush, February 16, 2006.

At approximately 10:05 as I continued work on my sketch, I was interrupted by a second phone call.

"Guess who, Tenderfoot. It's Horseradish." Damn. It was that Indian gangster, Hajji, from the Gansevoort. I had told him to call me on Monday. But with Ahmed in jail I thought I could shake him on my own.

"Right," I answered. "Hey, listen, I'm glad you called. Turns out, I'm not going to need your help anymore. What do you know? I found a manufacturer right here in Brooklyn! Can you believe my luck? Anyway, it's better this way, so—"

"You see the papers?"

"The papers?"

"C'mon. Today's paper. Extra, extra, read all about it. You'll be interested to know our friend got pinched."

"Why, I don't know what you mean. Listen, I really have to be going."

"Lucky lucky, rubber ducky. They didn't even mention you. Not a peep."

"I'm sorry . . ."

"Google this, Tenderfoot! U R fucked dot com! See what I mean? Now, how'd you like to stay out of the papers?"

"I don't follow." I was stalling. I realized what was happening. This bastard was blackmailing me.

"Keep things honky dory," he said.

I said nothing.

"Terror's bad for business, don't you think?"

"Can I call you back?"

"You do what you have to do. While you're doing it, think of a number between one and two hundred thousand. And I'll call *you* back."

"Two hundred thousand! Are you crazy?"

"Certifiably," he said, and hung up. Two hundred thousand dollars. This was the going price for Hajji's silence. Not knowing what to do next, I called Ben.

"Great news," I said. "I'm being blackmailed by an Indian gangster."

"Who? Don *Curryone?* Take an antacid, that's what I'd do. Ha!"

"That's not even funny. Racist, actually."

"Hey, no one's experienced the blunt end of the bigot's stick like the Irish. Tack my last name on the end of it, and you'll have a portrait of a man who knows something about racial prejudice."

"Seriously. I just got off the phone with one of Ahmed's associates. A man named Hajji. He's this little fucker who followed me the other night. Says he wants two hundred thousand dollars or else he'll go to the press and link me to Ahmed. What the hell am I suppose to do?"

"Let's go to the police."

"And tell them what?"

"It's extortion."

"What a mess. We go to the police, and then I have to tell them about this, that, and the other."

"This Hajji threatened you explicitly, right?"

"Well, not explicitly. It was implied."

"Let me have his number. I know just what to say to people looking for handouts."

"He's a pretty nasty guy. Bad dye job, long fingernails, the whole bit. He followed me to Philip's party the other night. He must know where I live."

"What's his number?"

I gave it to him.

"Listen, go take a nap, and I'll call you when it's finished. I'm going to make it clear to this asshole that he's messing with the wrong fashion designer. Ciao."

"If you say it just like that, I'm a dead man."

Midafternoon, Ben called me back. I hadn't left the apartment all day. I was crippled with worry, and so I'd locked myself in.

"The good news is I talked him down to 175, but you have to tailor him two suits now. The bad news is I got him very angry, and I think we should definitely go to the authorities."

"What happened?"

"Things were said. Threats were made—"

I had another call from another unidentifiable number. 555.

"Great, I think he's phoning me now," I said.

"Yeah, don't pick up. Let him leave a message. Maybe he'll say something stupid that we can hand over to the police."

"Jesus."

"I'll pick you up."

"Wait. Let me think."

"What's to think about?"

"I'm not up to this. Not today. I'm exhausted."

"Boy, this guy seems pretty dangerous. You said yourself."

"Yes, but I think we should do the right thing here."

"Which is?"

"I think you should call your friend George and make the

whole thing public. There's no point in hiding. If we say that Ahmed was involved with the label, then Hajji has nothing, and I don't have to be bothered with the police. It's bound to come out sooner or later. Better it comes from us."

"Good point. Qureshi's an *alleged* arms dealer, remember. You'll be connected to a suspect now rather than a convicted terrorist later. . . . If, god forbid, this thing is true. It's the lesser of two evils. And the quicker it'll blow over."

"That's what I'm thinking."

"I'll handle it," said Ben. "And I'll prepare a statement. Who knows, maybe we'll get lucky and end up having a laugh over the whole fucking mess."

Truly, we intended to come forth with the truth. Ben was to handle everything. Perhaps it was foolish to think that I could skirt around talking to the authorities by going directly to the press. Anyhow, it didn't matter. I was already out of time.

The Overwhelming Event

It is raining today in No Man's Land. The pelt against my window-pane is a phenomenon I associate with living in the city. Whenever it rained there I became hyperaware of sound. Cars splashing through puddles, the screech of the Second Avenue bus in the wet. The change of the traffic signals. The clicking inside the tin boxes that made the traffic signals switch. Everything operated with such efficiency, such timing, even in the rain. You knew what to expect at every crossing. When the red hand on the walk sign blinked, you sensed how much time you had by the other pedestrians. If there weren't any, then by the eagerness of the cars inching into the crosswalk. One learned to read the signs.

Here in No Man's Land nothing is certain.

When will I meet my personal representative?

When will I meet with my lawyer?

When will I be released?

You see, uncertainty is their greatest weapon. Not the chains. Not the cuffs. Not the SMERF squad. Uncertainty.

It begins with the knock on the door in the middle of the night.

You may be fixing yourself something to eat, a midnight snack perhaps, or dawdling however one chooses to dawdle. As it was in my case, you may be entertaining a former lover, answering the proverbial booty call that had been placed just a few hours prior.

Michelle had sent me a text asking me if I was home, and I had answered it with a text of my own: WOOD LUV TO HAVE U CUM OVER XOXO. I used these fairly obvious sexual innuendos to make sure we were on the same page. We were, for she responded: B OVER IN 20 –XXX. I found my skinny jeans to be too constricting for my state, so I changed into some lavender silk scrubs kept in reserve for such an occasion. Then I put some clean linens on the bed and sprayed the pillows lightly with cologne. It was Michelle's habit to reach for a tube of lubricating jelly during the act, and so I got that ready too, strategically placing it in the top drawer of the nightstand.

Michelle rang from downstairs and I buzzed her up.

(I almost forgot. The knock that you will receive is more of a pounding, not any ordinary knock. Such is the rapping of the authorities.)

I opened the door and waited. I listened to the echo of her footsteps as she clicked her way up the stairs from the main foyer, then along the concrete hallway. She was wearing heels. Her shoes made movie sounds. She must have come from a date that had gone badly.

"Thanks for seeing me," she said. She was fragrant, a blouse and a summer skirt. She took off her shoes at the door and slid into a pair of Havaianas. It was something familiar and automatic. We were the same size.

"Of course I'd see you. I want to see you."

"You know what I mean. I don't know what's come over me. I just couldn't stay at Nana's place tonight."

It was after midnight. I realized how late it was by the glaze in Michelle's eyes.

"What about your other friend?"

"Who?"

"The one I saw you with at DuMont."

"Really, Boy. I told you then that he was no one. That he was a friend. We hardly speak. He has a girlfriend. He lives in Queens. Should I keep going?"

"I guess I don't care."

"Do you have anything to drink?"

"There's a pinot in the fridge."

She disappeared into the kitchen and returned with two glasses of wine. It pleased me to know that she didn't have to ask where things were.

"The place looks nice. You cleaned."

"I have a woman come by."

"You've hired your own Filipina. Look at you."

"She's Polish from Greenpoint," I said.

"Even better. Anyway, it's clean. Give her a raise. Show me what you're working on."

We walked over to my worktable. Michelle had a very good eye for what she would wear and what she wouldn't. I still trusted her opinion and was flattered when she began flipping through some of my new drawings. "I like these," she said. "These I'm not so sure. I would rethink what you're doing. What are you doing?"

"Sometimes I don't know what I'm doing when I sketch. I just keep going until I have a pile. Then I go through the pile and gravitate toward what I feel is right. Then I have the beginnings of a collection without a name."

"Strange way to operate. You can't write a play like that. You can't just write and write and then choose scenes. Everything stands on what came before it. Things need to be obviously connected. So does a collection, if I'm not mistaken."

"It will be, but not at the beginning. At the beginning I just need to feel out what I'm doing. I need freedom. There's nothing being wasted when it's just pencil and paper. Only time."

"Not everyone has time."

"Everyone has time. What didn't you like about these?"

"They don't seem wearable yet. These do. These don't. But I only glanced at them. Show them to your friends. Take a poll."

"Wearable. I almost don't know what that means anymore."

"I don't mean in a Target way. This is New York. This isn't Paris or London. Wearable, you know."

"You're right," I said. "These aren't wearable." I took the pile of sketches and pushed them aside. I showed her patterns I was considering for the looks she had admired.

"I like these," she said. "Rudi Gernreich?"

"Rudi Gernreich for Target."

"That's funny." She laughed.

I kissed her. She wasn't expecting it and resisted with her mouth at first, hardening her lips, but soon she relaxed into it. She had already been drinking. I tasted gin on her lips.

Suddenly, she pushed me off.

"Where are your cigarettes?" she asked.

"They're in the kitchen. Right-hand drawer."

She went and got them. I followed. She turned the stove on to high. It was an electric with those hypnotic burners. "You want one?" she said. She took two out of the pack anyway.

"Yes," I said.

When the burner turned red she bent over and lit each

cigarette individually. She handed me mine only half lit, and it gave off a chemical smell. There was still tobacco stuck to the burner, smoking. I turned off the stove for her.

"I have to use the loo," she said, and disappeared again.

I moved both our wineglasses over by the bed next to the ashtray I kept on the nightstand. The prop was cinematic. Not the ashtray alone but the whole act of smoking in bed, before or after, it didn't matter. It never bothered Michelle to have one lit in the ashtray during, burning itself out. She once said it reminded her of Anne Bancroft in the movie *The Graduate*.

I sat down next to the bed on my Wassily chair, close enough to the ashtray to rest my cigarette, and waited.

Though I didn't know it, this would be my last moment of freedom.

What did I think of? Since each second of freedom we have is so crucial, so fleeting, I would like to remember exactly what was in my thoughts. I could certainly make something up, something as dramatic as the way the smoke lingered in the air, trailing away from my cigarette in the ashtray. And you would certainly believe me. But I honestly don't recall. Matter of fact, I don't believe I thought about anything of significance. Isn't that a shame? The last moment I had to myself and I had wasted it like spilled wine. I sat and waited. I waited for Michelle to return from the bathroom. I waited for them to come knocking on my door.

This space of time that followed was like the moment before a crash, or so I can only imagine. Caught in that fraction of a second, you're not anything. You are afloat. Time, space, perception are askew. Your life is secondary to the imminent event. The event is overwhelming. Even fear, which seems so crucial to the event, is somehow put on hold. I have read accounts of people getting mugged at gunpoint, how they are able to think with incredible clarity, how they are able to follow directions with composure. They do as they are told in the face of a loaded gun. I must have reacted similarly. Fear was not a concept to me in this space of time. I was nothing, as I said.

There was the knock at the door. A pounding. Three times, maybe, though the number is irrelevant. Because it was not a knock to be answered. The door came down before I could uncross my legs. I froze mid-uncross. The men were relevant, bursting through the light of the hallway into the dark of my apartment, and once they were in the dark it was hard to decipher how many there were. (One must remember too that the order of action has been transformed by the nightmares I've had since. However, this is as close to the actual event as I can recall.)

There was shouting: Get your hands up, get on your knees, get down on the ground, etc. Levels of sound were altered. When one thinks of traumatic experiences, one immediately assumes sound is drowned out, muffled, like under water. But that is not so. Levels are altered, but there is an acute awareness. I understood clearly what the men were demanding of me. I had already been reduced to a well-trained dog, and on command, I did exactly as I was told.

The number of men was more threatening than the guns being pointed at me, even though the gun-to-man ratio was equal.

They had me down on the floor when they shackled me. Both my hands and my feet. This was very painful. "Stay down." From the ground I could hear the search underway. I was becoming more lucid, perceptive of multiple things happening simultaneously. Michelle was crying. Though her crying was growing more prominent with each passing moment, she wasn't actually getting louder. Her screams and pants were simply coming into existence for me. Voices were taking their respective places in the room. A man's boot heel was on my neck, but I managed to turn my head to the side in order to get a better look at the surroundings. Once he understood I was able to move, he applied pressure. "Don't move." My atelier was being ransacked. But my concern was for Michelle, not for any of my things. I could see the men. SMERFs. Not the same SMERFs we have here in No Man's Land, but similar. Padding, vested, heavily armed. They continued to turn everything inside out. What were they looking for? I don't even think they knew. Racks of my dresses were tipped over. My worktable was turned on its side, my sketches scattered to the floor along with pens, needles, spools of thread. My sewing machine was picked up off the floor and taken away. Bolts of fabric were unrolled quickly in the air, like someone airing out a sheet in the yard. I heard tearing, and I knew my dresses were being ripped apart, most likely the unfinished ones that were still on the forms. I couldn't locate Michelle. I couldn't turn my head. I strained my eyes trying desperately to look beyond their capacity. By her far-off cries I assumed they had her confined to the bathroom. Because of what they were saying to get Michelle to calm down, I now understood that the men had not come to rob and kill. But I still did not understand that they were agents of the government who had come to take me away. I would not understand this for some time. The man with his boot on my neck applied more pressure. I wanted to say something along the lines of a question but I couldn't begin to formulate language.

Someone else asked a question. One SMERF inquired of another, "Any weapons?" For a designer of women's wear, you can only imagine my shock over the implication. That I would have weapons in my home like some common criminal. Surely, I thought, a mistake has been made.

I was hooded.

The hood had been doused with something chemical. No kidnapping is complete without the drugging of the victim.

When I woke up I was somewhere else.

War Crimes

I shall do nothing more today than transcribe my most recent reservation.

"You comfortable here?" asked Spyro.

"I've gotten used to it," I said. "But these are horrible conditions." I told him my theory about how one can adjust to anything. It amazes me still how quickly human beings can adapt to their circumstances.

Spyro acted uninterested.

"You know," he said. "You've been receiving preferential treatment. Not that I need to tell you. You're not stupid."

"How do you mean?"

"You're permitted to write in your cell. Sketch. No one else is allowed pen and paper. You get fresh soap, extra towels, blankets, that kind of shit."

"I get a pen and paper because you've ordered me to write my confession."

"I had it authorized. Everything you have is because of me. The magazines, newspaper clippings, the news about your play. Even time. You have time because I've bargained for it."

"Are you fishing for gratitude?"

"*Am I fishing for gratitude?* No. No, I'm not fishing for gratitude. Let me ask you something. Do you think you'll be able to ask that of a military interrogator?"

"What do you mean?"

"The others. The other detainees. When they're interrogated it is by the military, not by us. You must have noticed."

"They keep me in the dark mostly."

"Well, take my word for it. The others answer to the military. They are interrogated at all hours of the night. The others aren't allowed to sleep for very long. They're not treated like you. And this is all because of me."

"Thank you kindly," I said.

He gazed at me, calculating something. "My point is: It won't always be like this for you. Our time is coming to an end. I'll have to hand you over to the military interrogators. They will ask you questions pertaining to your arrest."

"Is that what has happened to me? I've been *arrested*?"

"You see, smart-ass things like that will get you in trouble. These guys don't fuck around. They'll ask you questions, the same questions I've asked you, only they won't be too friendly about it. You'll stand instead of sit. You'll meet at night instead of day. You'll be left alone for hours upon hours, and then you'll be forced to talk for twelve straight."

"Nothing I'm not already used to."

"And there are techniques to get you to talk. It will not be pleasant, I can assure you."

"I sense a big fat 'but' looming."

Spyro rolled up his sleeves. I could predict his movements before they happened. I anticipated the scar on his forearm, the dampening at his hairline, his physical tics. Fingers tapped, lips wetted, etc. How many hours had we spent together?

"I've read everything you've written so far," he said. "When I submit my report along with your confession to the convening authority in Washington, here's how they'll see it. You've consorted with arms dealers and known gangsters. Men on international watch lists. Men banned from certain countries. Your cover as a designer of women's clothing is a perfect front. Potentially, the money you were about to make from your business, projected over five years, could fund another 9/11. You have access to elite targets. New York Fashion Week. The New York Public Library, by way of Bryant Park. Your associates have connections with Somali terrorists. And you still say you're just a designer of women's clothing? There was only one other designer in history with connections like you, and that was back in 1943."

"Who?"

"Coco Chanel," he said.

"That's preposterous!"

"She was arrested and charged with war crimes for her involvement with the Nazis. I'd tell you to go look it up, but I'd be wasting my breath. Chanel was banging an SS officer from '39 to '43 or thereabouts. He had his *Schutzstaffel* so far up her tight ass that she'd do anything for him, including an attempt to broker a deal between the British and the Nazis for whatever was left of Europe. Needless to say, they arrested her couture ass."[1]

---

1. This is true, for the most part. Coco Chanel was in fact arrested for war crimes in 1943 for her involvement in the Nazi plot Operation *Modelhut* (Fashion Hat). However, she was later acquitted on all charges, due to an intervention by the British royal family.

"You're making it up. And the thing about the Somalis is nonsense. I never met a Somali. You know as well as I do."

"And just like Chanel, you're seen as a collaborator in all this. A terrorist sympathizer. A key financier. You, the fashion terrorist. They got you. Those in Washington are almost positive. But those in Washington want a confession."

"Those in Washington think the quickest way to connect two dots is to draw a straight line. I've given you my confession."

"We're almost out of time, Boy. I need you to start telling me what I need to know."

"I've done nothing but—"

"You've done everything but give me what I need. You've fed me a lot of shit."

"I've fed you nothing but the truth."

"Bullshit."

"I'm sorry you see it that way. I thought we were on a level of understanding."

"Will you stop it? Stop. Enough! Did you or did you not know about weapons prior to Ahmed Qureshi's arrest? Prior to May 25, 2006."

"The fertilizer?"

"Weapons. Weapons of mass destruction. Whatever that may mean to you. Ammonium nitrate fertilizer. Whatever. Did you know about weapons? Did you know about a deal?"

"No."

"See, you're lying. You did know about a deal. It says so right here in your confession."

"It says I suspected Ahmed was a liar. That I couldn't believe half the things that came out of his mouth."

"And you did nothing."

"I didn't do nothing."

"If you tell me now, you'll make it a lot easier on yourself before I give you over to the CO for another round of interrogation."

"Why do I have to talk to him?"

"Because I'm off. I'm done here. I'm sorry to say it, but our time together is through. Every good thing must come to an end. And when I'm gone, they're going to start all over again. All the shit you've written down so far gets filed away, and they take it from the top. So if you tell me now, you're going to save yourself a lot of time and anguish."

"I told you. I don't know about weapons. I know only what I've already told you. I was entrapped."

"That's a big word for you. Do you even know what it means?"

"I was set up. That's the only way I can deduce my being here."

"You weren't set up. You were given up. Your friend Ahmed fingered you out over everyone else. Qureshi talked. Your other friend Hajji, he didn't get pinched. He's fine. He's a cooperating witness. Ahmed fingered *you* when they put it to him. He *gave you up.* He said you're the brain behind all this. You're the money."

"The money came from him! It was all from him!"

"But you come from a rich family. A family of doctors, you said yourself. Private school, et cetera."

"My family doesn't have any money. Check them out. They supported me here and there when I got to New York, but that's all."

"You came to the U.S. and you set up shop. You sought out Qureshi and took up residence in the same building. You're consorting with known gangsters. The funds are all in place. Ahmed finds the buyers. Somalis. He gets the goods. Ammonium nitrate fertilizer is just the beginning. He makes promises to the Somalis for more weapons. RPGs, antiaircraft guns, night-vision goggles, tanks for Christ's sake. We've been following him for a year. Your name comes up on the tapes. Once you get the money you funnel it through your business, you produce women's clothes because it's very lucrative, and on the other end you have the Somali deal."

"You have it all wrong. It's the other way around."

"That's your defense? 'Your honor, it's the other way around. It was the chicken not the egg.' Look at it through their eyes. They see a textbook example of a terrorist ring at work. And I got to say, it doesn't look good for you, my friend."

"I want my lawyer," I said.

"Now you want your lawyer. You didn't need a lawyer when we started here. Why not?"

"Because I believed you. I thought you could help me. Only you're just a pawn like I was. So now I want my lawyer."

"Good news, he's on his way. He's still waiting for his security clearance. Should be any day now."

"I will say nothing else. It's all in my confession."

"Your confession has a lot of holes."

"I dare you to prove me wrong."

"Is that a threat made from a detainee to a special agent of the FBI? Do you know what can happen to you when I snap my finger! Before our time is up, and I give you over to the marines, I need to know, Boy. Listen to me, to them you're just another number. They don't care where you're from—Mr. New York City big shot who-gives-a-fuck. You are just a number." Spyro stood up. "Now I've treated you like a man. Like an honest man. And we're at the end of our road together. I'm leaving. I'm not coming back. So I need to know. It's your last chance to confess before I feed you to the jarheads. Did you know about any weapons prior to Qureshi's arrest? Prior to May 25, 2006. If you had any involvement and you confess it now, I'll give my highest recommendation to Washington. You have my word."

"I'm already a number. I'm prisoner number two-two-seven."

"Did you know about weapons before Qureshi was arrested, prior to May 25, 2006?"

"No," I said. "I've told you. What I knew I put in my confession."

"This confession stinks. I'm asking you here and now. For the last time. Did you know about weapons? Did you know about fertilizer? What did you know?"

I felt that complying with my interrogator at this stage would be to waste my breath. These were roundabout questions. Questions I had already answered.

I refused to gratify him with another answer.

On the Tarmac

On the night of the Overwhelming Event, May 30, 2006, I was deliberately hooded so as not to be able to identify faces, streets, landmarks. This should tell you right away that what has been done to me and others in my same situation is illegal. Even hardened criminals—murderers, rapists, drug peddlers, pimps, and thieves alike—get to see the faces of their captors. Those headed for No Man's Land do not.

Oh sure, I might have caught a glimpse of one or two of the SMERFs who came through my front door, but I can't possibly identify anyone. They've covered their tracks very well! If I wanted to bring charges against those who kidnapped me, against those who transported me here, against those who handled me so violently through the night sky, how could I?

The path to No Man's Land is kept secret too. Those who need to get here, my lawyer for one, are still trying to navigate their way. Everyone knows where No Man's Land is. One can easily point it out on a map. But passage into this place is an enigma. I couldn't even begin to tell you the way to the forbidden island. It was all done in the dark, with a hood over my head. At times they used noise-canceling headphones. Shall I create for you what it was like to be taken in the middle of the night and transported to such a place? Sure, I could go through all the sounds and voices that I heard during transport: the bumpy roads, the rivets in the bridges, the popping of my ears in the tunnels, and then jet engines starting up, and planes taking off. But I would only be speculating. The God's honest truth is that I don't remember how I came to be here. When you are taken as I was, and you are masked, all you pay attention to is your own breath. You become very aware that you are still breathing and that you would like to continue breathing. I wasn't wondering where I was headed. I had already accepted a fate much worse than the one I got—that I would not be breathing for very long.

Transport is your first introduction to solitary confinement, and so you retreat into your mind and try to endure the pain of your senses being suffocated. Imagine being in a coffin for thirty-two hours, buried alive, and at the end of those thirty-two hours (which is just an arbitrary number, for I wasn't counting) you will be let out, only you don't know it. What would those thirty-two hours be like? Why, I'll tell you. Every inch of air taken in is exhaled as if it were the last.

When did it occur to me that I was a prisoner? Perhaps as soon as I was let out of the coffin, when the sack was taken off my head and I could see light and breathe proper air.

I was grateful to the soldier who removed my hood. He gave me life. I cried at his knees as he sat me down in a chair and chained me to an I-bolt in the floor. He pulled me by the shackles, my wrists and ankles raw from so many hours in chains. Where was I beginning my new life? I looked around and saw that I was in a room. Just a room with four walls. Brightly lit. A table. Chairs. A door. He left the room through the door, while I sat at the table and waited for several hours. I said and did nothing.

The many hours I had spent hooded and transported here and

there—this is all part of the fear they want to instill in you. I really believe the Americans tried to simulate death. Transport, as I said, is your first taste of solitary, as it is a great big void of nothing. I must have been driven around, moved from place to place quickly. Drugged and carried, hooded and deafened.

Where did I end up?

Why, not far from where I started that night waiting for Michelle. When the hood came off I was in Newark, New Jersey. Only I found this out much later, when another soldier said so. I was too disoriented to be conscious of place. As far as I knew, I was in Cairo or Kandahar.

The hood was off and I was seated at a table in a room. It was a room used for questioning. For interrogation. All airports have these rooms. I can only imagine that after the great scare of 2001 they became necessary. After several hours of waiting in the room I met my first interrogator, nonmilitary, wearing a shirt and slacks. He had a clipboard and wore a neatly trimmed goatee. He appeared to be in his forties, though he could have been younger. He wheeled in a small cart with a polygraph machine and proceeded to attach me to it. Then he sat down across from me and began his inquiry.

Newark was where Ahmed, my alleged accomplice in all this, my "coconspirator," was arrested for selling fertilizer to an FBI informant, and where he talked about all the bad things that could, would, and should be done on American soil. For me to say from my cell in No Man's Land that I still can't believe Ahmed was capable of such things would be unabashed ignorance. He roped me into his game a scapegoat, and I took the bait.

"Are you Boyet Hernandez?" I was asked.

"Yes," I said. I was surprised by the sound of my voice. I hadn't spoken in some time.

"Do you go by any other names? Any aliases?"

The interrogator seemed to have something in his teeth, and so his tongue struggled between his cheeks and gums to free whatever was there.

"I go by Boy. I'm a designer of women's wear."

"Just answer the question."

"I don't go by any other names. No," I said.

He did not tell me why I was there and I did not ask, for I didn't have the nerve. I had assumed it was because of my relationship with Ahmed. I should have shouted for a lawyer, examined the investigator's identification, proclaimed my innocence, demanded everything and anything a proper prisoner gets, but I was too paralyzed by fear. My, how I wish I had done it differently! I wish I'd had the strength to tell them that what was happening was wrong. I should have demanded that they charge me with a crime or set me free! You know, I didn't even suggest to them that they had the wrong man. That's what everyone, I assume, insists as soon as they are captured. Not me. I went willingly. During my first interrogation I did nothing but answer the man's questions.

Within a matter of minutes the questions took a rather preposterous turn. I was asked why I was planning a trip to Pakistan. When I said I wasn't, the interrogator accused me of indeed planning a trip to gather materials. Then he read off a list of names. I was to answer whether I knew anybody on the list with a simple yes or no. I was not to explain my relationship with the names; I was just to acknowledge whether I knew them. Here is where I had trouble. My interrogator never properly defined what it meant to "know." I did not know if he wanted me to acknowledge whether I knew them personally or whether I simply knew of their existence. The interrogator did not ask the question: Do you know so and so? He only read the name, and I was made to respond. The list was even more preposterous than the allegation of the upcoming visit to Pakistan. As we began I experienced a great deal of confusion, especially with his little machine making its squiggly marks along a piece of paper.

Some of the names that were read to me: Osama bin Laden, Khalid Sheikh Mohammed, Aman al-Zawahiri, George W. Bush, Dick Cheney, Ahmed Qureshi, Habib "Hajji" Naseer, Michael Jordan, Mickey Mouse, Ben Laden, Philip Tang, Michelle Brewbaker, etc. The list was composed of about two hundred names. I was to simply answer yes or no. I was not to elaborate on my answers.

When we were finished with the list he unplugged me from his machine and left the room. That was it. I never saw him again.

Writing out my confession, I have tried to capture the essence of my life. Because everything I write about is in the past, I don't see myself as living anymore. This is what happens to you when you are arrested. The present is shifted instantly into the past, and what had once seemed unfathomable—torment, misery, profound suffering—is now actual. "An omnipotent actuality," my special agent would call it, quoting one of his beloved Russians.[1]

Now that I approach the end of my confession, I find that I am beginning to lose hold of my character. I have become removed from the hero of my own story, you see. To lose hold of your own

1. Aleksandr Solzhenitsyn, from *The Gulag Archipelago*.

character must be part of the natural order of things in No Man's Land.

All the same, I have tried to capture myself, or my character, as sincerely as possible. To re-create what it was like to live in my skin.

After several minutes alone in the room at Newark Airport, I was once again hooded and shackled by two unidentifiable men whose faces were obscured by the brims of their military caps. No headphones this time, just the black shroud over my head covering my eyes. The two men carried me outside. We were on the tarmac. I felt the wind and heard the noise of propellers as I was carried along. They placed me in the back of a van and sat across from me. I was getting used to the feeling of metal under my feet and around my wrists and ankles. The chains rattled against the floor as the van moved fast and smooth across the tarmac.

One of them said, "Don't say anything." He wasn't addressing me but the other man.

"Don't," the other one answered back.

I heard the click of a picture being taken with a cell phone. It was the recording of a click. A simulation. That's how I knew it was a cell phone and not a real camera.

"I'm taking it off," one said.

"Don't."

"Who will ever know?"

"If they ever find out it'll be our ass. Mine and yours. Mine because I let you do it."

"No one will know. We're already on the runway."

"Shut up."

"Like he doesn't know."

The man reached over and yanked the shroud off of my head. They were young, white, well built. The one holding the shroud covered his nose and mouth with it and waved a camera phone in front of me. I stared into the panel of his little mobile device, the tiny lens in its corner. It was a Samsung. He was trying to take a picture, but the van was swerving. We were speeding. The other guard covered his face with his hat.

"Welcome to Newark, you terrorist fuck," the guard with the phone said through his shroud. "This is your last moment of freedom. Say cheese."

"Don't look at me," the other one said. "Look at the camera." I was looking at neither. I was looking at the guard holding the camera, the one who accused me of being a terrorist fuck. I hadn't the faintest idea what he was talking about.

He took the picture.

Somehow I knew this would be my last opportunity to speak freely. "Where are we going?" I asked him.

"*We?* We're not going anywhere."

"Where am I going?" I said.

I could tell he was smiling behind the shroud. I could tell by the shapes his eyes made. "Somewhere . . . ," he sang. "Over the rainbow . . ."

This made the other guard laugh. The coward still hid behind his cap.

"Where?" I demanded.

The one with the camera looked at his colleague and then turned back to me.

"No Man's Land," he said.

Honor Bound

Today I received a visit from the colonel. He was much shorter than I had expected.

What had I done to deserve such an honor?

The colonel informed me that tomorrow I would be moved to another camp, where I would not be allowed the provisions I've been permitted here. It all sounded very official, like it was really going to happen. (By "provisions," I assume he meant my pen and paper.)

They have a saying here in No Man's Land, something of a greeting between a higher official and one of his subordinates. It's a call and response. *"Honor bound!"* the high official will say. *"To defend freedom!"* is the response given. Until now, I never gave it much thought. One hears it so often on the block that one forgets to listen. Only when the colonel greeted Win this morning did I start to contemplate the meaning of the phrase. Why now, all of a sudden? Why, it was the way the colonel said his lines, with the delivery of a powerful stage actor. He spoke to Win with such bravura, such authority—such grace!—that I thought he must have authored the words himself. "Honor bound, soldier!" said the colonel.

"To defend freedom, sir!" said Win.

Win saluted the colonel with a quick slice of the hand at a

downward angle, swift, precise. The colonel returned the salute; then with a nod, he motioned Win at ease.

In a few days, my tribunal will begin. When I told the colonel that I would like for my confession to be submitted as evidence in my CSRT,[1] he informed me that he would see to it, personally. "You have my word."

"Scout's honor?" I quipped.

"My word alone is enough. You will find that when I give my word, it produces results. Decisions are made; people move on my command. Lives are at stake—"

"Et cetera, et cetera," I said.

"Why don't you ask the private?" he said, nodding over at Win. "Private, what happens when I give my word?"

"Sir, decisions are made, sir," said Win. "People move ASAP on your command, sir."

"Why's that, private?"

"Sir, lives are at stake, sir!"

"You see. There you have it," said the colonel.

So far, none of my cohorts on the block have had their tribunals.

"It is quite a new process," said the colonel. "But you shouldn't worry yourself. The process is being perfected every day."

"When will I meet my personal representative?" I asked. "The one that I was promised."

"Any day now," he said.

"Before my tribunal?" I asked.

"Oh absolutely. The process requires it."

"And what if I choose to defend myself?"

---

1. Combatant Status Review Tribunal.

"That, of course, is one of your options, but it is not encouraged. It may hold up the proceedings to have to explain everything to you and so forth. It could be very confusing for all parties. Your representative in this matter will inform you of all you need to know."

"And what about my lawyer in New York?"

"What about him?"

"Why can't he defend me?"

"I believe he needs to be cleared by the Pentagon first. Even so, this is a military tribunal—a proceeding of the United States military. Nonmilitary personnel are prohibited. It is a matter of national security, you understand."

"Then I will defend myself," I said.

Something in the motto for this godforsaken place has got me thinking about my captors. They are men who have dedicated themselves to what they believe to be a just cause, a righteous cause, a cause buried in a few simple words. I say buried, because breaking the phrase into a call and response, punctuated with "sir, yes sir," confuses a fairly respectable ideology: "Honor bound to defend freedom." I am beginning to see how these words could be applied to my own situation. Be free or die trying.

"I shall defend myself," I repeated.

"That is your right. But again . . . it's not encouraged."

"Tell my personal representative not to bother coming."

"I don't think it will take. Your representative in this matter is essential so that you may better understand the process. Even if you were to choose to defend yourself, he would still need to be at the tribunal."

"But you understand what I'm saying, colonel. I no longer wish to meet with him. I'm through waiting."

The colonel didn't move. He just stood there, hardened, looking me in the eyes.

"There's a real shit storm brewing because of you," he said.

"Come again?"

"A shit storm. That's parlance for one fucked-up situation. You're back in the media again. Congratulations. A real Patty Hearst. America's heart bleeds. But I won't let you burn me. Mark my words. I'm a fair man, but I won't be walked all over."

"I don't—"

"I know you don't know what I'm talking about. But listen. Accept. To listen is divine—that's what I tell my men. And my men listen, comply, act. Lives are at stake. I am not one to be humiliated, son. I run a secure facility housing the worst criminal masterminds of our time. This is a place of routine and discipline. Hitler would be here today. So would Mussolini, Stalin, Pol Pot, Ho Chi Minh. Bin Laden himself will be here very soon. Wait and see. We'll get him. This will blow over. I don't mean the war, but this media shit storm we're about to enter together. It will not be remembered. With the right actions anything can be extracted from hearts and minds. Suppressed then forgotten. Mark my words. Whatever happens, mark my words."

The colonel turned swiftly and he was gone. Win came to attention and saluted an empty corridor.

Afterword

BY GIL JOHANNESSEN

I began my story where it ends. On the windward side of the bay, where the banana rats run rampant, where the iguanas live under a protected order like the American bald eagle, where men train other men to crawl like dogs, to eat and shit on command, and then to stand hind-legged for long, intense intervals. It's a controlled nightmarish evolution, a weird science of cruel and unusual punishment. For us bent over on the wrong end of the red-hot poker, it's madness and chaos. Delta's infernal inferno. Death. No, worse. Death uncertain.

—Boyet R. Hernandez
From "Closing Statement,"
Combatant Status Review Tribunal,
Camp Echo

I.

On the morning of November 11, 2006, at approximately 0400, Boy Hernandez was awoken by the sound of chains. It was Veteran's Day, an occasion celebrated in Camp America with an early morning ceremony scheduled to follow the Pledge of Allegiance. Two MPs arrived, dropping the shackles at the foot of Boy's cell door. Private First Class Jeffrey Cunningham, Boy's night guard, had dozed off for a few minutes and was startled awake. One of the MPs, a lance corporal, reprimanded Cunningham for snoozing on duty. He informed Cunningham of their orders, that they were taking the detainee to another facility. Cunningham knew that Boy was to be moved that day, though the transport was originally slated to take place after Cunningham's shift. The men had come several hours early. That was when one of the MPs whispered into Cunningham's ear a code word: "catwalk." Cunningham understood the order and stepped aside. He knew if this code word was ever spoken to him he was not to notate anything in the detainee's logbook. Hernandez would be taken from his cell without record.

When Private Winston "Win" Croner arrived to relieve Cunningham at 0600 as he did every morning, he found Cunningham guarding an empty cell. "They took him," he said to Croner.

Win Croner looked in the logbook for the latest entry.

"Don't bother," said Cunningham. "He's gone. My orders are to wait."

And so the two men waited through the call to prayer, the Pledge of Allegiance. They listened to the trumpets of the veteran's ceremony outside the blocks. No one came to explain to Cunningham what the next steps were, and he never saw Boy again. He left the logbook with Croner and went back to the barracks, frustrated. The next day Cunningham was reassigned to the isolation ward Quebec, where he guarded, among others, the Australian David Hicks and Omar al-Shihri.[1]

In December 2006, the Pentagon released an official time line of that day. The record indicates that Boy was moved to a new cell in Camp Echo and arrived on schedule at 1100 hours.

Camp Echo lies to the east of Camp Delta and was once the harshest camp in all of Camp America. During Boy's term it served as a holding facility for prisoners who were scheduled to meet with their lawyers, personal representatives, or interrogators. The ride from Delta to Echo on a good day takes approximately fifteen minutes by jeep.

The Pentagon's records are in opposition to the story Cunningham would tell me when we met in New York in the fall of 2007. After his deployment ended, Cunningham left the service and moved to New York City, where he has pursued a career as a male

---

1. Hicks was the first to be tried and convicted under the Military Commissions Act of 2006 and was released to Australia in 2007. Al-Shihri, who was also released in 2007, has most recently appeared in an al-Qaeda propaganda video in which he implicates himself in an embassy bombing in Saudi Arabia. Al-Shihri was released into Saudi Arabia's custody, where he underwent a rehabilitation program for former jihadis, only to fall in with al-Qaeda once again.

model. Cunningham possesses classic American good looks, a dimpled smile, and short-cropped blond hair. Boy, apparently, had turned his night guard on to the prospect of working in fashion. He had recommended a booking agent at Elite Model Management, which now represents Cunningham.

If the time line the Pentagon released were accurate—that Boy was in fact delivered at 1100 to his cell in Camp Echo on November the eleventh, and if what Cunningham told me was also true—that Boy was taken at 0400—then there are still seven hours from that morning unaccounted for.

Cunningham didn't speculate as to where Boy was taken in the interim. He said he stopped thinking about Hernandez once he was transferred to isolation ward Quebec. He did, however, hint at the practice of secret interrogations done in a facility off the map. When I asked who ran the interrogations, he laughed. "Take a guess," he said.

"The military?" I asked.

"OGAs.[2] Everybody knows that."

OGA is military parlance for the CIA.

II.

The picture that was taken of Boy by the MP, Lieutenant Richard Flowers, on the night of Boy's transport on the tarmac of Newark Airport is by now a famous portrait of human injustice. The dimly lit 1.3 megapixel snapshot was taken with a model LRT Samsung mobile flip phone. Boy's desperation in the photo is unnerving. His

2. OGA: other government agency.

hair is matted down, he has been sweating, his face is gaunt, and his eyes are concave from lack of sleep. His white shirt collar is stained yellow, either by sweat or puke. It took several months for the photo to finally surface, but when it did, Boy's story, which had been reduced to a short-run Broadway satire involving a vapid trust-fund brat and a fashion designer turned terrorist loosely based on Boy Hernandez, was once again headline news.

The photo's going public explains the appearance of Colonel Albert T. Windmaker, high commander of the Guantánamo naval base, in the final pages of Boy's confession. Windmaker was known to see prisoners only when there was discord on the blocks, or if the base was playing host to a high-profile guest. It is plain to see, as the colonel readily admitted, that his visit was inspired by the media situation in the United States that was about to become unruly. Within twenty-four hours of Windmaker's session with Boy, the detainee disappeared for an unknown block of time.

Whatever governed Lieutenant Flowers's intentions in taking Boy's photo on May 31, 2006, has by this point become completely diluted by political statements and apologies made on both individuals' behalf. The conclusion of Boy's memoir leads us to believe that it was Flowers's intention to humiliate his prisoner. Instead, the image became a symbol for everything that had gone wrong in America since January 11, 2002, the day the prison at Guantánamo Bay opened its doors. Boy's portrait surpassed the images that had already haunted us, those of men in orange uniforms down on their knees in the gravel, masked with blackout goggles and noise-canceling headphones. What Flowers did was put a face on the abused, the face of an up-and-coming designer of women's clothing.

Days after the photo's release, the artist Sheriff Michaels took the notorious photo of Boy and superimposed it with damp shades of red, white, and blue—"cartoonifying" it, as Michaels calls it (a process that only takes a few minutes) and stamping the word BEHAVE at the foot of the image. A poster boy for the decade was birthed. As Boy's long-delayed CSRT got underway, the BEHAVE image spread. It was stenciled on buildings and construction barricades throughout New York City, Miami, Chicago, Portland, Seattle, Los Angeles, St. Louis, and even Tallapoosa, Missouri, where, ironically, the Hernandez scandal had set off a minor scare just five months before.[3] BEHAVE was the antithesis to what Boy (the person) had symbolized for the presidential administration. Hernandez, the fashion terrorist who had been the administration's much publicized prized capture in the global war on terror, was now a martyr for justice.

III.

When I began to investigate Boy Hernandez's detainment, the officials at Guantánamo and the Pentagon had no comment to offer. No one at the White House press secretary's office would return my calls. In fact, as a fashion writer, I was not taken seriously by anyone (though this was something I was used to). *W* magazine wasn't even willing to publish my idea for a follow-up piece on Boy and his indefinite detention. The magazine deemed it far too political, even though it involved a well-regarded fashion designer, one who had graced their pages less than a year earlier.

3. "Panic in Tallapoosa," *New York Post*, June 4, 2006.

None of the other majors I pitched it to would back the project either. My intent at the beginning was to do a bit of investigative journalism, something totally different from the fashion puff pieces I was known for. Call it my own political awakening. I would say that I even felt an emotional attachment to the story, equating the news of Boy's detainment to word of an unexpected death of a friend. Indeed, when I began my investigation, it was as if the fashion world had simply accepted that Boy was already dead.

When the BEHAVE movement erupted, Boy's cause was coopted by the mainstream press, where I held absolutely no influence or clout.

Still, I pursued the trail, and in late December of 2006, one soldier, not Jeffrey Cunningham, finally came forward, calling me from a pay phone in Miami. The soldier, whom we will call Coco, was willing to talk to me as long as he could remain anonymous. I immediately boarded a plane for Miami.

IV.

There is an automobile in Camp America described to me by Coco as a white van with blacked-out, tinted windows. Many of the guards call it the "mystery machine," after the vehicle in the Scooby-Doo cartoons. Inside the van is a cage big enough for one prisoner. It is common knowledge among the guards that the mystery machine moves freely in and out of Camp America, transporting prisoners and OGA agents without being recorded at the various checkpoints.

It seems likely that Boy was moved in this van at 0400, when Cunningham says he was taken from Camp Delta. However, on

November 11, Boy was not driven directly to Echo, as the Pentagon claims, but to an off-site facility north of Camp America, known by some as Camp No. Camp No is its unofficial name; the government currently denies its existence. But according to Coco and two other guards who have since come forward, Camp No does exist, and Boy was held there not only for seven hours but for seven *days* before his transfer to Echo.

Boy arrived just before dawn. The cells in No are built for isolation. It is a solitary facility designed to break prisoners. Unlike the steel-caged blocks of Camp America, No's cells are made of concrete. Boy would spend the next several days in a four-foot-by-seven-foot concrete box with no natural light. There were two buckets, one for him to defecate in, and another to urinate. There was a spigot for cold water that was sometimes shut off, and a thin mat on the ground where he was to sleep. On the walls of Boy's cell was what appeared to be blood spatter. To him it must have looked like the last prisoner had been beaten to death.

He spent his first two days at Camp No in complete isolation and saw no one. At night, he was kept awake by the screams of other prisoners. Often it sounded as if men were being severely tortured; other times it sounded like a woman was being raped and beaten. These were simulations intended to break prisoners. Coco said this was an effective tactic the OGA interrogators used. They would claim that what the detainee was hearing was his wife or daughter in the adjacent cell when really it was a female interrogator acting out the part.

On November 13, day three of his isolation, Boy was visited by an OGA interrogator, a man in plain clothes. These interrogators, according to Coco, are usually white males in their midforties to late fifties. They wear black shoes with white socks. The OGA interrogated Boy on that day for approximately seven hours without break. Boy was then allowed to rest for one hour before the same interrogator returned, fresh and ready to begin again. The interrogator stayed on for another five to six hours before Boy was allowed to sleep. If there weren't screams keeping him awake, it was loud music coming from one of the neighboring cells.

The same interrogator visited Boy for three consecutive days on similar terms. One long stretch of interrogation without break, and then a second interval into the night. By day six of Boy's imprisonment in Camp No, Coco reported, the OGA interrogator seemed "extremely agitated." He was not as confident or alert as he was at the beginning of their sessions. Something seemed to be weighing on him, qualities Coco rarely detected in OGA interrogators at Camp No.

During Boy's final session, the same interrogator started early, at 0600, and came out of Boy's cell less than an hour later shaking his head. He looked "disturbed," according to Coco. The man walked down the dark corridor to where another interrogator on a break was smoking a cigarette. "This is a fucking reach around," Boy's interrogator said. "He doesn't know jack shit."

The smoking man made a gesture with his shoulders, indifferent, and Boy's interrogator said, "Get him the fuck out of here."

From what I've been able to ascertain, Boy was moved to Camp Echo not on November 11, as the Pentagon records attest, but on November 18, one week later.

The cells in Echo are divided into two rooms. One makes up the prisoner's living quarters, with a bed and a toilet-sink combo. The other half holds a steel table, two chairs, and an I-bolt cemented to the ground. This is where Boy would eventually meet with his lawyer.

Boy was without the pen and paper he had occupied himself with in Delta. Everything he'd been permitted to keep with him in his old cell had been taken away, including the English copy of the Qur'an that once belonged to the prisoner David Hicks. There were no longer any guards for Boy to converse with. And no one else could be heard on his new cell block. On November 27, after several grueling days in extreme isolation, and stripped of his ability to write or communicate with anyone, Boy tried to take his own life.

Using his towel and strips of cloth from a white undershirt, he fashioned a noose and tied it to the bars dividing the two rooms of his cell. He stuffed the remaining fabric into his mouth to stifle any noise he would make during the act.

When the guards, who routinely checked in on each prisoner every ten minutes, found Boy, he was still alive, struggling to hold on to the noose around his neck. He had one foot toeing the edge of the bed, barely keeping his body aloft.

The guards rushed in and cut him down.

He spent only two days in the infirmary under evaluation until he was deemed fit to return to his cell in Echo.

Boy's Combatant Status Review Tribunal was again delayed.

Ted Catallano first met with Boy in early December 2006. BEHAVE was now everywhere, and the Pentagon could no longer delay Catallano's requests to meet with his client. They were, however, able to delay the consultation just enough so that Catallano had only a week to prepare Boy for the CSRT that had been rescheduled. Catallano would not be able to defend Boy, because it was a military proceeding, but he was notified that Boy would be defending himself. This worried Catallano for several reasons. The CSRTs had been under contention since they were created. They have been considered "mock trials" by many reputable litigators involved in these cases. Catallano has said, "At any other time these processes would be illegal. And any time we make movement in court to shut them down, the administration overrides the ruling, which in my opinion is a disgusting abuse of executive power." What worried him even more was that Boy refused to meet with his designated personal representative, a request the command at Guantánamo honored without fuss.

When Catallano arrived at Echo, he brought with him a hot mocha latte from Starbucks, a Big Mac, french fries, and a vanilla shake. All of these he had purchased on the opposite side of the bay, where the litigators stayed. On their first day together, Boy was somber and not readily willing to cooperate. He felt betrayed by his federal interrogator, Special Agent Spyro Papandakkas, and he was traumatized by his time in solitary confinement and the stressful techniques he had been exposed to. The idea of going over his defense with someone completely new, just days before his tribunal, exhausted Boy. "He wasn't happy to see me in the least," said Catallano. "This man had been broken. In my opinion he was not fit to defend himself in a tribunal. I petitioned to get us more time, but we were denied. I had to win him over in a very short time frame." Catallano tried to convince Boy to accept the military's counsel but was unsuccessful. So with only a few days left, Catallano started to prepare Boy for the trial of his life. At night he read a copy of Boy's confession, a document that had been submitted as evidence, known during the trial as Exhibit 3B. Their preparation had been curt, but by the end he felt confident that Boy could handle it. "He was a public figure who loved the limelight. Once I was able to get through to him, I knew he'd step up. We had prepared his opening and closing statements, which he wrote himself. And from his words alone, I knew he could do it."

The tribunal took place on December 9, 2006, in a makeshift courtroom inside a trailer. Catallano watched the proceedings on a black-and-white monitor in a neighboring trailer set up for journalists and lawyers. Boy met his personal representative for the first time on the morning of his CSRT as he arrived at the tribunal.

According to the allegations given at the Hernandez tribunal, Boy's detention was due to the following:

(1) On October 9, 2006, a federal jury in Newark, New Jersey, found AHMED QURESHI guilty on five counts of terrorism and other felony charges, including his material support of a group of Somali terrorists known as the ASPCA (the Armed Somali People's Coalition of Autonomy). QURESHI was arrested in Newark, New Jersey, at a Sheraton hotel after bomb-making materials (ammonium nitrate fertilizer) were exchanged with a Cooperating Witness working with the FBI. (2) AHMED QURESHI stated that he cultivated a relationship with the ASPCA in order to sell bomb-making devices while having full knowledge of the group's intent: to target several highly populated spaces and landmarks in and around New York City, including Bryant Park during Fashion Week, among others. QURESHI stated that he had hoped to retain a relationship with the Somalis, who were interested in obtaining more bomb-making materials and other

weapons such as antiaircraft guns and Stinger missiles. QURESHI also stated that he had an inside man, a "sleeper," already working in the New York fashion industry. QURESHI identified the inside man as the Detainee, BOYET R. HERNANDEZ. QURESHI stated that HERNANDEZ was the "money" behind the "operation," that he controlled the funds and was known in certain groups as the "emir of Seventh Avenue." QURESHI also stated that HERNANDEZ was an associate of BIN LADEN (sic).[4] (3) A second Cooperating Witness stated that the Detainee planned to travel to Pakistan to acquire materials. On two separate occasions the CW transferred $50,000 United States dollars into the Detainee's business account for the Detainee.[5] (4) QURESHI stated that the Detainee was the facilitator of these funding requests and that the Detainee knew about the ASPCA and their targets. (5) The Detainee sent a text message to QURESHI in 2004 that read: "Took Rudy back to sleeper cell and introduced her to my leader." (6) The Detainee made a diary entry in 2004 in which he stated he would "wage war" against other "designers" in the United States. (7) The Detainee made a second diary entry in 2004 in which he stated he would demolish Fashion Week if he were not permitted to show his collection "this time." (8) QURESHI stated that the Detainee told him on one

4. I suspect that the administration purposefully left this typo in order for the charges to have more gravity. It is, however, amended at the end of the charges.

5. The second Cooperating Witness in the *Hernandez* case was later identified as Hajji, also known as Habib Naseer.

occasion that he was working on a "counterattack" with
BIN LADEN. (Let the record show at this time the
similarity between the Detainee's publicist Benjamin
Laden, aka Ben Laden, and OSAMA BIN LADEN.
Any confusion in this count and previous counts will
be clarified at this hearing.)

It is Ted Catallano's opinion that all of the allegations made
against Boy could have been cleared up in one afternoon at Federal Plaza and Boy's detention avoided entirely. But because the
climate after 2005 was so volatile, paranoia was infectious, and
actions were taken to the extreme. It was less than a year before
Qureshi's arrest that four suicide bombers had attacked the London transit system using ingredients similar to what Qureshi had
been dealing in: ammonium nitrate fertilizer.

"The allegations were absurd," said Catallano. "They would
never have held up in a U.S. court of law. It was cleverly disguised
hearsay all based on what one informant alleged while trying to
save his own ass. Qureshi was a known criminal prone to tell lies.
They knew that from the beginning."

The tribunal lasted a week. The verdict was decided by the
convening authority in Washington, not by the council of military
personnel present at the hearing. With the pressure on, the convening authority made their decision within a few days. They
determined that the evidence against Hernandez was insubstan-
tial, and there was "no credible information that Hernandez provided material support to terrorist groups." Boy's status as a
non-enemy combatant was made official. He would be returned
home.

V.

I wrote to Ted Catallano while Boy was still awaiting transfer back to his home country of the Philippines. Catallano had me over to his office on West Twenty-fourth Street, close to the garment district. He informed me that the Pentagon had placed Boy under a gag order, one of the conditions of his release being that he not speak to the media about his experiences inside the prison for the term of one year. It was the government's way of stifling any further embarrassment. I found it rather odd that America was keeping a wrongfully accused man under such a strict leash when he had been found innocent by their own tribunal. When I asked Catallano, he said, "It's a condition set by the military. We're working on getting it reversed. They've threatened to have him extradited back to the United States and prosecuted if he breaks the agreement."

"So he can't talk to me under any circumstances?" I asked. "Even as a friend?"

"Sure, he could talk to you as a friend, but if you were to publish anything that the Pentagon determined to be a breach of the agreement, they could go after him. And what they determine to be a breach of the agreement is exactly what's uncertain. You see, they've been making it up as they go along since the beginning. Each day we're waiting to see what they'll come up with next. Look at the Detainee Treatment Act. Look at the Military Commissions Act."

The Detainee Treatment Act of 2005 stripped federal courts of jurisdiction to consider habeas corpus petitions filed by prisoners. In the wake of the Supreme Court's decision in *Hamdan v. Rumsfeld*, which found that military commissions violated the Geneva Conventions signed in 1949, the Military Commissions Act of 2006 again authorized military commissions to try those accused of violations of the law of war, explicitly forbidding the invocation of the Geneva Conventions when executing the writ of habeas corpus.

However, at the time of my meeting with Catallano, I was unfamiliar with these developments.

"I'm unfamiliar," I admitted.

"Well, get familiar."

Catallano was rather gruff about the situation. He had jumped through hoop after hoop in the *Hernandez* case, and once he felt progress was being made, he'd suddenly get hit with a clause that had been reinterpreted by the administration, and which would delay his progress for months. Though he didn't say it, I could sense that Catallano thought my article trite and misguided. He felt I would be ignoring what was most important about the *Hernandez* case. And in a sense he was right. I was looking for the fashionable angle in Boy's story, a designer's life after prison.

"Just remember," he warned at the end of our meeting. "Whatever you write, now or a year from now, is going to be looked at by them. And a man's life hangs in the balance. So it'd better be worth it."

I still hadn't reached out to Boy directly. He had been moved to Camp Iguana, about a kilometer from Camp Delta, where non-enemy combatants were held while the United States negotiated for their release. This was a process that could take several months, even years. For instance, many Yemenis and Uighurs were stuck there indefinitely because of the political climate in their home countries. The State Department had to find hosts that would take them. Even though Iguana was lax by comparison to the other camps, a letter sent to Boy there would still need to pass inspection. I didn't want to endanger his release, considering the conditions of the gag order. And so I held off on any contact with him until he was home safe in the Philippines.

Boy spent eight weeks in Iguana, a short span considering how long the others were kept waiting. In Iguana the detainees wore white uniforms and lived together in communal cells. Many of them spoke English, having learned it from years spent in captivity. The camaraderie Boy experienced there was life changing, and he made many lasting friendships. He shared a cell with Abu Omar and Hassan Khaliq, two journalists from Islamabad who had been arrested by the Pakistani authorities. They had each been critical of the Pakistani government and wrote about it regularly. Boy also shared the cell with Shafiq Raza and Moazzam Mu'allim, who'd been captured in Afghanistan and sold for bounties of two thousand dollars. Each of these men had served three to five years in Guantánamo Bay before they were determined to be non-enemy combatants.

On February 17, 2007, when Boy stepped off the plane in Manila at Ninoy Aquino International, he received a presidential homecoming. The airport had laid out a red carpet for his return and set up barricades along the length of the runway for the hundreds of journalists from all over the world. The flash photography alone was overwhelming. He was met by his mother, who was accompanied by Ted Catallano. Boy's father had passed away earlier that year of stomach cancer. Ben Laden was there, standing alongside hundreds of extended family members on the tarmac to welcome him home. It was an emotional reunion for Boy. He walked arm in arm with his mother down the length of the red carpet, smiling and waving. Reporters shouted questions at him but he merely answered, "Thank you for coming." It was incredibly humid that night, and by the end of the carpet

Boy looked as if he were going to collapse. Catallano and Laden helped Boy's mother carry him into the terminal. The headline the next day in the *Philippine Examiner* read MANILA'S BOY RETURNS.

I sent an e-mail to Boy after his release, mentioning that I had been following his case from the day he was seized. "It's a gross injustice what has happened, and it makes me ashamed," I wrote. I expressed my deepest sympathy and let him know that if there was anything he needed from me, personally or professionally, he should not hesitate to ask.

My e-mail went unanswered.

Weeks later I received a letter under the guise of a pseudonym, a Ms. Ellie Nargelbach. It was an anagram for Gabrielle Chanel.

> Dear Gil,
>
> It would please me greatly to meet with you, but as you probably already know, I am under strict orders to keep as quiet as a mouse. A travesty *inhumaine*! For now my dear friend, I leave you with the idea of coming to Manila to cover the opening of the new Balenciaga store in Makati next month. There's a wonderful café nearby with a man-made pond and a gondola. Listening to an opera over an espresso dopio, two can pretend they are in Milano watching all the tight asses. Just follow the sounds of Puccini to the northwest corridor of the plaza. The café is adjacent to Bubba Gump Shrimp.
>
> Yours Truly,
> Ellie Nargelbach

In my reply to Ellie Nargelbach I informed her that I would attend the Balenciaga opening the following month, only my letter was returned to me two weeks later. It was not an issue. I had already bought a ticket to Manila.

The journey from New York was nearly twenty-four hours. I transferred in Narita to an Egyptian airline. Flying coach on the connecting flight, I had little legroom, and after about half an hour my legs began to cramp. For the first time I tried to imagine what it must have been like for Boy during his detention. I had read that detainees were placed into stressful positions for the duration of their transport; they were chained low to the ground with blackout goggles and headphones, deprived of their perceptive senses. I then tried to picture Boy in his cell, the man I remembered. I decided that I wouldn't have made it. As a test, I tried to remain in my seat while my legs went numb. But this alone was too much for me, and I had to excuse myself in order to stand up. One cannot simulate the conditions he had to endure. Boy coming out on the other end, not just alive but living a life somewhere, was a tremendous example of human endurance.

It was early evening when he appeared at the rendezvous point. Café Italia was just as he had described it, on the edge of a man-made pond in a high-end shopping plaza. There was a dark Filipino man in pinstripe and a straw boater hat wading in a gondola. An opera, not Puccini, played through a set of speakers hidden in a palm tree high above the courtyard. I had arrived at the café early that afternoon, since he hadn't specified a time in his one and only letter as Ellie Nargelbach.

It was not easy to recognize him at first. He was remarkably light skinned, pale in complexion, and wearing a white A-line skirt and navy blouse that looked to be Vivienne Cho. He had on a pair of Chanel flats, and his legs were freshly shaven. His face was masked behind oval vintage sunglasses, and a shoulder-length black wig with bangs covered his forehead. He looked like a sixties movie star. But what gave him away was the Marc Jacobs carryall. This was actually a men's item, a very expensive men's item, which I recognized.

He approached my table and put out his hand. "Ellie Nargel-bach," he said, casually. "So glad you could make it."

I was already on my feet and took his hand. Was this Boy's latest incarnation or a paranoid precaution? I must admit it was hard to tell. I decided I would play along. "It's nice to finally see you," I said. "Would you care to join me?"

"I'd love to. But I can't stay long."

"Please, sit."

"Do you have a Kleenex?"

"I have a napkin."

"That'll do." Boy took the napkin and wiped his seat clean before sitting. He looked around the plaza, at the shoppers who circled with large shopping bags from Gucci and Louis Vuitton, then glanced across the pond at the man in the gondola.

"I'm sorry, can I have another napkin?" he asked. Boy patted each of his eyes underneath his sunglasses. "I can't help it."

"It's fine," I said.

"I'm allergic to this place. The pollution. The smog. My skin is hideous."

"You look fine."

"Thank you, you're too kind."

He told me he had been suffering from insomnia as of late. Even the sleeping pills that he now took regularly would only put him out for two to three hours. Last week he had been awake for three consecutive days and had even considered having himself committed.

"We really shouldn't stay here," he said. "Best to get the check and go somewhere else."

He suggested we venture over to a club where his girlfriend, Star Von Trump, was performing that night. Von Trump was a transgender singer who performed at many of the city's popular karaoke clubs. She had a successful following in Manila.

I paid the check and we caught a taxi headed for The Fort, the city's Fort Bonifacio district (formerly Fort McKinley, a U.S. military base until 1949). In the cab Boy took off his sunglasses. It was approaching twilight. The early evenings in Manila were otherworldly; the smog created a vibrant, almost radioactive sunset.

Boy directed the driver in Tagalog, and there was a moment of confusion. The driver seemed to be ignoring him, and Boy became irate and started to raise his voice.

"What did you say?" I asked, once we were moving.

"I called him an idiot."

"Why?"

"He called me one first. He's an asshole and a homophobe. *Aren't you?*" Boy said to the driver.

"He proboked me, sir." the driver said, politely. "He proboked me."

"Oh shut up," said Boy. "Keep your eye on the road and drive."

The man did as he was told. The argument was over. The rosary beads dangling from the cab's rearview mirror swayed back and forth as we merged onto the highway. I tried to put on my seat belt, but the female part of the buckle was missing.

"Jesus saves."

"I'm sorry?" I said.

"Jesus saves," Boy repeated, pointing to an advertisement for a megachurch on the back of the driver's seat sandwiched between an ad for Reebok and a spectacular shot of Michael Jordan, air bound, advertising nothing.

Boy sat back in his seat and took off his wig. His hair was short, and I couldn't help but notice how thin it had gotten. I then tried to diffuse the tension in the cab by asking him about some of the designers we both knew. Boy immediately began to liven at the subject. He was like a different person when talking about fashion. The success of Vivienne Cho's fragrance line had surprised him. "It's actually quite good," he admitted. "They sell it here. She's in duty free." He admitted to buying a bottle for Von Trump. I told him Vivienne was planning to open several more stores in Singapore and Tokyo.

When the conversation turned to Boy's former classmate, Philip Tang, who had helped him significantly in New York, Boy just shook his head. He was bitter over something Tang had been quoted saying in the tabloids. "Oh, my fair-weather friend," Boy remarked. "I have so many of those now."

On the way to the club, Boy pointed out where he was living. It was a luxury apartment complex called Manhattan City, a small replica of Midtown Manhattan in the heart of The Fort. Manhattan City had five buildings, no one higher than thirty stories, each fashioned in the image of a different New York landmark. Boy's rented apartment was in the tallest one, a mini Empire State Building. There was also a mini Chrysler Building, a replica of Rockefeller Plaza, and even a MetLife building towering over an

ambitious and fairly ornate Grand Central Terminal (actually a
bus and train station called the GCT). Approaching The Fort district from the highway, one could see a mirage of the Midtown
Manhattan skyline, perhaps as Boy had seen it from Queens on
his first day in America.

He took out another wig from his carryall and admitted it was
Von Trump's clothing he was wearing now. "I borrow from her
when I have to go out. It's funny how I've made women's clothing
for most of my life and I still can't get used to dressing like this."

"You felt you needed to disguise yourself when you came
home?"

"No. It was after I got here. I moved in with my mother, into the
room I grew up in. After a few weeks I began to notice that I was being
followed by a white van wherever I went. If I went out shopping, there
it was. One night I even saw it parked outside my family's house."

"Did you call the police?"

"I didn't question who it could have been. I just left Manila for
Samar, the island where my mother was born. My family still has a
house there on the bay. The setting was familiar in more ways than
one. That's where I met Star, actually. She saved me, you know."

"How so?"

"I went out there with the intention of never coming back. My
father had a *banka* that I had played in as a child. It's just a small
dinky boat. I planned to take it out into the bay as far as I could."

"And did you?"

"No. It wasn't even there anymore. The sea had washed it away.
The caretaker had a *banka*, but I was too ashamed to take his only
one. I offered to pay him for it, you know, but he said just take it.
He wouldn't accept my money. He wanted to lend it to me. At this

stage the idea was getting complicated. The whole point of the boat was that it would be there when I arrived."

"Were you followed to the island?"

"No. I saw no white van, nothing out of the ordinary. And then I met Star. She was performing at a small club that my cousin owned in Calbayog City. The next day I saw her on the beach from my window. I went down and said hello. She stayed back on the island, and soon my idea of going out into the bay started to fade. Star was pushing me to come back to Manila with her, but I was reluctant. Then one night, when we were playing around, trying on wigs—she has the most fabulous wig collection—I said all right. Though I decided I would need to take precautions."

"And is it working? Are you still being followed?"

"I've seen the van, but not as of late. I take several cars at a time. One to the mall, Greenbelt, or the Galleria, and then I switch cars, or switch wigs in cars. If I do this when I go out, they can't keep up with me. Coming here I took three cars just to be safe."

Boy put on a short brown wig, a pixie look. He straightened it using the driver's rearview mirror.

"We're here," he said.

In the club we watched a few run-of-the-mill drag queens perform top-forty pop songs. The selections were typical of any karaoke bar. Von Trump was the club's headliner that evening. She was like an ideal woman seen through the eyes of a middle-aged American tourist: olive complexion, perfect breasts, a tall hourglass figure, long legs. Tonight she was blond; tomorrow she could be a redhead. She was beautiful in her own pretense. Though she didn't possess a great voice, she used it to a seductive effect. It bled sexuality. She closed with "Bésame Mucho" and did an encore of "Girl, You'll Be a Woman Soon." Now and again she looked over in Boy's direction. We didn't say much to each other during the set. We only watched and listened. After, Boy suggested we move to a private karaoke chamber where we could talk.

A hostess led us to Boy's favorite room. He was a regular. Von Trump had been performing at the club for several months now. She brought in the crowds, and Boy came once a week to watch the show.

The subject turned to his ex-girlfriend Michelle Brewbaker, the aforementioned playwright whose debut, *The Enemy at Home or: How I Fell for a Terrorist*, enjoyed a short run on Broadway before the BEHAVE movement eclipsed it entirely. Boy, as one can tell from his treatment of Brewbaker in his confession, was rather unforgiving when speaking about her. "In prison I spent a lot of time thinking about the two of us."

Brewbaker insists she intended for the play's title to be ironic. According to her, she didn't set out to make a grand statement on Boy's case. She thought she had written a topical character study of two people caught in the net of post-9/11 paranoia. Brewbaker, who is now seen as a right-wing darling, has made serious attempts to shake this image.

"Have you talked to her?"

"I'm too bitter to ever forgive Michelle for writing that play."

With the remote control he chose a song by Chloë, the actress-singer-songwriter who starred in the Broadway production of *The Enemy at Home*. For a moment we just watched the words of her hit single, "Chas-titty," fill the screen over a slide show of photos from around the world: London, Bangkok, Amsterdam, Helsinki.

"It baffles me how things turned out," he said.

"I'm sorry, Boy." It was all I could think to answer.

"I have a confession," he said.

This made me quite nervous. I was afraid he was about to violate the gag order, and even though I wouldn't write about it, I feared that the Pentagon would somehow find out anyway. "You don't have to say anything, Boy. I'm here as a friend. Not a journalist."

He laughed. "No, I wouldn't lay that on you, man."

What followed was the first I heard of the document Boy had been assigned to write for his federal interrogator. Catallano had been working on getting the Pentagon to release it into Boy's possession and was fairly optimistic about retrieving it, in part because it was used as evidence in Boy's CSRT and should be made public.

"I want you to read it for me," he said. "If you could, I'd like you to tell me whether it can be published. It's important to me that it's handled by someone I know . . . who knew me before all this."

The confession, as Boy explained, detailed his life in America leading up to the time of his capture. What I did not know was that it was also a portrait of the island prison during its most volatile period.

I agreed to help him.

Boy once again brought up the Brewbaker play. He couldn't come to terms with it being the only written work about his life as the fashion terrorist. If he could only get his confession out into the world, then his time in prison wouldn't be a complete waste. This was Boy's way to regain control, to take back the power his former captors still held over him. If his words had carried the strength to convince the convening authority in Washington of his innocence, then, he believed, they might also reverse his exile. For

Boy, the publication of his confession could be the first step in his journey back to America.

There was a knock at the door, and Von Trump joined us. She was still wearing the red sequined tube dress and blond wig from her show. After she introduced herself to me, she took a seat next to Boy on the plush sofa and placed her hands in his lap. Once again the conversation turned to fashion. He wanted Von Trump to know just how big he had been in New York, how his name had popped up in conversations, how his clothes had appeared in fashion editorials in all the major magazines. He wanted her to hear what other designers had thought of him, what I had thought of him, and he couldn't disguise his own need to hear it too. His mania and his momentum made it seem like he was bouncing around the carpeted walls of the small red room. Von Trump said she'd never seen him like this before. He put his arm around her and asked, "Gil, what was the piece you wrote about me called again? Tell her, I forget."

"It was 'The Fall of Boy.'"

I knew he hadn't forgotten. He couldn't have. But he needed to know someone else remembered. And then his eyes went distant, as if he were looking through me, imagining everyone who once knew him by his name.